BLOOD MAGIC

BLOOD MAGIC

MAGIC, LOVE, AND MISCHIEF BOOK 2

4 Horsemen
Publications, Inc.

KAIT DISNEY-LEUGERS

4 Horsemen
Publications, Inc.

4 Horsemen Publications, Inc.
1497 Main St. Suite 169
Dunedin, FL 34698
4horsemenpublications.com
info@4horsemenpublications.com

Cover by J. Kotick
Typesetting by Niki Tantillo
Edited by Kristine Cotter

Library of Congress Control Number: 2022951910

Paperback ISBN-13: 978-1-64450-796-4
Hardcover ISBN-13: 978-1-64450-797-1
Audiobook ISBN-13: 978-1-64450-799-5
Ebook ISBN-13: 978-1-64450-798-8

To Storm, who is not a romance reader but still demanded I write every new chapter immediately. #SisterLeugers

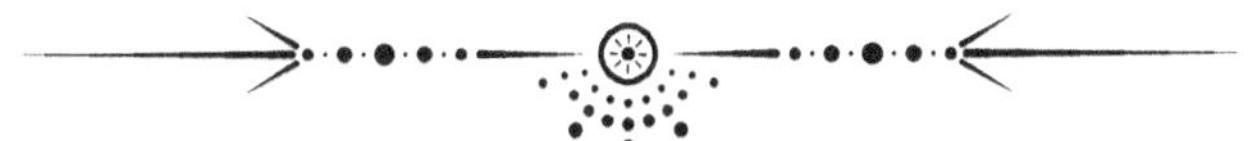

ACKNOWLEDGEMENTS

Book two, here we go! When I started writing *Antique Magic*, I wasn't planning on making it a series. But then Lily and Albert just wouldn't leave me alone, and I knew I needed to tell their story. Once again, Linda Stewart was there telling me to write more, that she needed more about my witch and vampire. So here you go, my friend.

Much love and many thanks to my editor, Kris Cotter, who believed in my characters and set me straight when I messed up on my pagan representation. Big thanks to everyone at 4 Horsemen Publications for being writers working for writers. You are such a kickass group of people, and it is an honor and a pleasure being a Horseman.

A special shout out to my Twitter writer friends, especially L.B. Black, who is the best source of all things vampire. I think that Albert and Lawrence would be besties and be awkward vampire nerds, totally crushing on their witchy ladies together.

To Greg, listen, I'm a peacock; you gotta let me fly! And to my kids, Artemis and Orion, I love you both to the moon and back, but man, you two made sure I didn't write when you were awake. It was worth it for all the hugs and cuddles, though.

I forgot to include Jordan Bunnell last time, so I'm doing it now. Thank you, friend, for all the dumb TikTok you sent that got me out of my own head for a while. I needed them, and I didn't even know it.

Finally, thank you always to my parents. Mom has told everyone she's ever met that I wrote a book, and I love her for it. Dad, I'm not dedicating a romance book with spicy scenes to you. It's weird enough when you force me to flirt with your dwarf characters in D&D whenever I DM; don't make this weird. You throw off my groove (but I still love you).

TABLE OF CONTENTS

CHAPTER 1

The lamp clicked on with a gentle snick, illuminating the bedroom in a soft glow. Dawn was still about an hour away, but it was time to get up and out the door. Lily Everett placed her feet on the floor, burrowing her toes in the plush carpet below the bed for a moment before pushing herself up into a standing position.

She would much rather stay in bed, but that wasn't an option. At least the air in the house was warm, unlike the bed, which was always a little chilled.

"Leaving already, darling?" a husky voice asked from the bed. Lily smiled as she turned and bent over to kiss her boyfriend, Albert Hsu. She intended for it to be a short and sweet kiss, but good intentions never stood a chance against Albert's kisses. He pulled her toward him, and she fell forward onto the bed, catching herself on her hands over his body.

She didn't try to pull away as he deepened the kiss and delighted in the shivers that ran through her body as his hands reached up to touch her. The coolness of his fingers did wonderful things against the flushed heat of her body. But then, Albert was always cold, one of the side effects of being a vampire. Lily was used to it by now, but the sensation of his cold against her heat was still wonderful.

Finally, he let her pull back just enough to answer the question she barely remembered him asking. "Yes, love, I have to. You need your beauty sleep, and it's almost sun-up, and I have a load of work in the garden before it gets too warm out." She slowly stood from the bed again, incredibly reluctant to go. She would stay in bed with Albert all day if she could, but he was at his most vulnerable during the day, so she opted to leave him be while he slept or hid out somewhere in his house.

She dressed quickly and kissed Albert again, reluctantly pulling away, and then headed for home.

The Everett family farm was already bustling in the pale dawn light. Her eldest sister, Rose, sat on the porch drinking coffee as Lily walked up the path to the house.

"Don't think getting home late from that vampire's place means you're getting out of dawn harvest. Mom wants us all in the morning glory plot in thirty," she said cuttingly. Rose had the ability to be a sharp-tongued bitch even at six in the morning.

"Fine." Lily smiled. Not even her sister's grumpiness could tarnish her good mood after a night with Albert. Besides, she was used to early morning harvests after a long night since she switched her focus to night-blooming plants to spend time with her vampire.

So far, her family had not been particularly supportive of the change. But then again, they weren't particularly supportive of her relationship with Albert.

Lily came from a long line of witches, and in her family's opinion, witches, especially from such an esteemed line as the Everetts, simply did not date vampires. Or any other magical beings that weren't other witches.

Lily walked through the house and into the crowded kitchen. Her father stood at the stove watching over a batch of eggs, while the rest of her family—her mother, her other older sister Ivy and her fiancé Jamie, Rose's wife Manu, her granny, and papaw—sat at the table. There was never a time when the Everett table wasn't full of people. It had been that way even forever; there were always aunties, uncles, and cousins around being as loud as possible. And that happened still, since all the Everetts lived around the farm, one house at each cardinal point, completing their family circle.

But there was one person who never got to sit around the family table. Not once had her family invited Albert to dine with them. Other than the Samhain party, Albert had not set foot in her family home, and that was almost a year ago. The two of them spent all their time out of the house or at his place. It wasn't lost on Lily that even though her family was welcoming to everyone, including her siblings' partners, they were not as welcoming to her own.

True, witches and vampires didn't mingle much, even if they were all part of the same magical community. But Lily never thought her family would harbor such prejudice against a vampire, especially since they hosted the Samhain event for the local magical community every year, and Albert had been coming to that for many years.

Lily took a seat at the table just as her father slid a plate of eggs and plant-based sausage in front of her, followed by an empty mug. As her father turned away, the carafe of coffee in the center of the table lifted and poured the steaming brew into the mug. A sugar canister floated to the mug and spooned out two spoonfuls on its own before replacing itself back across the table. Around her, the table was loud with chatter, and Lily focused on her food, letting the voices swirl around her.

"Out all night again with that vampire, Lily?" her mother asked, and there was an accusation hidden in her tone, which was unusual for Hyacinth Everett. Her mother was even more cheerful than Lily, which was a feat unto itself, as Lily had a reputation for being the most cheerful, easygoing person in the room.

Lily set down her fork and pulled her coffee close. "His name is Albert, Mom. And yes, we had a date last night, so I stayed over."

"You know, you could have dates in the daytime if you just dated someone normal. Then you could spend evenings with your family again. Besides, it's not like he can offer you any kind of future, except for when he finally snaps and drinks your blood," Rose jeered as she walked into the kitchen. She sat down next to her wife, who gave her a long glare. Manu didn't necessarily agree with Rose, but she never said anything in defense of Lily, either.

Arguing with her family left her without an appetite, which was a shame, since her dad was an excellent cook. "It's really none of your business, Rose. And I don't appreciate your insinuation. Albert isn't like that;

he only drinks from willing people. Which I've told you enough times. I don't understand what you have against him." She tried to keep her tone even and tried to stay calm. If Rose detected any trace that her words were getting an emotional rise out of Lily, she would pounce on it.

"You can't be serious? You're not that obtuse, Lily. He's a vampire; that's all I need to have against him. You are an Everett. You should be with one of your own kind, not some bloodsucker. Am I the only one who sees how big of a problem this is?" Rose turned her gaze around the table. Manu averted her eyes. She didn't want to be counted with Rose on this, but she also wouldn't go against what her wife said. Lily often wondered why Manu put up with all of Rose's shit, but she supposed love had a lot to do with it.

Granny and Papaw continued eating as if the conversation wasn't happening, which wasn't surprising either, as they rarely involved themselves in family squabbles anymore. Lily wished her granny would speak up, since she knew the old woman didn't have a problem with Albert. But her avoidance of family conflict was greater than her acceptance of Lily's choice of partner, and Lily didn't necessarily fault her for that. In the grand scheme of things, a boyfriend, no matter how much she loved him, wasn't that important to an old witch who already had to go through the whole issue of spouses with her own daughters.

"Lily, dear, your sister does have a point. In the times I've met Albert, he has shown himself to be a nice enough man, but he still is a vampire. And you are a witch, an exceptionally powerful one at that.

Maybe you should start thinking about your future in this coven." Hyacinth's tone was gentler this time, as if trying to coax a small child. There was nothing Lily hated more than when her mother spoke to her like that. Sure, she was the baby of the family, one that came much later after her sisters than anticipated, but she also wasn't a kid anymore. She was twenty-four and knew, for the most part, what she wanted out of life, and was clearly able to make her own decisions.

Lily abruptly stood from her chair and grabbed her coffee. "I'll be in the morning glory garden."

"Lilybelle, wait," her father called after her, but Lily left without turning around and didn't stop until she reached the garden gate.

She gulped down the rest of her coffee and then transfigured the empty mug into a woven basket for collecting. Her dad was going to give her hell about wasting another mug, but she couldn't find it within herself to care at the moment.

I'm so tired of this, she thought as she walked through the gate and into the garden proper. But she had become used to it since now that it had become a recurring fight between her and Rose over the last several months. Sometimes her mother made snide comments or tried to use her soothing words to convince Lily she was wrong. Ivy kept trying to set her up with random wizards and witches that either she or Jamie knew. And Jamie, Goddess love him, just turned off his cochlear implants whenever he wanted to avoid an awkward conversation.

She loved her family; they were everything to her. So, the fact that they didn't support her when she was so incandescently happy with Bertie made her feel awful. At the beginning of their relationship, her family seemed happy for her, with the exception of Rose, but Lily long ago gave up on ever getting Rose's approval on anything. But after six months of dating, things became more hostile toward Albert.

Because they finally realized we were serious. Lily supposed it was okay to sleep with a vampire, but not go steady with one.

Lily was at war with herself. It had always been in her nature to be cheery and to lighten a room as she walked in. No matter what, she wanted everyone around her to feel at ease and happy. Making friends came as easily to her as breathing.

Standing up to her family was where she faltered. And she worried that, eventually, they would push her enough that she would break it off with Albert just to keep them happy. Lily had always done what was expected of her to keep the Everett legacy strong. But when it came to Albert, for once, she wanted to be selfish. She wanted something for herself.

The two of them had danced around each other for a long time, ever since Albert changed his pick-up day at her friend Ezra's antique shop to match up with hers. For three years, she pined over him, made small talk whenever their schedules crossed, tried to spend time with him at the holiday celebrations. Now, finally, they were together, and it put her at odds with her family.

Lily sighed heavily as she put another white blossom in her basket. Maybe her family would come around and accept Albert one day. She would get through it. She always did.

CHAPTER 2

Albert hated summer days. They lasted so long that there was hardly enough night to get anything done outside the house. And all he wanted tonight was to see his girlfriend.

Tonight, he was finally going to ask her to move in with him. Not once in his long existence had he ever asked someone else to live with him, and his normally cool demeanor was thrown off.

In short, he was nervous.

What if she does not want to leave her family? For probably the hundredth time, the thought crossed his mind. Lily was close with her family, and her whole livelihood was tied up with that farm of theirs. He wanted her to know that moving in with him didn't mean she would have to completely leave the farm or her family. She would still have her work, even though she didn't need to work. Albert had more than enough money to take care of her for several lifetimes. But Lily wouldn't stand the idea of someone else taking care of her. Albert just wanted her to be happy and near him more, selfish as that was.

Which was why he was awake when the sun was up, dealing with the human embodiment of sarcasm that was Bridget St. James in his kitchen.

"So, I have the flowers in the left garden, mostly all decorative, but she'll enjoy those. Right garden is all hers. I have some starters out there and the bags of seeds if she wants them. Let her know that I can get anything she wants for that garden pretty quickly. Our supply chain has really picked up since switching suppliers." Albert could hear the pounding of the woman's heart and knew without a doubt that she had had entirely too much tea before coming over. Brie's racing heart had nothing to do with fear. She had never really been afraid of him.

When Albert had called the antique shop to ask her for help, her line of questioning was so pointed he felt like he was being interrogated. The two of them had never been friends, or even friendly, which he knew was his fault. He was nice enough to the human, for Lily's sake, and right now, despite his general indifference to her, Bridget was really helping him out.

"And this will be enough room for her to start her own garden here?" He had asked already, but everything had to be perfect for Lily. He wanted her to feel like this was her home. It wasn't nearly as large as her family's farm. *Maybe I should see about purchasing my neighbor's land.* Anybody could be compelled to sell with enough money thrown at them. Maybe he could buy up the neighborhood—let Lily set up her own farm.

A hint of annoyance flared in him as he watched the human's eyes soften when he turned his attention back on Brie. That was not how their interactions worked. "It's more than enough space. She's going to love it." She smiled, and that was just too much for Albert. But then she continued, "And hell, she might even want to stay with you. Not that I get that." There it was. They almost had a nice moment, but luckily, Bridget had reined in her friendly demeanor. That was just not how they acted around each other.

"You may tell Ezra I will settle up the bill when I pick up my next parcel. Now get out." He lifted a hand to indicate the doorway out of the kitchen. It was best to keep their usual exchange, lest either consider actually getting friendly.

Bridget shouldered her monstrous messenger bag. "There's the asshole I know and love. You're welcome." She walked out of the kitchen and out the front door without another word to Albert. He was suddenly grateful for the silence.

Things were about to change, and he planned to enjoy the last bit of peace he had before he poured his cold, dead heart out to his girlfriend.

A chime came from his trouser pocket, the modern mobile phone Lily had convinced him to get months ago so they could text. He still didn't understand all the features the phone provided, but he did enjoy the things Lily sent him, especially the images she called *nudes*. Those were his favorite.

With some difficulty, he pulled his mind from the images of Lily's bare skin before him on the small screen. What he should focus on was preparing the house for her arrival. Or preparing himself to ask for a change in their relationship. It was lucky he could no longer sweat, or else he would be absolutely soaked through.

[Lily: On my way, stopping by the butcher shop]

A wonderful, thoughtful woman, he thought to himself as he typed back a quick acknowledgment. While he preferred fresh blood straight from a willing source, any blood was nourishment enough, so a few pints from the butcher made the dining experience with her better.

After that, the real panic set in. He dashed around the kitchen, pulled the bottle of champagne from the refrigerator, and dug up the ice bucket he had stashed away long ago. He stood in front of the china hutch and agonized over which set of crystal flutes to use. One of the pains of being an immortal was that one tended to collect a lot over the decades and rarely got rid of anything. Which was why Albert had such a large house for one person, to fit all the stuff he accumulated over his long life.

Maybe when Lily moved in, they could work together to finally clear it all out. He wanted her to feel like it was her home, too. It didn't need to be full of his junk. It could be full of plants and Lily's scent. And *their* junk.

The turn of a key in the lock brought him back to the present.

"Babe, I'm so tired! Would you be open to rubbing my shoulders?" she said as she kicked the door shut behind her. Her hands were full of bags, stuffed with produce from the farm and groceries she had gotten on her way over from the looks of it.

Faster than Lily could see, he was by her side and grabbing the bags from her hands. "Bertie, you scared me." She jumped as he materialized beside her, and she swatted him with the back of her hand even as she laughed.

Her laugh became muffled as he leaned down, far down to reach her much shorter stature, and kissed her deeply. Lily's now free hands reached for him and pulled him closer. With as much care as he could manage without removing his lips from hers, he set down the bags and wrapped his arms around her. A human man would probably feel the pain in his back from bending over Lily's petite frame, but all Albert felt were the pinpricks of electricity wherever their bodies met. Kissing Lily truly was a full-body experience.

When they finally disentangled, Lily was breathless. Albert felt he would be, too, if he needed to breathe. "Well, that was a nice greeting. I expect that every time I come over now. You've set the precedent now, babe." She laughed as she picked up the bags from the floor and padded off to his kitchen.

"What's the occasion?" she asked, nodding toward the champagne and glasses as she set down her bags.

Remember to keep your composure, Albert. You are a gentleman, he thought as he rounded the kitchen island and pulled the bottle from the bucket, even though he was barely in control of his emotions.

He made quick work of the cork and poured two glasses, handing one to Lily. "Do I need an occasion to drink champagne with my lover?" A small smile formed on his face. Only Lily had seen those smiles.

Only she could coax them out of him. And he smiled so much in her presence. More than he ever had, even when he was human.

She took the glass and held it toward him. "To us, then." They clinked their glasses together. Even though the drink did little for him, Albert had always enjoyed the way the bubbles tickled his nose. And he savored that feeling now, a way to ground himself a little as he tried to keep his mind calm.

"There's something I want to show you." He took her glass, set down both flutes, and then tugged on her hand and led her out to the expansive backyard. Bridget really had done brilliant work in turning the mundane grass lawn into a garden of potential. Something for his Lily to cultivate, to make her own. Damn, now he would have to do something to thank the human.

Lily gasped at the sight before her. "Bertie! When did you do this? Is it for me?" Her golden-brown eyes were wide, and her mouth formed a surprised circle. He wanted to kiss her, to hold her close in her garden.

"Your troublesome human friend helped me. It's for you. I want you to feel at home here. Like this is your home." He was surprised how even his voice came out. Vampires were not supposed to be afraid of anything, and yet he was so afraid of her rejection.

Her beautiful eyes turned glassy and she looked on the verge of tears. "What are you saying, Bertie?"

This was it, now or never.

"Darling, would you perhaps want to move in with me? Here. In this house. Together." Heavens, he was losing his composure. He closed his mouth, lest he continue babbling, just saying words that involved "house."

For a moment, Lily didn't say anything, and then she launched herself into his arms. If he were a mortal man, he probably would have been caught off guard and staggered, but instead, his body was steady as he brought his arms around her. She pulled back just enough to grab the lapels of his jacket and tug him down to kiss her. She kissed like she was claiming him, imprinting her mark on his lips.

"Does this mean you will?" he asked as the kiss ended. Even with her reaction, a flash of uncertainty passed through him.

"Of course it does. I really want to live with you." She wrapped her arms around his neck and stared lovingly up at him. Yes, he had to hunch over significantly, but he did not mind if it meant she was holding on to him. If his heart could beat, it would be wild and soaring. Lily was his everything and now she would be there every day. The first thing he saw at night and the last thing he saw in the morning. Albert could face the final death right now and would die again happy.

They stayed wrapped around each other for several minutes, neither saying anything. Her heart beat against his chest and he lost himself to the rhythm of it. At one point in his life, that sound would have driven him into a bloodlust, but now it was soothing. He supposed he would have to thank his friend Ezra for that. Not that he would actually say the words, but Ezra would know.

"You saw this happening, didn't you?" *Why did I think I could keep a secret from a psychic?* Not that he wanted to hide anything from Lily, but it wouldn't matter if he tried; she would know.

She hummed against his chest. "Maybe, but hearing you say it in person is way better than one of my visions. I like the real thing." They lapsed into a comfortable silence and clung to each other as if letting go would break the spell between them.

Lily was the first to break the quiet moment. "Guess I'm going to have to tell my family I'm moving out. That's going to be a fun talk." She laughed lightly as she released him to wipe tears from her eyes. Albert brought his cold hands up to cup her jaw and brushed the last of her tears away with his thumbs.

"Do you want me to be there for that conversation?" He knew how the Everetts and their coven felt about him. He hadn't been invited to any of the family dinners Lily went to. The few times they had been assembled, they had basically ignored him or shot him sharp disapproving glances. And Lily's eldest sister was downright hostile toward him. But he would endure it for her.

Her laugh was louder this time, and she pressed her face into his chest. "Oh Goddess, no. No offense, babe, but that would definitely make things worse. Rose tried to hex you after we told her we were dating, and I'm pretty sure it will only get worse when I tell them you are whisking me off to your lair."

Albert sniffed in feigned offense. "I do not have a lair. This is a lovely house that will be made more so by my beautiful sweetheart moving in."

"Your sweetheart? You're so old-fashioned, babe." She smiled brightly up at him before pulling him down for another kiss.

"Now, how about we consecrate this garden?" she asked as she pulled him into her new haven, slipped down the straps of her overalls, and pulled her shirt over her head. They could retrieve their clothes before the sun rose.

CHAPTER 3

"I can't do it. Like, I can absolutely move in with Bertie; I just can't tell my family I'm doing it. Maybe I'll just slip out in the middle of the night and send a text to Ivy the next day. Or just start slowly moving things and then leave a note once it's done." Lily's head thudded against the wooden counter.

Her best friend, Brie St. James, shop assistant and unofficial co-owner of Spirit Antiques, patted her head in sympathy. "I don't think you can just ghost your family, Lils. You're going to have to tell them, and eventually, they will come to love Albert."

Lily lifted her head and gave the other woman a pointed look. "You don't even like Albert, let alone love him."

Brie held up her hands in defeat. "Yeah, well, that's because he's an asshole toward me. But I bet he's on his best behavior with your family. I mean, we don't have to be pleasant to each other, and we're doing just fine."

"I'm surprised you're not trying to talk me out of it." Lily chuckled.

Brie took a long sip of the tea in her cup, draining it. When she set it down again, Lily watched as the delicate cup refilled itself with more steaming tea. One of the reasons she always loved Ezra's shop was the casual magic about it—like a tea cup that just provided whatever the drinker needed. Or that the owner was an actual angel.

"I may not be your vampire bf's biggest fan, but he makes you happy, and that's all that matters to me. But just know if he breaks your heart, I get to go all *Buffy the Vampire Slayer* on him." Brie made a gesture like she was using an imaginary stake.

Lily's laugh filled the store front. "I'm not sure you would be able to catch him. I've seen you run." Her friend was many things; athletic was not one of them.

Brie joined in the laughter. "True, I am not fast. But what I meant was that I would make Ezra go all Buffy on his ass."

As if summoned by his name, Ezra appeared through the Storage Room door. "What am I doing with asses exactly, sweetheart?" He stopped next to Brie and leaned over the counter to rest on his forearms.

She patted his arm affectionately, and the two of them only had eyes for each other for too long. Lily was used to their total infatuation with each other, and really, she was partially to blame since she encouraged Brie for months to just go for it with Ezra. And it paid off in the end; her hedgewitch bestie and the angel she had known forever were head over heels in love.

"Albert's ass, dear, and you're kicking it if Lily says so. Otherwise, the only ass you need to worry about is mine." She chuckled as Ezra's cheeks pinked slightly.

Lily tried to hide her own smile at his embarrassment, but it did little good.

"And anyway, the real issue is that Albert wants Lily to move in and now Lily has to tell her family she's shacking up with a vampire for good." Brie shot her a sympathetic smile.

Ezra shrugged. "I don't see the issue. Isn't it a normal part of the courting process to move in together? The two of you have been together for a while now; it seems only natural to cohabitate."

The bell of the shop tinkled behind Lily, but she didn't turn. "Oh sure, you make it sound so easy. I just go home and say, 'hey, family, I'm moving out of the farm to go live with my boyfriend. You know, the vampire one who you all hate.' Yeah, that's going–"

"You're what?!" A shriek came from behind her.

Fuck!

Lily finally registered the wide eyes of her friends in front of her as they realized at the same time she did who had just entered the shop. The last thing Lily wanted to do was turn around and face this, but there was no avoiding it now.

Slowly, she turned from Brie and Ezra. "Hi Mom."

Hyacinth Everett stood at the door of Spirit Antiques, her face a mix of shock and anger. Her long, dark, tight curls were barely contained in a large scrunchie. She wore a similar pair of overalls to Lily's, only hers were khaki, a stark contrast to her deep dark skin. Lily always thought her mother was the most beautiful person in the world. Even now, as wrinkles had started to bracket her mouth, and a few strands of grey rushed through her curls, Hyacinth was gorgeous.

But right now, all Lily could focus on was her mother's thick brows narrowing and her eyes piercing Lily with an accusatory look.

"Lily Athena Everett, you can't seriously be considering moving in with that vampire!" Hyacinth stormed across the shop to stand close to her daughter. Lily might be just a little taller than her mother, but Hyacinth Everett was five and a half feet of terror when she was angry. And right now, going by the fire in her eyes, she was well past angry.

"Oh, I think I forgot something in the Storage Room." Brie's excuse was flimsy, and she quickly disappeared behind the door with Ezra on her heels.

Cowards, Lily thought as she raised her eyes. With a quick prayer to the Goddess and a deep breath, she prepared to face her mother. "Mom, I was going to tell you tonight. Albert asked me to move in and I want this. I love him, mom, and he loves me."

"I absolutely forbid it, Lily. You are a witch. He is a vampire. It's simply not done. You will stay on the farm, like every member of our family has before you. And furthermore, it would be better served for you to call it off with that thing and find a nice witch to settle down with. One that would respect our traditions." Energy crackled off Hyacinth, which always happened when she got worked up. Lily and her sisters had experienced it many times growing up, but it had been many years since Lily was on the receiving end of her mother's fury.

"Mom, I'm not a child anymore. You can't just tell me I can't move out. You never told Rose or Ivy who they could date. I don't know why you think you can do that with me." Lily really didn't want to fight with her mother in the middle of one of her favorite places, but she knew better than to stop Hyacinth. Knew better than to try to reason with her mother when she was like this. They would have it out right here in the middle of the shop, whether Lily liked it or not.

Her mother scoffed loudly. "Your sisters settled down with witches from nice families, not vampires. You are my child, and I can absolutely tell you what to do."

"Why do you hate him so much? You don't even know him; you haven't even tried to get to know him." She quickly congratulated herself for keeping her voice even, though she wanted to scream. Screaming at her mom had never ended well.

For a moment, Hyacinth's eyes softened, and even when the fire returned, the intensity was diminished. "I don't hate him. My sweet Lily girl, I want you to be happy. But you need to be with your own kind. He makes you feel loved now, but he'll never be able to give you sunshine and children. We witches live a long time, but we still age and die eventually, and he never will. Do you think he'll stay with you once you get old?"

Lily didn't want her mother to know her words hit on her secret fear. She wasn't naive enough to think she and Albert would live happily ever after forever. She would die one day while he lived on. Biological children would never be possible. And though Lily loved the sun, she would always be alone in the sunshine.

But she loved Albert. For years, they had shared lingering looks and awkward attempts at flirting. At every holiday, they had danced, shared food, or just stayed in each other's company. Really, their relationship felt inevitable; they were just too scared to do anything for so long. Now that she had him, she wouldn't give him up so easily. Not even if it meant rejecting the future her family wanted for her.

"Momma, I know what I want with Albert. I love him and that's all that should matter to you. It's my life to figure out and–" The bell tinkled over the door again, and Lily cut herself off. It was bad enough to argue in public with Brie and Ezra nearby; they didn't need to drag unsuspecting customers in, too.

"Can we not do this here?" She dropped her voice so only her mother could hear.

Hyacinth gave her daughter a long look before she responded. "We'll continue this at home, Lily. And I expect you to have gotten your head on straight and seen reason by then." Without another word, she turned and left the shop, whatever she had planned to purchase forgotten.

"Well, she seems cheerful today. Not even a parting slap on the ass for her darling Apollo," the newcomer said from beside Lily.

Lily liked Apollo; she really did. The golden incubus was a little much at times with his over-the-top flirting, but he was fun and had all the best gossip in New Britain. Right now, though, she really didn't want him around because, knowing him, all of the magical community would know she was moving in with Albert and her mother was not happy about it. And if there was one thing the Everetts hated the most, it was being at the center of community gossip.

She turned her attention to him fully. "Apollo, sweetie, you're going to keep your big mouth shut this time. Please, for me." Better to just cut right to it than deal with niceties. Lily was always nice, but this was damage control.

Apollo's Cheshire cat grin was enough to flood her with doubt. "My sweet Lily, I would never run my mouth about your personal affairs. I'm a gentleman."

"You are literally texting right now!" She watched as his phone appeared in his hand and his thumbs flew across the screen.

"Completely unrelated, just a friendly group chat." Apollo grinned again, but he didn't look up from his screen.

And, of course, not a minute later, Lily's phone buzzed with a text in her pocket. Followed by another, and then several more. She pulled out the offending device to see a slew of texts from coven members. There were a lot of exclamation points. A text from one of her teenage cousins just had an eggplant emoji. Sometimes the speed of technology annoyed her, and she had a pretty good feeling the messages were going to be coming in all day.

"I hate you sometimes," she grumbled and put her phone back in her pocket.

"Alright, you out," Brie shouted from behind the counter. Lily hadn't heard the door or her footsteps.

She's spending too much time with Ezra.

Brie never could stand Apollo, even though he had been there to save her last winter and he was sort of seeing her brother. Not that Brie was very happy about that, either.

"Little lamb, sunshine of my life, what did I ever do to deserve your ire?" Apollo batted his eyelashes at Brie, but she crossed her arms tightly and scowled at the incubus.

"You're obnoxious and screwing my brother; you more than deserve it. And you are bothering Lils and blasting her personal shit on the group chat. Here's your shit. Get out." She threw his package at him and he caught it with a *mmfph*.

He sulked on his way out and didn't bother to keep up the banter, but that could have been more to do with his ceaseless texting. Lily was grateful for her friend's intervention, though it wasn't enough to stop Apollo. By now, the whole of the New Britain magical community knew what was going on. Hell, probably the whole east coast magical world knew already. Goddess, he was the worst sometimes.

Lily groaned loudly and scrubbed her hand over her face. "Can I stay here tonight? Thanks to Apollo, it's not just going to be my family; it'll be every witch in the tri-state area. Please let me crash on your couch." Part of her really hoped Brie would say yes, even if it was only a joke.

You have never run from your problems before and you are not starting now, she chastised herself.

"That's what your new house is for. With your boyfriend. But the couch is always open if you need it. Or we can ask the Storage Room for an actual bed. Actually, if you want to hang out in there and let the Storage Room fuss over you, that would be great. It's getting a little baby crazy and driving me nuts." Brie sighed. Despite her words, Lily saw the happiness in her friend's eyes. She had been through so much in the last year. The shop and Ezra had been good for her healing.

"I should go see Bertie soon. Let him know that all Hades is about to break loose," Lily said as she bent to pick up the canvas bag she had dropped on the floor when she first entered. The sun was still up, but she really didn't feel like going home.

Maybe I could just not go home ever? Or at least until they forget that I'm dating a vampire.

But really, that was wishful thinking. Lily could never leave her family, and the Everetts had a long memory.

"Don't tell him I said hi. I filled my nice quota for the year with him this week," Brie said as she sat on the stool behind the counter and pulled a large ancient book toward her.

"Thank you for that, by the way. It was gorgeous and so thoughtful of Bertie to have you help." Lily's smile was large and genuine, like one of her usual smiles when she wasn't being crushed under the weight of her family's disapproval.

Brie waved her off. "It was nothing. Albert and I might not get along, but we both love you and that's all that matters. Now, stop avoiding your problems and get out of my shop."

"You know, some days I miss the old Brie, the one who didn't know about magic and was nice to me." Lily laughed and headed for the door.

"Yeah, well, that Brie got killed by a crazy-ass warlock. And it's called tough love, babe. Now go get your man." The bell tinkled as Lily exited the shop, the sound of her friend's laughter in her ears.

Spirit Antiques was like a second home to her. She had been coming to visit since she was very little. But now she had a real second home to get to, one that held someone she loved very much.

Her sky-blue bicycle sat locked in front of the shop, waiting for her. The forest green basket on the back was empty and she flung her canvas bag in before hopping on the bike. Lily loved the thrill of riding her bike. This one especially, since it was enchanted with a teleportation spell. All it took was a little powering up with pedaling, and then she could zoom off to her intended destination in a blink. She much preferred it to her car, which she seldom used unless absolutely necessary.

With the incantation muttered quickly and softly, she started to pedal down the street toward Albert's house. One moment she was pedaling down the street near the shop, and then she reappeared just down the block from Albert's house, the trees on either side of the road creating a shadowy canopy with filtered green light making patterns on the ground.

The house was dark when she pulled up; not that it wasn't always with the shutters and black out curtains, but Albert always left the porch light on for her in the evening. So, he clearly must have slept today and wasn't up yet. She left her enchanted bicycle on the porch and let herself into the house.

If she woke Albert, he would know quickly it was her, but she decided against waking him, though she silently wished he would wake and find her. She longed to have his chilled body wrapped around her. Instead, she settled with tea, directing her magic to fill the electric kettle and start the boiling process. The vampire's house was stocked with plenty of human essentials just for her. They were supposed to also be for non-vampire guests, but Albert never had guests over, so it was basically all for her.

The tea collection in the cabinet was extensive, a few in labeled tins from her favorite tea shop that Albert bought for her, but most were in sealed glass jars with Lily's own blends. A rose tea would help with the anxiety that whirled through her without making her feel sleepy.

Once the warm brew was in her hands, she stood at the kitchen counter debating how long she could put off going home. More than anything, she wanted to crawl into Albert's bed and snuggle close to him. Albert didn't always sleep, but when he did, she couldn't bring herself to wake him prematurely. So, she stayed in the kitchen until her vampire appeared some time later.

Her second cup of tea sat cold and half-finished beside her as Albert walked up to her and wrapped his arms around her from behind. "What's bothering you, my darling?" His chin rested on her shoulder, lips pressed against her neck. Sharp fangs skated over her throat gently, not enough to break the skin, but it did send a delightful shiver through her body as heat pulled low in her stomach.

Albert had never bitten her, never even brought it up with her. She was actually grateful for that. As much as she loved Albert, even loved the feel of his fangs over her skin, there was something about him actually biting her, pulling blood from her body, that just completely wigged her out. It wasn't an intimacy issue, or that she thought Albert would get carried away. Maybe blood play just wasn't her kink. And Albert didn't seem to mind. They were perfectly happy trying other things in the bedroom.

The feel of Albert's body pressed against her was enough to drive off some of her anxiety. She leaned her head back and sighed. It would be so easy to lose herself in him now. There was nothing wrong with that.

"Let me help you take your mind off it, love." His cool breath scattered her thoughts. One slender-fingered hand skimmed up her covered stomach to grasp her breast, pulling a gasp from her. The other made quick work of the buttons on the side of her olive-colored overalls to slip his fingers into her clothing and down between her legs over her underwear. Her gasp turned into a loud moan as his fingers pressed against her, and she arched her back into his touch.

"You ... don't ... even ... know what's on my mind," she panted as the hand between her legs began to tease her through the cotton material. The hand on her breast got to work teasing and pinching her nipple into a stiff peak.

Albert let out a small groan as he felt her grow more aroused. "You can tell me after I take care of you, my love." He kissed her neck again.

To hell with it, she thought as she let the feel of Albert's hands wash away her worries. She focused on what his hands did to her body, playing her like an instrument, plucking her just right. And on the large bulge pushing against her back, subtly grinding into her from behind. He was clearly enjoying himself.

Nimble fingers pushed aside her underwear and Albert ran one cool finger through her wet, inviting center. They moaned together; their panting echoed through the kitchen.

"So ready to be pleasured, my Lily," he growled in her ear as he slipped one finger into her. His thumb moved to just the right spot, and he began a leisurely caress back and forth. Slowly, he began to pump his finger in and out.

The hand on her breast moved, and she nearly cried out at the loss of touch until he made quick work of flicking open her overall straps one-handed, the showoff, the clip of them unfastening loud in the room. With nothing to hold it up, the front of her overalls bent in half and the whole of the garment slumped down on her hips. The hand between her legs did not cease its tantalizing thrusting. In a moment, his free hand was back on her, burrowing under her bra to palm her bare breast, cool skin against her raging heated flesh.

"Please, Bertie, I need–" Her words cut off into a long, loud moan as he thrust his finger deeper.

Albert soothed her with soft kisses against her jaw. "Shhh, darling, I know what you need. Now," he pushed a second finger into her, "ride my fingers like the good girl you are."

It was all the prompting Lily needed and she rolled her hips against where he was pressed deep inside her. The more she moved, the faster his fingers plunged in and out, the tighter the circling of his thumb grew.

Her teased nipple was hard and verged on pain, but she relished it.

As her body climbed higher toward her peak, her mind felt more grounded. She acutely felt every place that Albert touched. But there was so much more beyond their bodies. Every green thing inside the house was tied to her. The soft damp earth seemed to be just under her feet. Earthy scents of dirt and leaves, blossoms, and herbs. Eyes closed to the sensations around her, she felt her connection to her surroundings grow still more solid.

When her orgasm hit her, she was completely unaware. Her responding shout left her breathless and her body shook from the aftereffects. When she was finally back in her own head after several long moments, she leaned back against Albert's chest and just let him hold her up for a moment more. He slowly removed his hand from her intimate place and returned to wrap his arms around her middle and pull her close.

"You bloomed again, darling." He kissed her cheek and pulled away.

"I did?" Lily reached up into her halo of black curls where her fingers met the silk of flower petals. She pulled it from her hair, a whole swath of lily of the valley clutched in her hand. "Not again! This is your fault, Bertie. You and your fucking magic fingers!" It didn't happen often, but on certain rare occasions, Lily would sprout some type of plant that reflected her emotions. When she was little, it happened all the time. Her wild curls were always full of flowers and greenery. As she got older, the flowers appeared rarely, but seemed to find a way to bloom, especially around Albert.

At least it happened in private this time.

Albert tugged on her shoulders so that Lily faced him. When he kissed her, there was a smug grin on his face. "And here I thought you were the magical one in this relationship."

Lily gave his chest a playful swat. "Don't get cocky. You know you're good at what you do." Playful banter with her boyfriend was nice, but as the effects of her orgasm receded, the anxiety and dread began to creep back in.

"My mom knows about me moving in. She found out by accident and now the whole coven is probably waiting at home to ambush me," she blurted. She covered her face with her hands and tried to hold back her tears. Whenever her anxiety spiked, or on the rare occasion she got angry, tears came unbidden. And right now, her anxiety was through the roof.

"Darling, I need you to take deep breaths." Albert's voice broke through the panic in her mind. She didn't even realize she had started to hyperventilate. A deep intake of air and a slow exhale did little to actually slow her breathing, though.

Albert left her side for a moment, and her anxiety skyrocketed in that split second as she thought he was leaving her to her panic attack. But before she could finish her thought, he stood before her, holding out an orange pill bottle. "Take one, darling. I'll make you some more tea."

Lily took the bottle of Lorazepam and shook out a pill into her hand and swallowed it. She had been on the anxiety drug since she was a teenager when her panic attacks started to be triggered by everything. Her mother didn't necessarily approve, but despite the magical skill of her family, there wasn't much they could do for mental health issues. So traditional human medicine succeeded where magic failed.

More deep breathing and a cup of tea started to ease her anxiety. "We'll figure it out together, Lils. But that is tomorrow's problem. Tonight, you need food and your new garden." Albert kissed her deeply, and while her panic was still there, his attention took the edge off.

CHAPTER 4

Daylight approached quickly as Albert lay in his bed wrapped around Lily.

Their bed now.

He gently ran his fingers through her hair as she slept curled up against his chest. His body offered her no warmth, but she pressed herself close, anyway. Tomorrow would be a long day for them both. She was going to face the rest of her family and probably the whole coven. It was for the best that he stayed back at their house.

Am I hiding? Maybe.

But that meant he would need to spend his time preparing to fully move her in. Maybe he should clear out a room for her use.

Albert had spent the evening attempting to give Lily as much comfort as he was able. He made her a meatless version of xiao long bao using a modified version of his mother's recipe. As he made the little soup dumplings, his thoughts had strayed to his own family, his human family. They were long gone, killed in the San Francisco earthquake of 1906, lost and forgotten under the rubble like so many in the city's Chinatown.

The smells of the cooking food had him closing his eyes as memories flooded him. He could still clearly see his mother and grandmother working around each other in their tiny kitchen. His father would sit in the parlor reading the daily issue of *Chung Sai Yat Po*, the only thing worth reading, his father always claimed.

He had quickly driven those thoughts out of his head. There was too much pain in their memory, even over a century later. Besides, there were more pertinent family issues to worry about than the ancient history of the Hsu family. Lily's family was very much alive and seemed ready to keep her locked up at the farm just to keep the two of them separated.

Once he had fed her, they went to his room. *Our room*, he reminded himself, and with all the tenderness he possessed, he had brought her pleasure over and over again until she had finally fallen into a peaceful sleep.

At the start of the night, her phone had gone off repeatedly. But every time it did, she had looked at the screen, sighed, and placed the phone back into her pocket. Every single one was a call or text from a family or coven member. She sent one message to her mother to let her know she was okay, and then turned off her phone. Albert didn't push her to do more than that. Lily would never cut out her family, and he would never want her to, but setting boundaries with them was going to be her next obstacle, especially now that she would be moving out.

The plan was for her to head back to the farm with Brie and Ezra, who had offered their moving vehicle when Lily texted Brie earlier in the night. The three of them would bring her stuff back while Albert remained at the house and he would help her unpack later. Lily thought it best if Albert was not there when she confronted the rest of her family. And though Albert would never admit it, no vampire would, he was terrified of facing the wrath of the entire Everett coven of witches and their attempts at an intervention. Ezra and Bridget would help more as a buffer and get Lily back out quickly. Well, Ezra would help; Bridget was a powerless human who got on his nerves. But he was grateful for her assistance, anyway. The human could at least pack.

Soon Lily would rise for the day while he hid away from the sun and from his in-laws. No, as much as he wanted to be there for Lily, his presence at the farm would only escalate tensions.

He would just have to wait it out until she returned. Sleep would not happen, though; he already knew that. He didn't necessarily need to sleep, but he had been in the habit for so long now, it was just part of his routine. Besides, he wanted to be awake when Lily returned home.

There was no possibility of going out, not with the late summer sun. The best course of action would be to start to clear space for Lily's belongings. She would need room in the wardrobe and drawers. The bathroom cabinets would need to be arranged for the rest of her toiletries. She already kept a small collection at the house, but the rest of her stuff would undoubtedly take up the majority of space. Not that Albert was without his own collection. Stuck in the youthful form of a thirty-two-year-old man, that did not mean he didn't keep up a regular moisturizing regimen and use a light concealer to disguise his ghostly pallor. Clearing a room out for her own space seemed the best idea.

The kitchen was already stocked with stuff for her use, so not much was needed there. Except dessert.

I should make her dessert.

It was still a few weeks early for moon cakes, but his NaiNai used to make them for him and his siblings whenever they begged long enough or when one of them was sick. There was no greater comfort food; it was just what Lily needed. NaiNai would have encouraged him to make them now.

Why was he thinking so much about his family? It had been well over a century since their death. They were never coming back; he would never see them again.

But it was easier thinking about them, his human family, than it was to think about his other family. His vampire family. He left them thirty years ago and had few regrets about doing so. Especially now that he had his own circle and his Lily. He didn't need the toxic vampire cult he called a family for decades. Not anymore. He wasn't that Albert. That Albert, the one driven by bloodlust and hedonist tendencies, had met the true death.

The new Albert that emerged found salvation in Ezra's shop. He found a friend who made sure he lived a better life, a healthier life. Ezra picked him up, showed him he didn't have to be a monster, that he could be useful to society. And because of him, he found Lily, his guiding star. He found friends, even the annoying human, Bridget, though he would never admit it to anyone. His life was better, more fulfilling than it had ever been, even when he was human himself.

"You're thinking really loud, babe. Everything okay?" Lily's sleepy voice floated through the dark. She burrowed herself closer to his chest, breath warm against his skin. If only he could pause the moment and keep her close to him in their bed without the fallout that would soon happen once she left her family's house.

"It will be soon, darling. I'm more worried about you. Are you ready for today?" He kissed the top of her head just below the rim of the silk cap that covered her beautiful curls while she slept.

She chuckled against him. "No, I am absolutely not ready at all. I haven't even allowed any visions through because I don't want to know how they are going to react; it'll just make me chicken out. And that's harder than it sounds. But I still have to face them and get my stuff."

"And then what?" he asked as he scooted his body over just a little and tilted her chin up to look at her.

Lily let out a deep, sleepy sigh. "And then I hide here for a while until it all blows over with my family and they love me again. That shouldn't take longer than a decade or two."

Albert immediately kissed her, hoping it would ease her anxiety. "They will never stop loving you, Lily. No matter what, your family will always love you. Just like I will always love you."

There was a flutter in his stomach as he said it. They had said I love you plenty of times over the course of their relationship, but for some reason, this felt like more.

It's because I want her to be my mate.

The thought surprised him, though he knew it shouldn't have. Loving Lily was the easiest thing in the world. It shouldn't scare him.

But it did.

Because though a witch lived an extended life, Lily would not live as long as he did. One day, he would have to let her go forever. He had never loved a human in his immortal life; it was all so new to him, all the feelings inside of what it meant to love someone with an expiration date.

"You're doing it again, babe." Lily moved to sit up and rubbed the sleep from her eyes. She was a bleary-eyed dream, and she looked at him with such love and concern that it physically hurt for him to look at her.

Albert suddenly realized it had been several moments since he had said anything to her. He was too lost in his own mind to focus on the present. "I'm sorry, darling. There's just a lot on my mind. But once you are all moved in, I know my mind will clear itself. Especially since I plan to keep you in our bed for many, many days."

Lily's smile was devious. "Clothed or unclothed?"

He returned her smile with a full-fanged grin. "Oh, my darling, how about I give you a taste?" With vam-piric ease, he flipped her under him and she squealed in delight as he showed her exactly what he planned to do once she was home again.

CHAPTER 5

"We should have done this when everyone was sleeping and I didn't have to face anyone," Lily whined as she and Brie climbed out of Ezra's latest vehicle, a large blue pickup truck with a crew cab—one that he most definitely didn't know how to drive well. Her hand was numb from clutching the handle.

Brie hefted an empty canvas bag over her shoulder. It was dingy from use and not much larger than a backpack. "That's the coward's way out, and since I know you are one of the bravest people ever, being a coward doesn't suit you. That's what Albert is for."

"He's not a coward. It's just we both agreed his coming along would cause more problems. You know how my mom gets." She had to at least defend Albert's honor.

Lily focused her attention on the bag to avoid talking about it further since she definitely wanted him to be with her for this, even though it was a bad idea. "Are you sure that's going to be big enough to hold my stuff? That'll hold maybe a drawer of clothes. I thought you said you were bringing boxes."

"Oh, it's more than enough. This is Gary Gygax's 'Bag of Holding.' This bad boy can fit basically everything and then some. Well, so long as it's not living." Brie gave the bag a pat like she was selling a used car.

"Who's Gary Gygax?" Lily asked.

Ezra sighed as he shut the truck door behind her. "Don't, please."

Brie shot him a look. "Ignore him. Gary Gygax was the creator of Dungeons & Dragons. One of the magic items in the game is a 'Bag of Holding,' which is like a pocket dimension you can carry. Which is what we have here." She patted the bag again for good measure.

"Oh, my Goddess, you're a total nerd, Brie." Lily laughed. "Why am I just now realizing this?" The trio started to walk toward the house, feet crunching against the gravel drive.

"One, you should have always known this since I'm willingly paying to go through a Ph.D. program in history. Two, Wes started hosting a game recently with that pixie who owns the bookstore and some of her friends. I got roped in as part of my sisterly duty. You should join us; it's on Wednesday nights." Brie flashed her a bright smile; Lily always had trouble saying no to anybody.

"Don't let her talk you into it. You'll be stuck going forever. The only thing that gets me out of games is council meetings, which have become *so* interesting lately," Ezra deadpanned, though the effect was ruined when he gave his girlfriend an affectionate gaze.

Brie bumped his thigh with her hip; she was too short to reach higher. "Ignore him. He loves it." Lily chuckled at the banter between her friends. Not that

Lily would ever take credit for their relationship, but she did spend months trying to convince the two idiots to just kiss each other before they finally got down to it. And even if Brie's smiles came out a little thinner since her ordeal in the winter, she still lit up around Ezra. And her oldest friend, Ezra, looked as if the ginger-haired woman hung the moon personally for him. It was the sweetest thing she could think of.

They reached the door of the Everett farmhouse. It was quiet on the other side, which was definitely not a good sign. The house was never quiet; there was always something happening within its walls.

I'm in some deep shit.

With a deep breath in and a slow exhale, Lily pushed open the door and led her friends inside. The lights were on throughout the house but remained silent as they entered. Knots twisted in Lily's stomach. The door clicked behind Ezra as he was the last through. Then her mother's voice called out, "Come to the kitchen, Lily." Her voice was thin and strained, and the summons to the kitchen was a bad omen. Only the most serious of topics were discussed in the kitchen. It was the beating heart of the Everett house, where all household debates were settled, important decisions made, and announcements were broadcasted. She didn't know the extent of what she would find in that room, but it was certainly going to be a major event in the Everett household.

"They are so going to disown me," Lily whispered to her friends. Brie gave her a tight smile as they walked through the house toward the kitchen, the only comfort she could offer.

Upon entering the room, though, it was so much worse than Lily had imagined.

Not only was her immediate family gathered, but so were her aunts, uncles, cousins, distant cousins, family friends, and of course, the rest of the coven.

It was standing room only, with one chair left ominously open at the table. "Have a seat, Lily. We have something to say." Her mother indicated the empty chair. All eyes were on Lily. She felt their judgment like a physical touch. The crackle of magic that radiated off several of the congregated made the hairs on her arm stand to attention.

A hand on each shoulder grounded her enough. One hand was small and warm, the other large and heavy. Brie and Ezra's touch gave her strength. She would get through this. She would face them all and soon enough would be home with Albert.

"Don't you think this is overkill, Mama?" Her voice was stronger than she felt. The wooden chair she took a seat on creaked at the added weight, but that wasn't new; everything in the house creaked from age.

Several of the elders assembled narrowed their gaze on her, their disapproval clear on their faces. "This is underkill if you ask me," her sister Rose muttered, arms crossed tightly over her chest, a scowl on her face. Beside her sat Manu with their daughter Violet on her lap. Manu looked at Lily with sad, sympathetic eyes. Manu, while she never directly said she approved, had told Lily on many occasions that she was happy for her. That was the best she could hope for from her sister-in-law, at least with Rose within earshot.

Hyacinth shot her eldest daughter a disapproving glare before she turned her attention back to her youngest. "Lily, we called the coven for support on this matter. We're worried for you, my sweet girl. We've indulged this dalliance you've had with that vampire for long enough. It's time for you to reevaluate your loyalties and see reason." Her mother's words were warm, not patronizing. Nobody could say she didn't care for her daughter. And Lily knew her mother was coming from a place of love. It was just misguided.

Lily's eyes moved around the room and took in the faces of the assembled. Noted right away was the absence of her granny and papaw. It wasn't at all surprising, especially since she didn't know what her grandparents' feelings were toward her relationship with Albert. If it was like the rest of her family's, they wouldn't approve. But she couldn't know, since neither shared with her.

She forced herself to look again at her mother. "What do you mean by 'reevaluate my loyalties,' Mama?" Lily had a good idea of what her mother meant, but she wanted her to say it in front of everyone.

Hyacinth frowned at her daughter. "You need to be with your own kind. You are a witch, Lily—from a long, prestigious line of witches. You should be with another witch, not wasting your time with a vampire."

"It's unnatural!" one of the elder coven members, Agnus, shouted. Not that she needed to; the room was eerily quiet; the woman was just almost completely deaf and shouted everything these days. There was a chorus of agreement from the other coven members. A pang of betrayal hit Lily directly in the heart.

These were people she had known her whole life, ones that had watched her grow, taught her how to use the magic that lived inside of her. And rather than be happy, or at least indifferent, here they were trying to make her feel shame for her whom she chose to love. They were trying to make her feel like a bad witch.

They will never be happy for me.

It was a sobering thought, one that broke her heart. "There's nothing unnatural about two people loving each other." Her voice was soft, softer than usual. Lily wasn't a demure person, but she would be lying to herself if she said she wasn't cowed a little by the weight of their judgment. Her whole life, she strove to make her family proud, to make her coven proud. Their disappointment weighed on her and part of her wanted to give in, to please them all, even if it destroyed all of her happiness. It was a defeatist thought, and Lily had never been a defeatist.

Rose snorted angrily through her nose. "Are you kidding me right now? Love? He's not even a person; he's a leech. And you are just food to him. Do you think he'll stay with you when you get old and withered? How many times have you let him bite you? Goddess, I can't even look at you knowing you let that bloodsucker drink from you."

"But I haven't. He's never bitten me. He hasn't even asked to. And I'm not saying we'll stay together forever. We love each other, but love isn't a guaranteed thing. So just let me live my life, please." If her voice was pleading, it was because she couldn't help it. They would have to restrain her or lock her in her room to keep her from going home to Albert. Before today, that wasn't something she would ever consider her family doing, but the looks on their faces, on everyone's faces, made her question everything she knew about them.

"Even if he hasn't, he will one day. And Lily, what's to stop him from draining you, killing you? We love you, and we want you to be happy. But there are better ways, better people to find love with. Just let us help you and we can find you a wonderful witch who will love and accept you just the way you are. Even with your romantic history." Her middle sister Ivy's voice was gentle and Lily knew it came from a place of love. But her words cut through Lily like a knife. Did Ivy mean that she was now somehow tainted for being with Albert? She had always been closer to Ivy than Rose since they were closer in age. Ivy had always been in her corner.

Until now.

"What's your problem? There's literally nothing wrong with her dating Albert. For fuck's sake, he looks at her like she's the center of the universe. It's almost nauseating how in love they are. You're all her family. You should be happy for her." Behind Lily's chair, Brie was outraged. Outraged for her. Brie gripped Lily's shoulder possessively, her shield against the onslaught.

The sharp eyes of the coven turned their attention to Brie. "This doesn't concern you. You may have been the host of our Lady, the Morrigan, once, but you are no longer. Humans have no business in witch affairs." A middle-aged witch with short blond hair sneered, but that was typical; Evelyn was a bitch on the best of days.

A raised hand from Hyacinth ceased further outbursts from all. "Brie, dear, I love you like one of my own, but this is a coven issue. I think it would be best for you and Ezra to leave."

"That's not going to happen, Hyacinth. Lily needs someone on her side, and I can vouch for Albert's character. I've lived longer than everyone in this room combined, and it is by no means unprecedented for a witch and vampire to form attachments." Ezra's voice took on an authoritative tone, one belied by his angelic power. The room seemed smaller, or maybe it was Ezra's power filling the room, Lily wasn't sure. But Ezra had been a figure in most of the lives of the assembled, even the most ancient of crones, and they knew his nature.

"This isn't a coven matter; it's a family matter. And we're family. So, we're staying for Lily." Brie kept her hand on Lily and Lily nearly wanted to cry from the relief it brought her.

"If the vampire wanted his character vouched for, he should have shown up himself. Faced the coven. Not cowered in his lair like a coward," Nona Ester rasped. She was the oldest person in attendance, though Lily's granny was the oldest in the coven. But as an elder, Nona Ester's opinion held the most weight. The room grumbled their agreement.

"He didn't come because he thought it would make it worse. And he was right. All of you would have torn him apart and not listened to a word he said. None of you have to like it, but you do have to accept that I will make my own choices. So long as it doesn't hurt the coven, why is it a problem?" Lily wanted to scream at the absurdity of the whole situation. But she didn't. She couldn't. If she showed any form of weakness or a shadow of defeat now, the coven would pounce on it.

"What has gotten into you, Lily? It isn't like you to be combative. You have always been the good-natured one in the family. You've always wanted what was best for the coven. It's why we chose you to train Brie when our Lady's spirit inhabited her." Her father sounded incredulous. Damien Everett was the heart of their family. Kind and soft-spoken. He was more prone to feed her than chat, and his kitchen magic was unparalleled. He and Lily had always shared a special bond. More than anyone else in the room, his look of disapproval hurt the most.

Her mother spoke next. "You don't see it, but this does hurt the coven. Our reputation with the rest of the Connecticut covens is strong, but there has been talk as of late. The other covens worry we don't have a firm hold on the area anymore. If we can't control one witch from opening the door to the destruction of our coven, how can we be a leader in the state's covens? Do you want to be responsible for bringing ruin on us all?"

Lily's whole body shook, her mother's words piercing through her like a shard of ice. She couldn't bring herself to look at anyone. The words were a shock to her. Never before had she considered that her relationship with Albert would bring into question the coven's stability.

Have I been so blind and selfish that I didn't see the strain around me?

No, she hadn't. Their coven had always been stable, had always been seen as a leader among the Connecticut covens, even the ones in Hartford. But was that reputation so fragile that her relationship with a vampire would destabilize it?

The slow tap tap of footsteps behind her drew her thoughts back toward the room. "Hyacinth Diana Everett, I will tolerate many things. But I will not tolerate lies." Her granny's scratchy voice seemed to fill the entire room, though she spoke at a normal volume. Her mother looked past Lily to gape at her own mother's entrance. It was surprising to see granny; she never involved herself in coven business unless she absolutely had to.

"Mamma, this doesn't concern you. Let me deal with it." Hyacinth tried to placate the older woman to no avail.

Granny stopped next to Lily's chair but didn't face her granddaughter. "The girl's love has nothing to do with the coven's reputation. I've heard of enough covens out there that don't mind intermingling one bit. And here you all are pushing medieval thinking on a young woman. Shame on you all. But especially shame on you, Hyacinth. I raised you better." Hyacinth had the good sense to look ashamed, and she averted her gaze from her mother's.

Now that her child was properly chastised, Granny turned her attention toward Lily. "The coven's reputation has nothing to do with you or your vampire. And everything to do with how the coven responded to that damn warlock last year. It is not your concern. Now, go pack up your stuff, girl. Your new home with your man awaits. As for the rest of you," Granny turned her attention back on the coven, "you all should be ashamed of yourselves. You all allowed that dangerous man to run loose, to threaten one of our own. It was your inactions that caused this coven to lose prestige. I'm disappointed in all of you."

Then, just as quickly as she had arrived, Granny was gone again. Lily sat in stunned silence for several long moments. The rest of the coven remained silent as well, not meeting each other's gazes or just simply staring at the floor. Her own family had a mix of emotions. Hyacinth looked properly ashamed even while Lily's father comforted her with tight hand squeezes. Ivy's face was covered by her hands and Lily couldn't tell how she was feeling. But it was Rose who had the worst reaction. She was seething. Lily could practically feel the anger roll off her sister in waves. Rose glared at Lily, eyes narrowed. Beside her, Manu's eyes were big and sad again. Lily didn't bother to look at the rest of the coven.

"Let's get out of here quick," Brie said next to her ear. Lily wasted no time lingering in the room. The three of them quickly left the kitchen, which exploded into noise and shouts the minute they cleared the threshold.

On the second floor, where Lily's room was, Lily, Ezra, and Brie began to place Lily's things in the Bag of Holding. It was quite the sight to see all of her things, no matter how big or small, easily disappear into the ratty old bag without effort. They didn't speak as they packed up. Lily wasn't even sure what she could say.

Sorry my family and coven staged a love intervention?

Yeah, no, the whole thing had been so bizarre. Now Lily just wanted to get out quickly. Things would be better once she was home with Albert.

She sighed deeply. She was already thinking of it as home.

Their home.

CHAPTER 6

Their first week living together should have been happy, full of shared meals that he would mostly watch her eat, cuddling up on the couch, and passionate sex in their bedroom.

But instead, it was quiet meals that Lily barely picked at, quiet snuggling on the couch where she was distant, and early mornings of Lily clutching him tightly in her sleep.

Then there were the apologies. So many apologies. Lily felt guilty for every emotion she had. Albert knew how upset she was with what had happened with her family. He didn't blame her for the sadness she felt. He just wished he could do more for her, comfort her better, fix what was damaged.

But he couldn't.

For one, her family didn't like him, and there was no way they would speak with him on Lily's behalf. Then there was the undeniable fact that Albert just wasn't good at comforting. Sure, he held Lily close, gave her all the physical affection he possibly could. It was the words that failed him. Feelings and emotions were not something he was taught to deal with. Not as a human in his strict family home and not as a vam-pire, where he was taught to just give in to whatever he desired and to stifle any other emotions.

The sound of her sniffles out in the garden brought him to the patio door. He clutched a glass of lemonade and a plate of coconut macaroons as he walked out toward the garden. If words failed him, he would use his own love language, food, to comfort her. Time and food were the best healers.

"Care for a snack, darling?" he asked and tried not to fixate on the tears Lily hastily dashed away.

Her eyes found the lemonade and cookies. "All that for me?" Her smile was bright, but it didn't meet her eyes. She tried to put on a front for his sake.

He waited until she took a sip from the lemonade before responding, "My NaiNai always said the best way to care for someone was to care for their stomach." The smile he gave her in return was big, with his fangs on full display. It always made her laugh, his white fangs showing through his grin and his dark brown eyes lit with mischief. But this time, all it earned him was another watery smile as she grabbed one of the macaroons.

"Darling, I–"

"I'm sorry, Bertie," she interrupted. "I know you're worried about me and you want me to stop apolo-gizing, but I'll be okay. Eventually. It's just hard for me to not be with them. They keep trying to contact me, but I'm not ready for all that yet. Just, please be patient with me."

He kissed her gently, trying to pour all the love and understanding he could into that one gesture. She was hurting, but he knew she didn't blame him. So, he would be her rock and hold her until she was strong enough and ready to face her family again. And hopefully, her family would come around, and even if they didn't accept him, maybe they could be okay with their relationship. But he wouldn't count on it, even if they knew it would make Lily happy. He had experienced enough discrimination in both his human life and vampiric life to know better than to hope.

When they parted, her wild curls were adorned with white orchids. He reached out with one long finger and brushed a petal. "What do these mean?"

Without pulling one out of her hair this time, she responded, "Orchids for an apology, strength, and enduring love. You give me strength and love, and I'm sorry I've ruined our first week of living together."

Cool hands cupped her cheeks. "Darling, you didn't ruin anything. We'll get through this together. And when things get better, when your family has calmed down, we will go see them together and make everything right again. We are a united front, and we should have been from the start."

Lily let out a soft giggle. "When did you get to be such an optimist?"

Albert sniffed with faux indignation. "I'm not. And don't you dare tell anyone that I am. It's your bad influence." He smiled at her again and brushed an errant tear from her cheek. "Let's go inside and watch a movie. Lady's choice." Albert led her into the house, where he covered her in blankets on their spacious couch. It was his job to take care of her, and he would give her his strength to face whatever came their way.

And when she fell asleep with her head on his shoulder, Albert hugged her closer, surrounding himself with the fragrant herbal scent of her dark curls.

"You're late," Brie deadpanned as Albert walked into the shop. She held out his customary envelope. He took it and handed her his own envelope with the payment inside.

"Charming as always, Bridget," he snarked. Rationally, he knew he should be nicer to Lily's best friend. But this had been their repertoire for so long that to change it now seemed disingenuous. He liked the human well enough, even if, at first, he enjoyed frightening and antagonizing her. Now that he and Lily were living together, he assumed he would be seeing more of Bridget.

The annoyance melted from Brie's face in an instant; she also was not in the mood for banter. "How's she doing? I know I just talked to her yesterday, but this has been really hard for her." The worry in her voice was clear.

Lily is lucky to have her as a friend. What his lovely girl needed right now was people who cared for her.

"Better than last week, but I believe this is the longest she has gone without speaking to her family and it's taking its toll." They weren't confidantes, but he found himself continuing, "The only thing I've been able to do is feed her. It's the only thing I'm good at when it comes to comforting."

The human gave him a pensive look, like she was absorbing the information he just gave. Albert was used to people staring. No matter how much he tried to hide his ghostly pallor, people still would do a double take passing him on the street. The magical community was still wary of vampires, and the humans in the city seemed to think he was an oddity or a weirdo.

But that wasn't the look he was getting from Brie. No, she looked at him now like not only did she absorb his words but was trying to deduce if they really came from him. He supposed he couldn't blame her; it wasn't like they ever talked about their feelings to one another. Or really anything personal, for that matter. The closest they had ever come to being almost friendly was when Albert was part of the group, led by Ezra, to save Brie from the warlock Moloc last winter. Coming back from the dead could have that effect on people.

Other people, anyway. When it was him, though he didn't exactly come back alive, he felt less endeared to the vampire who brought him back. Sorrow and rage were all he knew as he stared at the rubble that had once been his city, as he stood before what used to be his childhood home, seeing nothing but tumbled bricks and splintered wood. At least for a time, he felt that way. But his maker was persuasive and showed Albert all the wonders of being a vampire and how attachment to the human world only weighed him down. And he had lived that life for so long, he sometimes still wondered if he made the right choice in rejecting that life. It was simpler.

"Well, food is a love language; nothing brings more comfort." Bridget's voice drew him from his own thoughts. He had forgotten for a second what they had been saying. "I think it's the coven keeping her family away. They spouted a bunch of bullshit about your relationship hurting the coven's reputation. Really, though, they are just a bunch of bigoted old crones." The conviction in her tone was inspiring. She really did care for Lily and her family. Whether they got along or not, Brie still defended Lily and his relationship.

Albert suspected much of the same but had so far refrained from sharing that idea with Lily. Her coven was just as part of her family as her blood relations. But she knew her parents and sisters loved her and the only way they wouldn't reach out was because the coven was preventing them from doing so.

"I fear you might be right. I just don't know what I can do to fix this other than to let her go, and I am far too selfish for that." That was the most honest thing he had ever said to the human, and it wasn't horrible to admit.

"Lily will make her own decision. Don't make it for her," Brie cut in before he could say anything further. She was right, of course. If Lily wanted to be done with him for the sake of her family and coven, that would be her decision. He would never purposefully push her away for her own good. He simply loved her too much.

I've lost so much of what I love in my long life.

Albert decided to direct the conversation elsewhere; he and Brie had started to get too chummy. "Where's Ezra?" His voice was indifferent again.

Brie shot a thumb over her shoulder to indicate the Storage Room door. "Inventory. Though, it's probably pointless since he has so much stuff and just keeps getting more. Do you want me to get him?" She started to pull what looked like a seashell from her pocket; the "shell phone," as she called it, much to Ezra's chagrin.

Albert waved the shell phone away. "No, that's quite alright. I should head home to Lily. Hm, thank you for this." He held up the envelope that contained the contact information for a willing and contracted blood donor. It was his way of feeding. More ethical and safe than just preying on unsuspecting mortals and killing them. At least these mortals knew what they were getting into, and he only took what he needed, easing them into death if they wanted. Many did.

"Ew, don't be nice; it's weird." She wrinkled her nose as if even the idea of it repulsed her, though she had a slight grin on her lips. She made a shooing motion with her hands and Albert left without another word. His focus was on getting home to Lily.

Lily was in her garden as usual when he arrived back at their house. The moonlight in her hair gave the wild curls an ethereal shine. With her hands in the dirt and her eyes closed in concentration as she poured magic into the roots, she looked like a goddess—like Gaia herself, breathing life into the earth.

Below her palms, green sprouts started to push through the soil. In a low voice, Lily chanted a spell, working her magic to give the plants resistance to disease and weather. Her magic would give the plants a head start, but then she would let them grow on their own. The magical properties worked better when they grew naturally, or so Lily said.

Albert was still learning about the various plants Lily grew. She tried to teach him about all of her beloved greenery, but Albert still struggled with most of them. He was more familiar with the language of flowers. But he did know her plants were sought after for all sorts of magical workings. Even with the turmoil with her family and coven, orders for her plants and herbal preparations were steady. So at least the coven wasn't punishing her business; they just wouldn't speak to her. He did have plenty of money to care for her every whim, if she needed.

"Are you just going to stand there staring at me, Bertie?" Lily didn't open her eyes or move her head at all.

He realized he had indeed been staring at her for several minutes, unmoving at the patio door, mesmerized by her movements. With graceful steps, he moved toward her but said nothing. He kept his movements slow, forcing himself to walk at a mortal pace, though he longed to be by her side in an instant.

When he finally reached her, he knelt in the dirt, for once in his life not caring whether his clothes got dirty. Albert was by nature meticulous about his appearance. But with Lily, kneeling in the dark earth was expected. He wrapped his arms around her middle from behind and rested his chin on her shoulder while he nuzzled against her hair. There was no way to avoid a face full of her curls when he did this, and he wouldn't have it any other way. The heady scent of summer blooms and soft rain was intoxicating and so very Lily.

After a moment, the magic dissipated and Lily leaned her body back, dropped her head, and leaned against the hard planes of Albert's chest. "I should take you right here, surrounded by dirt and magic. I've heard plants respond well to music. Why don't I make you sing, my darling?" he whispered into her ear as he let one hand travel up her body to cup her breast. She responded with a low moan and arched her back. Lily was definitely enjoying herself.

"That," she sighed, "was a terrible line, Bertie." She said nothing further as he began to trace kisses against her neck. A kiss to the spot behind her ear had her squirming, and he felt bold enough to move his other hand farther down toward the waistband of her shorts. Not overalls this time, which made him grateful for easier access.

She stopped his hand before he could do more. "Bertie, stop, please." He instantly removed his hands and pulled just far enough away to give her space, but not enough to make her think he was leaving.

A little awkwardly, she turned on her knees to face him. The desire in her eyes faded just as quickly, and he knew something had happened while he was gone. "Lily, what happened?" He cupped her cheeks and looked deeply into her dark hazel eyes, searching for answers.

Instantly, her eyes turned watery and tears threatened to spill at any moment. "Ivy called me. It's the longest I've gone without hearing from her. She wants to meet up tomorrow."

"That's good news, right? You miss her. Why wouldn't you want to see her?" He pushed one hand into her hair and tangled his fingers in her soft curls.

"What if she hates me?" Lily averted her gaze from his and a few tears escaped down her cheeks, but she made no attempt to brush them away.

With a tug on her wrist, Albert pulled her into an embrace. Her arms wrapped around him and she clutched tightly to him like he was a lifeline, the only thing keeping her from drifting off into a sea of anxiety. The floodgates opened then, and she cried in great, heaving sobs. His shirt soaked through in moments, but the only thing he cared about was comforting the woman he loved. If only he could hold all her pieces together just by keeping her in his arms, he would dedicate his life to the task.

"Nobody could ever hate you, my darling. You are too sweet. Ivy loves you. Perhaps she just misses you or is willing to talk to the coven. You should go see her." He debated whether to ask her if she wanted him to go as well, but held his tongue. If she wanted him to go, she would ask. Only if she didn't ask before the meeting, then he would offer. Lily likely just wanted the time with her sister.

Lily's tears began to slow, and her breathing started to come under control. "I said I would meet her. I want to see her. It's just, for the first time in my life, I'm really fighting with my family, and I don't know what I'm supposed to do." She looked tired and so defeated. Albert hated what the coven had done to her. Lily was a bright star, one that lit up a room just by walking into it. And they had diminished her just because she chose to love him. *I don't deserve her. But that doesn't mean I'll give her up.*

The kiss he gave her was sweet and tender, with none of the lust from minutes before. At that moment, all he wanted to do was tell her that he would be with her, that they would get through it all together. But what he could not say in words, he put into the kiss, hoping she would understand.

"Let me feed you," Albert said as he pulled them into a standing position. Lily's laugh was loud, and she sounded like herself for a moment.

"Kind of feels like you are trying to fatten me up, and I don't really need any more of that." She poked her stomach for emphasis. Lily was curvy in all the right places, curvy and perfect.

Albert slung an arm around her waist and pulled her close as they walked back into the house. "I absolutely love your body. Besides, food is my love language, so I am going to keep feeding you, darling."

At the patio door, he let Lily go through first before stepping behind her. Then, he froze. A feeling was at the back of his mind, like he was being watched. There was a familiarity in the feeling, like something once known intimately and was now forgotten. No, it was something he had not forgotten, just chose not to think about. He turned to look over his shoulder, quickly scanning the dark yard for movement.

"Bertie? Are you coming in?" Lily's voice drew him back, and he turned to focus on her.

"Sorry, yes, I'm coming." He closed the door behind him and stared through the window for half a second more into the darkness beyond, knowing, but not seeing, that something lurked nearby. Something he had not seen in a long time.

CHAPTER 7

Lily had been standing outside the cafe for fifteen minutes already. She had texted Ivy five minutes prior that she was almost there, needing the extra time to center her thoughts. Her sister sent back a thumbs-up emoji.

Before she left the house, Albert offered to go with her. It wasn't that she didn't want to ask him to come along necessarily, but since it was the middle of the day, it would have been tricky to get him to the café and she didn't want to put him at risk. Then there was Ivy. Lily really had no idea how her sister would respond if Albert were there. So, she insisted she go alone. It was the safest route to take. Albert had convinced her to take her Lorazepam before she left, and she was thankful for that because before she was even out the door, she could feel her anxiety rising to critical levels.

Though now, as she stood outside the cafe, she wasn't sure the anxiety medication would be enough. Maybe she could have found a way to make it work so Albert could be with her. At least then she could draw on his strength. It would have been better to meet her sister together and maybe win her to their side. Not that Ivy had much sway in the coven, but she could talk to the family, and they would have one more person in their corner.

The vision that came to her during breakfast was less than helpful in determining what to expect. There was no sound to the vision, just the image of her talking to someone at a table. She couldn't see the other person, but Lily had been smiling a little, though she didn't look quite in focus enough. There was no way to know if the meeting with Ivy was going to go well or end in total disaster. And her vision had done nothing to assuage her fears. Most of her visions lately hadn't been particularly helpful in divining the future, or the present, for that matter.

Maybe all this stress is messing up my gift.

With that thought and one more deep breath, Lily opened the door and walked into the café. The place was fairly busy; there were no open tables that she could initially see. She scanned the crowd for her sister but didn't see her. Maybe Lily got there first. She headed for the counter to order a latte and hoped that would kill enough time for Ivy to show up.

But as she stepped up to the counter, she was intercepted by a tall, boxy man. He had chocolate-colored hair and bright green eyes, and his light skin was just tan enough to show he had spent a considerable amount of time outside. He was handsome in a conventional sense, and Lily felt her neck strain as she stared up at him. *Maybe tall is an understatement. Yeah, crush my ribcage, you load-bearing behemoth.*

"Hi, are you Lily?" he asked with a gentle smile. His voice was deep and charming, with just a hint of a Boston accent. The voice/smile combo was perfectly made to immediately make him charming and trustworthy, and it was almost working.

Lily took a half step back. "Yes?" She wasn't going to let her panic ratchet any higher, but it was hard not to when a giant of a man she had never met somehow knew her name. No matter how smiley and friendly he made himself appear.

"Sorry, I'm Cameron. I'm Ivy's friend. Hope you don't mind; I already ordered us some lattes. Ivy told me what you liked, so I have a hazelnut latte with almond milk over at my table." He indicated the table behind him, which did, in fact, have two paper cups sitting on top. But that still didn't make the situation any clearer.

"Well, that's very nice of you." She tried not to sound suspicious. At first blush, Cameron seemed very friendly and open. And he knew Ivy. But that didn't mean he was trustworthy.

"Here, let's sit down. I'm hoping we can get to know each other." His smile was blindingly white and so wide that a little crinkle appeared at the top of his nose. It was, admittedly, adorable. Lily let him usher her toward the table with the coffees. He pulled out a chair for her and didn't take his own seat until she was situated.

Lily immediately began to fidget with the paper cup, not taking a drink. "So, how do you know Ivy?" That seemed like a good conversation starter while they waited for her sister to arrive. Though why she sent Cameron ahead to meet her was a mystery.

Cameron took a large gulp from his cup before responding. Now that he was seated, he looked a little nervous, and the chair seemed too small to hold him; he was just a solidly large guy. "Oh, we went to college together. And now she's a regular here. I supply all the baked goods for this place." The nervousness dissipated for a moment, and his whole face lit up with pride. Lily already felt herself relaxing in Cameron's presence. He was clearly one of those people that instantly made you feel at ease. He was a lot like her in that regard.

And then realization hit her, and she frowned. "Cameron, I don't mean to be rude, but is this supposed to be a date?"

His smile slowly fell from his lips and Lily found herself feeling guilty about that. A self-conscious hand rubbed the back of his head. "Oh, wow, am I that out of practice? Sorry, it's been a while. But yes, Ivy said she wanted to set us up. She said you were looking for a serious relationship, and I've been looking to settle down. I come from an old witch family, if you're worried about that. I'm sorry. Again, it's been a while. I have completely embarrassed myself, haven't I?"

The poor man just couldn't seem to stop himself. So, Lily took pity on him. "Listen, Cameron, I think that we've both been misled. I thought I was meeting Ivy to talk. I'm actually already in a loving and committed relationship."

Cameron's eyes went wide. "But then why would she try to set us up? Unless you are polyamorous.

Which is totally fine," he added quickly. "It's just not something I'm into. Totally monogamous here."

Lily finally took a sip of her latte to calm herself and collect her thoughts. "No, it's nothing like that. It's just that, well, my whole coven doesn't approve of who I'm dating." She paused, unsure if she should divulge anything further. Cameron was, after all, a stranger.

What if he's one of those old-school crazies, too?

No, she wasn't going to hide Albert from anyone. "Because he's a vampire." Her eyes met Cameron's, and she fixed him with an unflinching gaze, daring him to say something. But then he surprised her by smiling again.

"The heart wants what the heart wants. Not sure why your coven would have an issue, though. Witches have been on decent terms with vamps for a while now. Heck, I dated a vamp for a bit back in college. Schedule gets weird, but I had afternoon classes and had plenty of time to see him after. My coven never had a problem with that."

She found herself gaping at Cameron. Not only did he not care that she was a witch dating a vampire, but he himself was a witch who had dated vampires before. And the world didn't end. Ivy thought she was setting her and Cameron up to date and fall in love. That wasn't going to happen, of course. But Lily knew she was going to get more out of this meeting than her sister realized.

"Cameron, I'm sorry my sister got you here under a false pretense. But I think she did introduce me to a new friend, if that's okay with you?" She gave him her winningest smile. Her mother always called it her magic smile. For the first time in days, it wasn't forced.

Cameron grinned back and that adorable crinkle on his nose changed his whole face. "I would like that very much, Lily. I promise I am a lot less awkward in friend mode than I am in flirting mode."

Lily's responding laugh was infectious, and Cameron began laughing, too. "You sound like my friend Wes. He is the most awkward person until he gets to know you. Well, I won't keep you any longer. I've already wasted your time. I have a loud, angry phone call to my sister to make. Not because of you. You are great and I'm glad I got to meet you. But this was low for her. Let's trade numbers, and Albert and I can have you over for dinner sometime. Promise we won't try to bring you into our polyamorous fold. Which, again, totally not our thing." They both laughed again as they exchanged numbers.

Then she was back on the sidewalk outside the shop, cursing Ivy's name.

The door slammed shut behind her as she stomped into the house. She didn't bother trying to muffle the noise she made. Albert would be up anyway, wanting to know how things went with Ivy. She doubted he bothered to sleep at all; he had been sleeping less overall.

She found him in the living room, all the drapes shut tight to block out the afternoon sun. He stood from the couch where he had clearly been watching reruns of *Criminal Minds* again at her entrance. Worried eyes turned toward her. "How did it g–"

His words cut off abruptly when Lily quickly crossed the room and smashed her lips against his. There was nothing tender in her kiss. It was about claiming him. She reached up and held the back of his neck and pulled him closer. Cool hands rested against her waist, but she needed more.

As her tongue traced the seam of his mouth, waiting for him to open in response, she pushed her body flush against his. She wanted no space between them. As their tongues mingled, she moved her hand from his neck and let it trace down his shoulder, his chest, his stomach, and still lower.

She used both hands to open the button of his black slacks. He pulled away just enough to speak. "Darling, what's going on?"

But she didn't want to talk. She was too over-whelmed, too angry, too much of everything. The only thing she wanted now was him. "Take off your clothes," she ordered and stepped back just enough to give him room.

The lust in his eyes cooled slightly as he looked her over, the concern returning. "Lily, I think–"

But she cut him off again. "Take off your clothes, Albert. Please. I need this." Lily was tired of being nice, of accepting things because that was what was expected of her. Right now, she wanted to take charge of her life and not let anyone mess her around. But she wouldn't push Albert into doing anything with her. Not like that.

Something in her eyes must have said it all to Albert because he began to slowly undress without another word. Too slow for her liking, but he kept his movements languid like he was teasing her. Even now, following her directions, he didn't give up control.

When he stood before her, clad in nothing save his watch, she stared and stared and stared. Albert was tall, lean and had sharp planes and angles all over his body. His skin was white as death, which was the norm for vampires, but it gave him an unholy kind of beauty. His dark amber eyes were almost completely eclipsed by his blown-out pupils. His usual pristine black hair was already tousled from her hands and probably his own worrying earlier. It now hung in long wisps around his forehead and ears.

With a reach into her magic, she pushed it out to shove Albert onto the couch. A small oomph escaped his lips and his eyes were wide. Never in her life had Lily been so assertive when it came to sex, but right now, she needed something she had a measure of control over. Something that didn't make her life feel like it was crumbling before her eyes. Now, with Albert naked and willingly at her mercy, she felt powerful and sexy.

Lily mentally congratulated herself for wearing a dress today as she shimmied off her underwear. The length of him responded to her, and she felt a surge of pride that she could so easily elicit a response from him.

"Darling, please." He wasn't begging, he was demanding, because Lily hadn't moved. Instead, she stood before him, just out of reach with her dress still on.

His command turned her on even more, and she decided to ease his torture, if only a little. With more grace than she usually had, she glided to the couch and straddled Albert's lap. Though vampires didn't need to breathe, it was something Albert still did, if only to appear more human. And now he took a sharp intake of breath as she lowered herself down, letting him just brush against her entrance.

His arms slipped around her, holding tight to her hips. Lily responded by sliding one hand into his hair while her other pressed against his chest. She fisted the strands and pulled just enough to tilt his head back, keeping him on the line of pain and pleasure. "Tell me you're mine, Albert." It came out sounding desperate. She barely recognized herself; maybe she was desperate to know she was loved.

The hands on her hips squeezed tighter. She was sure they would leave bruises and that sent her head spinning further into an all-consuming lust. "I'm yours forever, my darling." His voice was husky as he looked at her like she was the moon itself.

It was all Lily needed to hear as she adjusted her seat to slowly sink down onto him. They both moaned loudly once he was sheathed to the hilt. There was a little discomfort at first because even though she was extremely turned on, she wasn't quite ready for him. But Lily pushed the discomfort aside and focused on the feel of Albert inside her.

"Darling, please move. I need you to move." He threw his head back against the couch and closed his eyes. She rolled her hips once, and his accompanying groan was the sweetest reward she could ask for. There was something powerful and sensual about her being mostly clothed while he was completely bared to her.

The rhythm of her downward thrusts quickened. "Look at me, Bertie. I want to see your eyes when I make you come." Goddess, what possessed her to sound like that?

"I'm going to touch you now," he choked out as he stared deep into her eyes. When she gave him a small nod, he brought one hand between her legs and began to rub at that bundle of nerves that sent her head reeling. His fingers were deft, bringing her to the precipice of her pleasure in seconds. The surge of magic within her was almost overwhelming and she could just see the red camellias blooming in her hair. *A flame in my heart—that's what he is to me.*

Then she was there, pitching over the edge of ecstasy. As her brain whited out in starbursts, she surged forward and bit him hard on the junction where his shoulder and neck met. His responding roar filled the entire room and he exploded within her.

Lily's body slumped against his. A sheen of sweat covered her, but he was still cool to the touch. He always would be.

Plush lips moved up and down her neck, planting kisses and sucking on her pulse points. He wouldn't bite her back, and she didn't know whether to be disappointed or relieved.

Relief won out. Biting and sharing her blood just weren't for her.

"You'll be the death of me, darling. That was incredible," Albert breathed against her neck, bestowing one final kiss before pulling back to look into her hazel eyes.

"Technically, you are already dead. But semantics and whatnot. Thank you for that. I really needed it." She found herself blushing all of a sudden. The sexually bold Lily slowly faded, and now she felt a cold dread settling low in her stomach.

Slowly, she lifted herself off his lap and settled on the couch next to him, not caring if there was a mess. He tucked her close, slinging an arm around her shoulders, still completely naked. "What was that all about, Lily? What happened today?" With his fingers stroking her arm, she relaxed into his embrace and settled her head on his chest.

"Ivy didn't show up. But the very nice witch she was trying to set me up with did. Nothing happened. I told him I was unavailable, obviously. He seemed very nice, and I think we could be good friends, but I'm so mad at my sister. She won't answer my calls or texts because she knows she fucked up. But that's not the point. It's just ... why can't they just let us be happy? Why did my sister resort to underhanded tactics? Did she actually think that would work? That Cameron would sweep me off my feet and I would just leave you? Yeah, let me just ghost the love of my life for some awkward dude I just met." It all came out in a rush; there was just so much inside her and her thoughts were overwhelming.

Albert's hand absentmindedly moved to her hair, and he wrapped a curl around one long white finger. "Was he more handsome than me?" She heard the laugh in his voice, though it sounded strained.

She lightly smacked him in the chest with the back of her hand. "I don't need to stroke your ego. But no, you are more handsome. Though you both are equal levels of awkward."

"How about I get on my knees and show you just how not awkward I can be for you, my darling?" This time, she looked up and saw the large grin on his face.

She laughed, full-bodied and light. "How about you feed me first and then maybe you can eat?"

His grin turned predatory, with his fangs on full display. "That sounds like a deal."

CHAPTER 8

As they lay in their bed close to dawn, Lily wrapped up tightly in his arms, Albert felt it again. The sensation that something was watching them. Watching him. And it felt so familiar. No, that wasn't right. It didn't feel familiar—it *was* familiar. He would know that presence anywhere.

Somewhere close by, his maker was watching him, stalking him in the night. And not just him, but the rest of his vampiric family, who once long ago he called his brothers and sisters. It had been thirty years since he left, but it seemed they had found him at last.

He easily disentangled himself from Lily's sleeping form, pulled on his discarded pants, and walked outside to the back garden. A figure stood in the predawn darkness between the trees.

"Albert Hsu, as the night is long. It has been an age," the voice said with a polished English accent. Though Albert could not say from where his maker originated, he knew the accent was more an affectation.

"Simon. It has been too long and yet, I find, not long enough." Albert crossed his arms tightly over his bare chest as he stared at the other man. Despite being a vampire for centuries, longer than even Albert knew, Simon still had a hint of the sun-kissed skin he must have had as a mortal. Pale blue eyes that could show unending caring, but could just as quickly turn into sharp chips of ice that could cut just by look alone, were framed by long dark lashes. Thirty years ago, he wore his dirty blonde hair in wavy, chin-length curls, but now it was styled short to his ears and expertly tousled to appear no time went into it. His style hadn't changed much—a white v-neck t-shirt with a black vest buttoned over the top and black jeans slung low on his hips. Too many necklaces hung around his neck, and small gold bands wrapped seven of his fingers. One gold ring for every vampire he had made. Albert had been the sixth, which meant that Simon had already replaced him with a new child.

Simon tsked, a patronizing sound that Albert had heard often in his younger years. "Is that how you greet an old friend? I thought your manners were better than that?"

Albert wouldn't give this man an inch. "We are not friends, Simon. That was made pretty clear when I left."

"True. Then, is that how you greet your lover?" Simon's fangs flashed in a grin. He was a man who liked to play games.

"I have a lover, and it's not you," Albert shot back too quickly. He cursed himself because, of course, Simon was goading him, and he had just given away his weakness. Not that Simon didn't already know if they had been casing his house for a while. Simon would know everything by now.

That full-fanged smile of Simon's took on a shade of malice. "Yes, I know. The little witch. Really, Albert? How low you have fallen since you left us. Word is that you no longer kill, either. I thought I made you harder than that."

Albert's spine stiffened. If Simon even hinted at a threat against Lily, he would end him right there in the garden. "Keep away from her, Simon," he growled, making his threat clear with every syllable.

"Oh, Albert, such dramatics. I have no interest in your little witch. Not yet, anyway. What I want is you. Come see us tomorrow night at the Hotel Nosferat. We have so much catching up to do." Simon gave him one more dangerous smile, and then he was gone. Simply gone. Disappeared before Albert's eyes.

For several minutes, Albert stood in the garden, trying to collect his thoughts. The encounter with his maker after so many decades had left him more shaken than he wanted to admit, even to himself.

He would have to go, of course. He shouldn't. But he needed to. As much as he didn't want to heap more complications on Lily, he would have to tell her about Simon's visit and what he planned to do. And she would most definitely insist on going with him. But that was simply too dangerous. Simon would have no qualms about hurting Lily just to get to Albert, and he would do it right in front of Albert without issue.

Using his vampire speed, he raced inside, found his mobile phone in their bedroom, and was back in the kitchen before the door even finished closing to their room. He pulled up the number he needed and dialed.

A clear voice answered because the person on the other end didn't sleep either.

"Ezra, I need your help."

Lily awoke later than usual. She came down to the kitchen after ten. Albert had used that time to make her a large brunch. They had a lot to talk about and everything was done better over food. At least, that was how his family always did it. His human family. Every major event was told over a heavily ladened table prepared by his mother and grandmother.

"Ugh, why did you let me sleep so long?" She stretched her arms up above her head as she walked into the room. Albert had heard her moving around a few minutes before, so the table was already set for her arrival.

He walked over to her while she was still in her sleep shorts and tank top and handed her a cup of coffee. "I thought it best to let you sleep. Yesterday was a lot." He kissed the top of her head. She sighed and leaned her head against his chest for a moment while he wrapped her up in a one-armed embrace. Then her eyes settled on the food.

"Are you feeding an army this morning?" She marveled over all the dishes, and he watched with pride as her eyes jumped from delicacy to delicacy. He really did enjoy cooking, even though the food did little for him. Nothing pleased him more, though, than feeding Lily.

He pulled a chair out for her and waited until she sat before joining her at the table. She filled a plate with a little of everything and began to eat. Albert said nothing until she had devoured half of the contents on her plate.

"Darling, there's something I must tell you. And it won't be very pleasant. I need you to just sit there and enjoy the food, though. That is non-negotiable. If you have questions, I will answer them." Albert straightened in his seat. Though he longed to reach for her, it was for the best if he composed himself enough to get through it.

Lily stared at him with trepidation. She set down her fork and watched him intently. Albert gave her fork a pointed look and then shifted his gaze back to her. She took the hint and continued to eat, albeit slowly.

"I was visited last night by Simon, my maker. It was brief, but he wants to meet with me tonight, and I assume the rest of his brood will be there as well." He didn't break eye contact with her, wanting to see her full reaction.

Her brow furrowed. "Are you going? I know you left them a long time ago, but you never told me why."

Dread flooded through him. He was prepared for this because, of course, she would want to know. Deserved to know the whole story. "Yes, I'm going. I... I think I need closure. My departure was abrupt, and to be frank, I hid from them for many years. I didn't want to be found." He ran a hand through his hair, mussing it up but not caring.

"Why, though? Aren't they like your family? Isn't that how vampires work?" She truly knew little about vampire customs. Judging from her family's reaction to their relationship, he wasn't surprised. He doubted very much that the Everetts put much stock in teaching their children vampire lore.

The sigh was deep and reflexive, but he knew he needed to press on. "First, you should know that this is all in my past. I've had no contact with any of them in thirty years. I want you to understand this so you don't question how much I love you." He hesitated. It wasn't like she wasn't aware that he had had lovers before. He was over one hundred years old; of course, he had. And he knew he was not her first, either. They just never discussed it before, and for the most part, he planned to keep it that way.

Lily rested a warm hand on his forearm. "Bertie, you can tell me anything. Your past is your past, and it doesn't affect us now." She smiled so warmly that his heart melted a little at the sight. Guilt hit him like a punch to the gut because he hadn't told her that Simon had basically threatened her.

He covered her hand with his own. "Simon was not only my maker, but we were lovers for many years. Under his direction, I did a lot of terrible things because I would do anything for him back then." He paused again and averted his gaze. How could he look her in the face as he told her of his past romance and all the terrible things he did?

"Did you love him?" Her voice was low, but not judgmental.

Eyes on the floor, he responded, "Yes, I did. At the time, he was all I had. Him and the family. He was my whole world since I had nothing left in it. At Simon's instruction, all beings were ours to drain. I killed so many. And I didn't discriminate on my kills. Men, women, even children. Simon told us they were ours for the taking and I believed him. He encouraged me to embrace my bloodlust, and it was so easy to give in. There was no rational thought when I was like that. I was a monster. I am a monster."

Tears welled up in his eyes, but he didn't deserve to cry. No matter how repentant he was now, he relished in the blood, in the killing. It was enjoyable. It was like a drug, and he was addicted. And even though he had changed for the better, worked every day to be better, he would always know what it felt like. He would always crave it a little.

Lily said nothing, waiting for him to continue at his own speed. Her hand remained where it was, and she gave his arm a little squeeze for comfort.

"I killed witches. So many witches. Simon drilled into us that witches were our enemy, that they would use sun magic to kill us on sight, so we had to destroy them first. But I know now it was only Simon's personal vendetta against witches. He used us, used me, to exact his vengeance." Albert never questioned Simon's hatred toward witches; none of them did.

There was silence for several agonizing moments when he paused again, unable to go on until she said something. But he still couldn't look at her, too afraid to see her judgment, her disgust.

The hand on his arm slipped away, and he closed his eyes to wait for her to leave. She probably should leave. But then Lily's arms were around him, holding him close to her body.

He turned his face toward her stomach, wrapped his arms tightly around her waist, and hid his shame. Her cheek rested on the top of his head and she just held him, saying nothing.

"I enjoyed it then. I still think about the high of the kill even now. Every time I feed, I think about taking just a little too much because I know how satisfying it can be. But the regret is always there. Simon may have molded me into being his creature, but I made those choices. I chose to kill, to murder, and I let myself enjoy every moment. I don't want to be that creature again," he choked out. His face remained buried against her and she didn't lessen her hold on him.

"You're a good man, Albert. You made the choice to walk away and have tried every day to be better. Simon can't touch you now. You're under my protection. And Bertie," she lifted her head and pulled him away just enough to cup his cheeks and draw his eyes up to hers, "I will do everything I can to keep you safe from others and from yourself if I need to. I love you."

It was too much. This woman loved him with every fiber of her being, and he didn't feel worthy of her love. But of course, he would take every ounce of it, anyway. She was his sun when all he had was darkness.

"I don't deserve you, my darling," he finally managed to say, reveling in the feeling of her warm hands against his skin.

She laughed loudly, breaking the gloom that had infiltrated the room. "Of course you do, love. Now, about tonight, I'm coming with you. No offense, but I definitely don't trust Simon around you."

"Do you trust me around Simon?" Lily still held his face in her hands and Albert couldn't bring himself to avert his eyes from hers. He wanted her to look into what was left of his soul and see his truth. That he loved her, that she could trust him to handle the demons of his past, that he would do anything to keep her safe. That he would never betray her.

Her lips pressing against his brought him out of his own head, and he let himself forget all doubts, all concerns about Simon, and focus solely on Lily. It was a slow and passionate kiss, his favorite. Without words, she told him how much she trusted him around Simon. Soft lips and an exploring tongue told him how much she loved him. Gentle fingers sliding into his hair told him that she claimed him as her own. Soft breaths against his cheek as she pulled away told him he was everything.

"Just let me know when it's time to meet Simon. We'll go together, okay? I love you." She kissed him on the forehead and drifted out to her garden before he had a chance to say anything further. He sat there in silence for a long time, filled with worry and guilt, while the memories of his past haunted him.

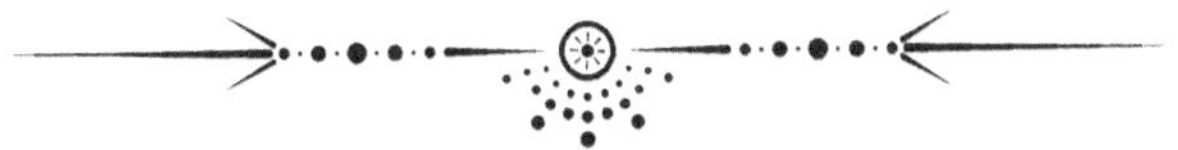

As the sun finished setting, Albert and Lily climbed into his car. The second love of his life was his car, a 1955 Mercedes SL300 with gullwing doors. He bought it brand new as a treat for himself and he just never had the heart to get another. It was his pride and joy, even now when it cost a fortune to get repairs done.

Lily hated it. More accurately, she hated Albert's driving in that car.

"Can't we take my car, Bertie?" she begged as they climbed into the sleek silver vehicle.

Albert gave the dashboard an affectionate pat. "Don't listen to her, baby. There's no other car with your style."

"There are no seatbelts, Albert. This thing is a death trap!" Even as she shrieked at him, she conjured up her own makeshift seatbelt with a quick spell. She did the same to Albert, though he didn't see the point. Even if they wrecked, which they wouldn't, because he was an excellent driver, he would be fine.

He pulled out of their driveway and headed down the street before turning to flash her a grin. "Well, I'm already dead, so I'll go out with my beloved automobile." She laughed as they continued to drive, though her hand gripped the handle tightly. But the sound forced a leaden ball to the pit of his stomach.

Before they had left, he had tried to convince her not to go with him. Begged her to stay so he could face Simon on his own. But she had insisted, "I don't trust this guy. I don't want him to just like abduct you," she had said. There had been a smile on her face, though Albert saw through her false bravado. He had planned for this, though. He just hadn't told Lily yet.

"Mind if we make a stop at Spirit? I need to speak with Ezra before meeting Simon," he asked, but his eyes remained on the road, so he couldn't look at her. She would see the worry on his face. Lily could read him so easily. As a vampire, he always thought he had a stoic look, a good poker face, as they say. Not when it came to Lily; she could see through it all as if he was speaking it aloud to her.

"Sure, that's fine." Lily gritted her teeth as she clung to the side handle for dear life. Albert had to remind himself to ease off the accelerator. Driving his car just made him want to go as fast as possible—something Lily was absolutely not a fan of experiencing. He shifted gears and brought the vehicle speed down closer to the speed limit.

They were outside Spirit Antiques in minutes with his driving. The street was still busy, though nobody walked through the door of the antique shop. He was around the car in a moment and helped Lily exit before gently shutting the door behind her. They twined their fingers together and walked into the shop. From the sidewalk, it looked as if the place was closed; the lighting was so dim inside, but even without the open sign on the door, they both knew Spirit Antiques kept late hours for its diverse clientele.

A little bell tinkled overhead as they entered the old shop. Across from the door and behind the large wooden counter sat Brie with the ancient ledger book beside her and a computer in front of her. Her head shot up as they entered and while her eyes brightened, her face couldn't decide between a smile for Lily or a grimace for him. "Hey, guys, what brings you in tonight? It's Monday, and neither of you usually comes in today. Shit, is there a special order? The Storage Room shelf was empty last I checked, but I can just pop back there and yell at it."

Lily tugged Albert closer to the counter and he let her lead him. "Nah, Bertie said he needed something from Ezra, so we just popped in before we head out. What are you doing here on a Monday?" Lily smiled brightly at her friend. Albert did not smile and Brie didn't bother to look at him. It was okay; they didn't need to be friends, but they could be cordial.

"I was bored sitting at home and Wes is out with Apollo, so I thought I would hang around and get something done that wasn't my thesis. Let me just give Ezra a call, and he can get whatever you need." She pulled out her shell phone from her pocket and flipped it open to reveal two glowing pieces. She held it up like a cell phone and began to speak. "Shell phone one to shell phone two, Lils and Albert are here to see you, babe." She grinned wickedly.

A deep sigh came through the shell. "Sweetheart, how many times do I have to ask you not to call them shell phones?"

"Oh, you'll keep asking and I'll keep ignoring. You made the mistake of giving it to me. Now get your ass up here. Shell phone out!" She snapped hers shut just as Ezra let out another long-suffering sigh.

A few seconds later, Ezra stepped through the Storage Room door. He was a stark contrast to his paramour with nearly a foot of height on her, light brown skin while she was nearly as pale as Albert, and his expression was set in a slight frown, whereas Brie still wore a bright grin. In his large hands, he carried a simple yet well-crafted box with a hinged lid.

"Lily, Albert, nice to see you, as always. I have what you need, Albert." He set the box on the counter and opened the lid toward the pair. On a velvet platform sat two vastly different necklaces.

One held a single large Nazar in blues and whites, shaped into an eye. It was beautifully crafted and hung on a silver chain. The other was a string of beaded Nazars, each with blues, whites, and golds. "Protection from the evil eye, probably the best thing I have against vampires on short notice. These are Ottoman, originally owned by the poet Mustafa bin Mehmed Cinani, so they are especially potent against the dead. Better against jinn, maybe, but most of the stuff I have for vampires is for killing them."

"Thanks for the history lesson, professor." Brie nudged him with her hip playfully.

Ezra's ears grew pink at her teasing. "You are a history doctoral candidate. I thought you would appreciate it." Ezra turned his focus back on Lily and Albert. "You're going through with your plan, then?" he asked Albert.

It was a loaded question since there was a lot to his plan, but he needed to do this. "Yes, it's the safest thing to do," he said solemnly.

Ezra nodded, his face neutral. He lifted the amulet and handed it to Albert. "Keep it facing out; it won't be much good if it's covered." The other necklace, with the beads, he handed to Lily. She took it and slipped it over her head without question. "Lily, yours has a few extra spells on it for your protection." Again, his face was neutral as he said this.

Ever the professional, thought Albert.

Lily fingered one of the beads. "I can feel the magic off these. It's strange, though. There's the ancient magic of the Nazar, but did you put some divine magic on this, too?"

"Yes, Albert asked me to. Like I said, extra protection for you." Ezra looked her right in the eye and didn't flinch away as Lily gave him a quizzical stare. Albert knew her sight had been vague lately, and it was frustrating her to no end. It was the only way he knew this would work; otherwise, she would have found him out quickly.

He needed to do this now.

"Darling, I'm sorry. But I'm going alone tonight. I can't risk Simon thinking he has a chance to get to me. He would kill you just to spite me, Lily. You need to stay here." This was his last chance to reason, and there was a hope, small as it was, that she might listen.

Lily whirled on him, her beautiful open face turning accusatory. "I'm going. We've discussed this and you don't get to dump me out of this now. I can handle myself, and now we have these fancy magic necklaces for the extra boost. Let's get going." She grabbed his hand and nearly dragged him back toward the door. "Thanks for the magic buff, Ezra. Brie, let's do a movie night s—" she called over her shoulder but then stopped with a soft exhale as if she had run into something.

Albert moved a step forward and stopped just before the door. On the ground between them, shimmering on the wood, was a glowing white line. Lily looked down at the magic on the floor and then back up at Albert in disbelief. "Bertie, what did you do?"

It felt like his heart was cracking in two. "What I had to so that you would be safe. You don't know

Simon like I do. You'll be safe here with Ezra and Brie until I get back. It is the only way to keep you from harm because I know you would follow me no matter what."

"You're damn right I would! We're supposed to be a team; you can't just leave me behind." The tears forming in her beautiful eyes almost undid him completely.

"I'm sorry, darling. I love you." And like the coward he was, he fled through the door as she screamed his name.

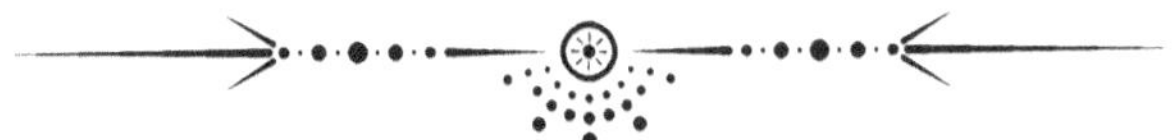

Albert arrived at the Hotel Nosferat an hour after sundown. The hotel catered exclusively to vampires, offering lightproof window shades for the day and a blood lounge full of willing donors. They strictly enforced a "no killing on property" rule, which even Simon would be forced to adhere to.

Once through the doors, he gravitated toward the open blood lounge, which beckoned hotel guests from its prominent placement in the lobby. It would be where most of the guests of the hotel congregated and a perfect meeting spot so that Albert couldn't make a scene. He didn't need to feel the tug of his maker to know that was where Simon was waiting, but the tug was there all the same—a constant reminder of his link to Simon. There was no way for that feeling to go away; save for the death of one of them, it would only dampen with distance.

It didn't take long for Albert to find Simon once he entered the lounge. Even in the dim lighting, his maker stood out amongst the pale of the gathered vampires. He sat nestled in a corner of the lounge, the center spot in a large booth, a sun god among the dead, already surrounded by his other children. There were only four of them at the table now. Albert had never known Robert and Rosalind, the twin vampires Simon had made centuries before him. They walked into the sun together fifty or so years before Albert's rebirth. Simon always mourned their deaths.

As Albert approached, he looked over the assembled party. Simon was much the same as he was before dawn that day. To his right, always on his right, was Celia, his first child. Celia was almost a cliché of what a vampire should be, deathly pale skin, raven hair that hung in long waves around her waifish body, and a black dress that hugged tight enough to be a second skin. Her red lips spread into a smile, a cruel smile, as Albert approached.

Next to Celia was Aron, tall and broad and handsome. He and Celia had been lovers off and on for the whole of their immortal life. Aron was brawny and blonde, his features rougher than most vampires Albert had met. Aron was also one of the most stupid beings Albert had ever had the misfortune of knowing.

To Simon's left was Sam. They were small and hauntingly beautiful, with androgynous features. Even before it was fashionable, Sam did not confine themselves to a gender; they just were, existing somewhere in between and nowhere. Their suit was well-tailored and black with silver buttons, and a wine-red shirt with the top three buttons left open to show white skin with blue veins. Their light brown hair was cropped short and tousled perfectly.

That left the newest child, the one Albert didn't know. She was young, perhaps early twenties at most, when she was turned—Japanese by the look of her. She was the same pale as the rest of them, with pink hair done up into two messy buns on the top of her head. Her hair was the only bright thing about her. She was dressed entirely in black to match the rest of Simon's group. *How cliché,* thought Albert. They were all like characters from a vampire movie. It was absurd, really.

"Our dear Albert, finally home," Celia purred as Albert approached the table.

"Celia, what a surprise to see you. I wonder, who's guarding Hades in your absence?" Albert narrowed his eyes at her. He and Celia had never gotten along for reasons neither of them actually knew anymore, so it was best to just keep up the animosity. She was Simon's creature through and through.

Celia laughed, but it was a harsh, grating sound. "Oh, how I've missed you, little brother. Such a wicked tongue you have."

"Can't say the feeling is mutual," Albert deadpanned. He didn't move from the edge of the table, preferring to remain standing so that Simon would know he wasn't staying.

But of course, that would not do for Simon. "Play nice, Celia. Come, Albert, sit and join us. I believe they have a young virgin on tap. That always was your favorite."

"I'd rather stand and I'm not here to drink. Just speak your piece and I'll be on my way." Albert didn't want to draw this out. He never wanted to see any of them again.

"No, he prefers witch blood these days, don't you, Bertie?" Celia licked her blood-red lips and smiled mockingly at him.

"Leave her out of this, Celia. Or I'll have to rip out that pretty throat of yours." It came out like a growl, full of menace and promise.

Simon held up a lazy hand before Celia could respond, and she snapped her mouth shut. Celia would never defy any order issued by Simon. She didn't get to be the right hand by questioning—obedient as always.

Simon was not so easily quelled. "Sit, Albert. It's not a request. We have much to discuss."

CHAPTER 9

Against his better judgment, Albert moved to sit at the end of the booth. Even though Albert had run from this mockery of a family thirty years previous, defying one's maker was still against vampire nature. Even if he wasn't compelled by his nature, he would still follow Simon's command; their bond still ran deep whether Albert wanted it to or not. And he most certainly did not want that bond.

Simon stopped him before he could sit. He pointed his finger at his newest child. "Eiko, Sam, move." The young one, Eiko, sullenly slid out from the table, Sam right on her heels with a bored expression, leaving the booth open for Albert to slide in close to Simon. He knew it was a bad idea, that it would leave him trapped beside his maker, but there was little choice. If he didn't face this now, face all of them, they might come for him again. Or worse, they would come for Lily to force his hand. Simon always made good on his threats; he was reliable like that.

So Albert went against all of his screaming instincts and slid around the table to sit next to Simon. Sam and Eiko resumed their places at the table, completely trapping him in.

Simon studied him for a long moment, his pale eyes assessing him, stripping him down to his bones. The elder vampire always did have a way of making him feel like he was looking into his soul, even if none of them actually had one—not anymore.

Albert knew better than to make the first move. Though every bit of his willpower focused to keep him from squirming under Simon's gaze. *No sign of weakness. Give him nothing.* He was literally surrounded by ruthless and bloodthirsty monsters. And he had betrayed them by walking away thirty years ago—not just walking away, but disappearing. He should have known Simon would never give up on what he owned. And he did own Albert. Simon would always be a part of him.

"I've entertained your youthful rebellious streak long enough, Albert. It's time for you to come home." Right to the point, of course. Outwardly ostentatious, Simon had no patience for long-winded conversation. The point was made promptly and his will and judgment were immediate.

Albert would not be intimidated by Simon, not again. "No, I have a home here. I'm content to stay." He would not give further explanation. It was best to be firm. Though how much that tactic would work was new territory for Albert. When he left the family decades ago, he had done it the coward's way— he disappeared into the daylight while they slept without a word. He took only the essentials and a magical trinket that allowed him to daywalk for a short time.

Beside Celia, Aron snorted. "Having too much fun fucking your witch whore." He took a drink from the glass in front of him. Aron rarely drank from the source, preferring instead to have the blood drained into whatever absurd drinking vessel he favored at the time. They were always impractical and often jewel encrusted. Ostentation ran in the family.

But Albert took any mention of Lily as a direct threat. He bared his fangs and hissed as he arched across the table toward Aron. Fingernails elongated to strike and slash with wicked speed.

Two things happened at once. Simon's palm pressed against Albert's chest with such easy force that Albert was thrown back into his seat, while Aron flung himself back out of Albert's reach, spilling nearly the entire contents of his cup onto his shirt and lap. "Don't even mention her. I swear I will tear you limb from limb and use your own hands to applaud your demise." Albert could feel the bloodlust rising within him as he struggled against Simon's hand, still holding him back. He felt feral, like he could tear the whole room apart for merely hinting at Lily—and he would. Brick by brick, he would tear the place down if it meant keeping her safe.

"Why you son of a—" Aron shrieked as he held his shirt away from his body, but Simon cut him off with a look.

Without removing his hand from Albert, Simon turned his attention back to the restrained vampire. "Now, now, dear Albert. I won't have the family fighting tonight. It's been so long since we've all been together like this. And you have yet to meet your youngest sister."

Simon waited for Albert to relax against the back of the booth before removing his hand. Not that Albert was actually relaxed. His whole body tensed, every muscle ready to spring him out of the booth and back to Lily, where he would beg for her forgiveness. It was a mistake to come.

"Now then, Eiko comes to us from New York City. It's been, what, ten years now?" Simon began, like he didn't know the exact time. He probably knew the exact minute he took her human life and changed her into the bloodsucker sitting at the table.

"Ten years this past May. Best day of my life." The young woman smiled with her fangs on full display. Her voice was girlish and cheerful. From her tone and demeanor, Albert concluded that she felt no remorse over becoming a vampire. Then again, in his experience, this generation romanticized vampires to an extraordinary degree, thanks to Anne Rice and Twilight.

Pale blue eyes gazed at her affectionately. "I had hoped you would return sooner, so I took my time before making another. But when you didn't return, I thought Eiko would make a fine addition to our family. She has proved to be a most dedicated student."

He beamed at the young vampire, and she batted her eyelashes at him, her smile even wider. Then he turned his focus back on Albert. It was easy for Albert to remember how that approving smile was enough to make him do anything for Simon. Even now, his charm was familiar and easy to fall into. The sweep of his eyes over her body was like a caress they could all see. Then his words shattered the illusion. "Actually, I made her for you."

The words shocked him to his core. He was disgusted, but there was also shame and sadness.

A life was cut short because of me. Because Simon couldn't let me go.

It was only a matter of time before Simon found him; Albert always knew that. And in that time, Simon found one of the few ways that would get Albert to stay.

Guilt.

Guilt caused him to leave thirty years ago. And now Simon counted on guilt to bring him back. His hands clenched into tight fists, nails digging crescents into the meat of his palm. "How could you do this, Simon?" He forced the words through clenched teeth, though he wanted to scream.

While Albert fought with himself, Simon's lazy smile morphed into a smug grin. He knew exactly the type of game he was playing, and Simon only started games he was guaranteed to win.

"Oh, relax, Bertie. Simon gave you a gift. Just like he gave me Aron." Celia's mocking tone grated on his already frayed nerves. "Now you have one of your own." She caressed Aron's cheek, asserting her ownership over him, as if anyone else would want him.

"Fuck you, Celia," Albert spat. He hated them. Hated them all.

"Simon has taught me very well. I promise I won't disappoint you." Eiko batted her lashes now at Albert, a suggestive tone in her girlish voice. Albert wanted to vomit.

He pushed himself up onto the bench, as there was no room to stand in the middle of the booth. "I'm leaving," he said and leaped across the table. Nobody made a move to stop him. They were letting him go, for now.

"We'll be seeing you soon, Albert. It's good to have you home." Simon's grin was white and gleaming. But there was also malice behind it. That malice had always been there. It was only now that Albert could see it properly.

"Leave me the fuck alone." Albert turned and sped toward the exit. It took all his willpower not to look back at the family surrounding the table. But he could hear their laughter as he left and his blood boiled.

CHAPTER 10

Lily sat in the staff room, though why Brie and Ezra bothered calling it that made no sense. Brie was the only one who used it. Then again, she was the only staff member Ezra employed. She cradled a crow-painted teacup in her hand, which she had been drinking heavily from for the last hour. She drained the last of the cup and waited the whole five seconds it took for the cup to refill itself.

"You should probably slow down, or you're going to be off your ass by the time Albert comes back," Brie said, looking at Lily with concern on her face. The two of them sat on the padded wicker couch at opposite ends. Lily had been drinking teacup after teacup of rum since Brie settled her in the room. Whatever one needed, the teacup provided, and Lily needed alcohol.

"Oh, I'm going to be a lot more than off my ass when Albert gets back. I am going to fucking destroy him." She was close to shouting but had lost the capacity to care the moment Albert had walked out the door, leaving her behind.

"I can't believe Ezra didn't tell me what was going on. I would have told him it was a terrible idea. And

fuck Albert for thinking he knows what's best for you."
Brie was trying to help, Lily knew that. But she was at
war with herself.

Of course, she was absolutely furious at Albert, for
lying, for tricking her. Even if his intentions were to
keep her safe, he hadn't been honest with her. Hadn't
communicated with her. But she was also worried.
Albert didn't speak about his maker much or the vampire family he left behind. She knew his past wasn't
good and wasn't something he liked to revisit. Still,
a part of her worried they would take him away or,
worse, hurt him.

No, it was better for her to stay angry at him than
to think of the worst-case scenarios. Albert would be
back soon enough, and when he was, there was going
to be hell to pay. And he was sleeping on the couch
tonight—maybe for a few nights.

"So, like do vampires leave a corpse behind, or do
they just dust like in Buffy?" Brie was still talking, but
Lily barely heard her. A war of anger and worry raged
inside her. Brie was just trying to help keep her mind
off what could be happening with Albert, and Lily was
grateful for that.

"I don't actually know. I can't say I've ever seen
a vampire killed before," she said offhandedly. The
mechanics of vampire death were not exactly covered in her witch education. Actually, very little was
taught about the magical community outside of the
witch covens.

Brie made a thoughtful noise. "Well, if he dusts,
that means less work for us, since we won't have to
hide the body. Just vacuum him right up." She laughed

to herself since Lily wasn't in a laughing mood. They lapsed into silence again. Lily felt restless; she wanted to get up and pace or move or just do something, but that wouldn't help calm her down.

Finally, after several long minutes of silence, Brie spoke again, "Lils, why aren't you using your sight? I'm sure it would help if you had an idea of what was happening." Concern completely clouded her friend's tone.

Why hadn't she used her sight? Especially after Albert told her of the meeting earlier in the day. Her sight was second nature and had always been useful, even for seemingly small things. But the visions had been blurry and unreliable lately.

Since her last clear vision, which she knew now was about meeting Cameron, Lily hadn't tried to understand her visions. Her visions had always been such a large part of her life. There was no reason they should fail her when it came to Albert. If he needed her, how would she know? Her sight was incredibly powerful and here she sat, moping and angry and worrying when she had the ability to know something. Hopefully. Maybe it was all the stress in her life. Between her family and Simon, she was certainly being crushed under the weight of it all. Stress had even started to affect her sleep, and Lily was a great sleeper normally. It stood to reason that stress would also impact her visions as well.

Goddess, she was an idiot. When you have perfectly good eyesight, you don't put on a blindfold and then complain you can't see. The only reason for her visions failing was because she was letting them. Since her visions started, she had been taught how to master the visions as best as any witch could. She knew how to trigger them when needed, knew how to stop them from overwhelming her and dragging her into them. Lily had control over visions, knew how to use them.

So why am I not using them? She couldn't help yelling at herself.

"Ugh, I don't even know what I'm doing anymore. You're right. I should have been using it, even if they've been garbage lately," she cried out, gently setting the teacup on the table in front of her finally. Her head felt a little lighter than she cared for, but she would have to work through that. Hell, maybe it would help.

Brie pulled her legs up to sit crisscross on the couch and faced Lily. With her back straight and her feet planted on the floor, Lily closed her eyes and grounded herself. She felt the room around her drift away, and her mind went searching.

The sight was never the same. Depending on the answers she was looking for, or if a vision came upon her unbidden, the experience was different. Sometimes it was hazy, like looking through fog and she could make out shapes and sounds, but nothing detailed. Other times, she saw everything in minute detail but heard nothing, just watched lips move, or actions happen. Then there were times when she saw nothing at all and there was just a feeling. Something that didn't belong to her, but she still felt it so intensely. But every time, it was different, giving much or withholding just enough to cause exasperation.

This time it was hazy, but not unlike the others recently. She stood in a space of moving smoke; there was nothing around her. No noise save her own heartbeat, which seemed so loud in the endless space. She was alone.

Maybe I'm just a little too drunk for this.

Just as the worry set in that her gift was broken, she felt a hand stroke her hair, fingers tangling lightly in the curls. She whirled around, but there was no one. Just more swirling smoke in the dim light. But when she turned back around, a man stood before her.

No, not a man. A vampire.

She knew at once who he was. "Simon," she breathed, and her heart started to race.

The vampire smiled, and Lily had to suppress a shiver. "So you're the little witch that is keeping my Albert from returning. Yes, I think I understand now. You are quite the beauty. Were you not a witch, I would take you for myself, I think."

Simon's eyes roamed over her body, and Lily wanted to vomit. His gaze was predatory and she felt he was detailing every flaw. "You need to leave Albert alone," she said with more bravado than she felt. As much as she wanted to look away from Simon, she kept her eyes locked on his, refusing to be the first to break the contact.

Simon didn't seem to care about the challenge. "Oh, little witch, you have no power here. And he won't stay if you are dead." Before Lily could react, Simon moved with such speed that he was nothing but a blur. And then he was there behind her, ringed hands grabbing either side of her head, and with a sickening crunch, he snapped her neck. Everything went dark.

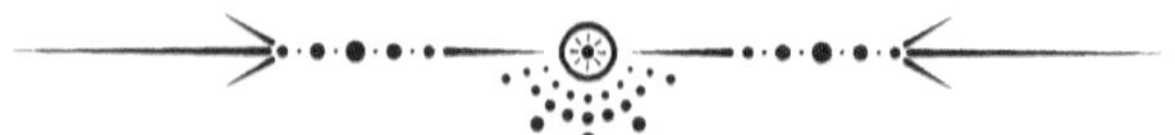

A scream filled the room as Lily came to. It took her a moment to realize the scream was her own, and she was now lying on the floor next to the wicker couch in the staff room. Brie hovered next to her on the floor, holding her hand tightly in her own while yelling for Ezra into her shell phone.

The angel burst through the door just as Brie helped Lily sit up. "What happened?" He rushed to Lily's other side. Her head felt heavy and the sound of her own neck snapping rang continuously in her ear.

Ezra's warm hand on her shoulder was like an anchor. Lily had been coming to Ezra's shop since she was very little and even though she teased him, he was still basically a member of her family and she appreciated both his and Brie's concern.

Lily took a moment to steady herself and let Brie and Ezra help her back onto the couch. "It was Simon," she said, covering her face with her hands.

"You saw him with Albert?" Ezra asked.

Lily shook her head, pulling her hands away from her face. "No, I mean he was there, talking to me. It wasn't like a normal vision. We interacted. There was nothing else but us in this void. And then he... he killed me." She took a sharp intake of breath, trying hard not to think of that feeling, of that sound.

"Well, that's just ... weird. Right? Like that's never happened before?" Brie sounded confused. Brie didn't come from magic. She hadn't even known the magical world existed until last year. So, she would have no idea how Lily's visions worked entirely. Not that Lily knew completely how her visions worked, since she had never spoken to anyone in her visions before.

"I usually just see a scene or get a feeling. Sometimes I hear things that will happen. But someone talking to me, interacting with me, touching me? No, that's totally weird. And deeply unpleasant." She rubbed her neck. She could still feel the sharp pain there, dimly. The cold feel of Simon's hands on either side of her face seemed burned into her skin.

Beside her, Ezra nodded his head. "Yeah, I've had my neck snapped a few times; unpleasant is putting it mildly." His tone was so nonchalant, like it was an everyday conversation to talk about necks being snapped.

"Ezra, no, that's not helpful. And also, if you had your neck snapped multiple times, you definitely deserved it." Brie shot her boyfriend a sharp look. "You want another drink from the teacup?" She turned her attention back to Lily, who nodded at her question.

Brie put the teacup in her hands, and she took a large pull and spluttered a little as the liquid hit the back of her throat. "I thought I was drinking rum. That's definitely not rum." She recovered quickly and drained the cup, anyway.

"The cup has a bad habit of producing whiskey whenever Brie uses it." Ezra took the cup from Lily and flipped it over on the saucer so it wouldn't fill again.

Brie only shrugged, and Lily let out a small laugh at her friends.

The door to the back room flung open suddenly, banging hard against the wall. And there stood Albert, eyes wide and frantic.

"Lily," he breathed and Lily could visibly see his tense body relax just a fraction. But when he went to speak again, a large burgundy-black flower covered his mouth, staunching his words.

"Black Dahlia, oh man, Albert, you really fucked up this time," Brie mocked, giving Lily's hand a squeeze before she pulled Ezra from the room.

When her friends were gone, the door shut firmly behind them, Lily turned her full attention on Albert. "Sit down and don't talk." Her voice held an edge of anger that even she was unfamiliar with. She felt more anger than she ever thought herself capable of.

At least, Albert didn't even question, or try to question, anyway, and walked to the couch.

At least he has the decency to look ashamed, she thought as she watched him cross the room, his eyes on the floor and his shoulders slumped.

Lily didn't know what she was going to say; her thoughts were a scattered mess of anger, worry, and sadness. It was all too much to process at once. She decided anger was the best route to start because anger would fade quicker than her sadness at his betrayal.

"What the hell were you thinking? You lied to me. And you used Ezra to lie to me. We're supposed to be partners. We're supposed to communicate and help each other. And not only did you take advantage of my trust by making me think we were in this together, you trapped me. You made it so that I couldn't make my own decision. You betrayed my trust and took away my choice. That's not what partners do." The anger was already fading as her eyes started prickling with tears. Albert didn't meet her gaze as she stood over him, and it took so much strength for her to continue to stand looming over him. Her knees felt weak and she wanted to collapse into one of the chairs.

How do people hold on to anger for so long? It's exhausting. Even if she wanted to, her anger wouldn't last.

She wanted to hold Albert close to her, but at the same time, she wanted to shake him and scream. And then there was a part of her that just didn't want to see him at all because it hurt her heart too much.

A wave of her hand disappeared the black dahlia in his mouth. "Now, speak. Explain yourself. And don't you dare try to play the white knight routine on me, Albert Hsu, or the flower goes back in and I'm leaving."

Finally, her knees couldn't take the shaking anymore and she crumpled onto the couch, as far from him as possible. Albert still didn't look at her. Instead, his eyes remained trained on the ground. He was capable of remaining deathly still, but his hands fidgeted in his lap instead.

"Darling, I'm sor—" he began, but Lily didn't want to hear it.

"No, don't you dare start off by apologizing. No excuses, no trying to make me sympathetic. You will be honest with me now." Lily had never been so forceful in her life, but the last thing she would tolerate was Albert preying on her good nature to get out of trouble.

He looked at his still fidgeting hands. He couldn't even look at her, and somehow that made her angrier. But she listened patiently when he began his explanation. "I didn't want you around Simon. To say he's an asshole is an understatement. He's dangerous and he would hurt you without a thought if it meant getting me back. I'm terrified he'll hurt you, or worse. I know I shouldn't have lied. I should have just been honest and told you I didn't want you anywhere near the family. I regret my deception, but I do not regret keeping you here where you were safe."

Lily couldn't help the scoff that escaped her throat. "I'm well aware of how dangerous Simon is. Our first meeting resulted in him snapping my neck."

Albert's head whipped up so fast that were he human, it would have probably made him dizzy. "What do you mean?"

Lily crossed her arms tightly over her chest and tried not to imagine the feel of Simon's hands, the sound of her neck snapping. "I used my sight to try and find you. But instead, I met with Simon somewhere in between. We had a lovely little chat before he decided my neck was better out of alignment."

"But that's impossible. I didn't think that's how your sight worked." He stared at her and lifted one hand as if to touch her, but then thought better of it and dropped it back into his lap.

"Whether it's impossible or not, it happened. Simon didn't just threaten me; he all but promised to kill me to get you back. So, you need to tell me what happened tonight." She kept her eyes on him and waited for him to speak.

Albert hesitated before speaking again, but at least he was looking at her now. Then he told her about the club, about Eiko, and Simon's intent to get him to come home with the family.

"Great, so now we both have family problems. But we should tell the Council and my family, just in case." She was going to be pragmatic about this. The disagreement with her family would have to be put aside for now, since she was sure Simon would come after them as a means to hurt her and Albert. The Council should know, and as one of the vampire delegates, Albert would be listened to. Not that the Council would do much. They were more about monitoring than actual action and would recommend they be watched rather than remove them from the city.

Still, her family knowing would be a good idea. There was no denying she and Albert were in danger, and a powerful coven could provide ample protection for them. Well, for her, anyway. Somehow, she would have to convince them to include Albert in that protection. Which, considering the state of things lately, would be a hard sell.

But then she had a thought. "Does it seem odd to you that after nearly a year of dating, suddenly my family is entirely against you and Simon returns? I mean, my family hasn't been thrilled, but they have been cordial enough until now." *Except Rose*, she thought before continuing, "And suddenly, after thirty years, Simon just shows up, finds our house easily, and just waltzes right into our backyard."

Albert seemed to quickly grab onto the opportunity to speak on something that wasn't his total fuck up. "The timing is quite strange. You don't think they coordinated this together, do you?"

That was the last thing Lily wanted to consider. Just a few weeks ago, she would have dismissed the thought that her family could ever betray her like that. But that was then. And now... well, she wasn't sure what her family would do to get their way. Maybe they would find a way to contact Albert's maker to get him out of the way. But then there was an even bigger question to consider. Why? Why would they go through the trouble? Why wait nearly a year into their courtship before lashing out?

There were too many questions and no answers. "We need to talk to my family. I have to know if they did this. I have to... oh Goddess, I don't even know." She finally collapsed in on herself and buried her head in her hands. It was all too much to consider. All her life, she was proud to be an Everett. Proud to be from a family of such esteemed witches. But more than that, she was proud to be a part of a family that loved each other unconditionally. They were a loud and loving bunch, and her family was everything to her. Every fiber of her being wanted to reject the idea that her family would try to completely destroy her happiness because all they had ever wanted, what they had told her for her entire life, was for her to be happy.

She pulled her hands away from her face, thankful that Albert knew better than to try to reach out and comfort her. As much as she loved him, she really couldn't handle his affection right now. "I'm still mad at you. And I'm going to be mad at you for a while. But now there are other things to worry about.

Tomorrow, we're going to see my family. Together. Like we should have already been doing. No more running off alone, thinking you know best. Okay?"

"Of course." He nodded. "I'll follow your lead on this. Should we... that is, should we go home?" His eyes shot back to the floor; he looked absolutely dejected.

Like he thinks I won't come home.

"Yeah, I've had enough of the shop today. I want my bed now." She stood and stretched. Her neck popped and she cringed at the sound. There was no way she was getting over the experience with Simon any time soon. Hell, she would be lucky if she could sleep at all now that she knew what it was like to have her neck snapped.

Brie and Ezra were waiting for them when they stepped back into the front of the shop. "Everything okay?" Brie asked, her question directed only at Lily before she shot a hard glare at Albert. Lily gave her a small nod. Brie and Albert might never get along, but Lily was grateful for her human friend, even if she looked two seconds away from staking Albert.

"For now. We've made a plan to see my family tomorrow to figure a few things out. And then we'll have to deal with Albert's vampire family." She sighed, already feeling exhausted at just the thought.

"Well, if you need help dealing with the vamp fam, just let us know. I'll send Ezra." Brie hugged Lily, squeezing her tight.

"Why are you volunteering me?" Ezra asked as he wrapped his arms around his girlfriend from behind.

"Oh, because you can get your neck broken and it's totally cool. You'll just walk it off. I get my neck snapped and it's kind of a permanent thing. I've already used up my extra life, thanks." Her laugh was strained, though. Brie was able to joke about it now, but the whole ordeal with Moloc and dying last year had really taken a huge toll on Brie.

Lily gave her friend another hug before she started for the door. "You're welcome to stay with me and Wes if you need. You can have my bed," Brie whispered into her ear before pulling back. A small smile and a shake of her head was Lily's response. Tempting as the offer was, she really wanted her own bed tonight.

When she turned from Brie, Lily noticed that Albert reached out his hand as if to take hers, but she pulled away, sending a clear message that she was still angry. So instead, he followed behind her and said nothing.

When they reached the door, Brie called out, "Text me when you get home, so I know you're safe. And Albert," she stopped and waited for him to turn, "go fuck yourself!" She stood there smugly, Ezra rolling his eyes above her. Albert said nothing; he just turned away from them and walked out of the store. Lily waved and then followed him out.

They drove home in silence. Albert kept his eyes trained on the road, still driving way too fast for Lily's liking, but she said nothing. Her eyes fixed on the passing street lamps of the city. The orange glow blurred as they sped down mostly empty streets toward the residential area of town. Neon signs soon turned to soft lamps in windows as they rolled through tree-lined streets until Albert pulled into their driveway.

Once inside, Lily trudged up the stairs to their room. She could hear Albert's footsteps behind her, slow and deliberate for her benefit. But she still couldn't quell her anger around him. Right now, she needed space. After spending a large part of the night worrying about him, she couldn't stand to be around him now. At least she knew he was safe at home. Safe with her.

When she made it to their bedroom, she slipped inside and firmly shut the door behind her. His footsteps stopped outside the door, but he clearly took the obvious hint and moved away again. But as he did so, she still heard him whisper, "I love you," before he shuffled off down the hallway and back down the stairs again.

CHAPTER 11

Lily stayed in her garden for most of the next day. Albert stood in the shadows of the kitchen and observed her, wishing more than anything that he could just hold her. He would spend the rest of his immortal life in repentance for what he'd done if it meant she would smile at him.

Lily was his other half, his match in every way. Maybe he had made a mistake in cutting her out in this instance. She let him into every aspect of her life, let him make choices about what to be involved in when it came to her family. But he didn't give her the same consideration. Lily wasn't a weak thing in need of protection. She was a powerful witch. He had seen how formidable she could be last winter when they had stormed the stronghold of the warlock Moloc. She had taken down a full-grown ravenous werewolf so easily. He had been in awe of her power.

But he still didn't fully regret his decision to leave her behind in safety. Lily was capable, but Albert knew Simon was ruthless and had his own protections against magic. That bit of uncertainty was enough to justify his actions. Yes, Simon had invaded Lily's vision, but snapping her neck in a vision and her remaining alive was a better outcome than the alternative. "Do you need to feed before we go tonight?" Her voice filtered through his thoughts. She stood in the kitchen with him, her hands and overalls caked in dirt. A smudge of dark earth crossed her cheek under her left eye, like she had wiped away a tear with her dirty hands.

Had she been crying?

Albert shook his head at her question. He would have to feed sometime this week, but they had other things to worry about, and he wasn't in danger of losing control to bloodlust. "I'll be fine. I'll keep to my usual day. What are we going to say to your family?" At least she was talking to him, concerned about his needs. It was an improvement, at least; she hadn't spoken a word to him all day.

She shrugged, her gaze fixed somewhere over his shoulder. "I don't know yet. I don't want to accuse them of something I don't actually think they've done. My family loves me and would never do something like bring Simon into our lives just to break us up. They clearly have a thing against vampires, so it doesn't make sense for them to work with one." Lily went silent for a moment; her gaze shifted to the floor. When she lifted her head again, her eyes had gone distant again. "Anyway, I'm going to go shower before we leave." She started to walk out of the room.

"Lily," Albert choked out before she could fully leave the room. She stopped at the doorway into the hall, but she didn't turn. "Darling, I'm so sorry. I don't expect you to forgive me; what I did was inexcusable. I'm not good with words, but I love you, and I will work to be a better partner to you." How he longed to reach for her, to pull her close against his body, and appreciate every second of it. But he didn't. He wouldn't until she was ready. If she was ever willing to let him touch her.

Lily's sigh was deep as she slowly turned back toward him. His heart nearly leaped from his chest when she crossed back to him and cupped his face. "Bertie, I love you, too. But I'm allowed to be mad at you, and you'll just have to wait until I'm over it. I will get over it, though. Just give me time."

She kissed him gently, and he didn't push for more, just let her lead. It was over too quickly, but he didn't chase her lips when she pulled away like he wanted. But his heart was hopeful again. Of course, she could and should be mad at him, but knowing she wouldn't leave him over this was enough.

Without another word to him, she left the room, and a few minutes later, he heard the shower start. He sagged against the kitchen island counter and closed his eyes.

With a practiced hand, Albert shifted gears as he turned onto the gravel drive of the farm. From the corner of his eye, he watched as Lily worried at the strap of the canvas tote on her lap. If this was a normal night, he would have reached out and taken her hand, but instead, he left it on the shift stick, aching for her touch.

"Did you see anything on the ride?" he asked, if just to break the silence. He knew she had used her sight before they left to see if there was anything they could prepare for, but all she saw was her family's kitchen and little else. Her gift was really giving her the bare minimum lately, and he knew it frustrated Lily to no end.

Lily stared out the window as her family's farmhouse came into view. She didn't turn when she spoke. "No, just the same thing. The family around the kitchen table speaking to me, but I can't hear anything. Guess we're going in blind."

He parked the car next to the cluster of others that belonged to the Everetts. Using a little of his vampire speed, he raced to Lily's door and offered her his hand. *I'm just being a gentleman*, he thought, though he would be lying if he said his motivation wasn't to just touch her. He was surprised when she slipped her hand into his and let him help her out of the car. They stood for several seconds holding hands, staring at each other with unspoken words. Albert could hear Lily's heart beat faster.

"Don't let go of me, Bertie. Please. I need you tonight," she pleaded. Albert would do anything to drive that note of panic from her voice.

He gave her hand a squeeze. "I'll always hold on to you, darling. I'm never letting you go." Without warning, she threw her arms around him and held him tightly. Albert didn't hesitate to wrap himself around her shorter frame. Holding onto her was like holding onto the sun itself. So bright and warm, and he needed it more than anything else.

"Just so we're clear, I'm still mad, but I'm willing to work past it because I really need you tonight. I love you, Bertie." She stood up on her toes and kissed him lightly.

Albert gave himself a moment to savor the kiss, to sink into the feather-light touch of her lips before she drew away. "Darling, you can be mad at me all you like. I'll still be here for you. Now, I believe it's time we faced the wolves." He turned them toward the house.

Lily gave his chest a light backhanded slap with her free hand. "Don't talk about my family that way." But she was laughing, though it was a nervous laugh, as she said it, and he couldn't help the smile he shot her.

"You mistake me: I was referring specifically to your sisters. Especially Rose." Her eyes sparkled with mirth as she laughed with him at his words.

"There is a statistical chance she'll try to stake you upon entering the house, but don't worry, I'll save you." She leaned her body against his arm and the heat radiating off her was almost enough to warm his chilled blood.

Albert gave her hand another squeeze. "My bold knight in shining armor." He wished they could stay like this, with the easy banter and the touching. Wished they could take the time to ease back into their repartee without the drama of their respective families. But now was not the time for that. Now he would appreciate every smile, every touch, every gentle word she gave him and be grateful. And when all of this was over, he would hold her, worship her like the goddess she was, and never again let her doubt his love and respect for her.

"Here goes nothing." Lily took a deep breath as she turned the handle and entered the house. Albert followed right behind her, their hands firmly pressed together. He could hear the bustling sounds of cooking coming from the kitchen and loud thumps from the workroom at the back of the house where they bottled potions and stored the dried herbs from the garden. All around him, he could hear noises of a lively family going about their evening rituals.

As they moved farther into the house, Lily's sister Ivy appeared on the stairs. "Lils? You're home!" She all but flew down the remainder of the stairs and threw her arms around her younger sister. Not once did she spare a glance at Albert.

Lily hesitated at first. She and Ivy had not spoken since the coffee shop incident, something that had weighed heavily on Lily. But then she dropped Albert's hand and squeezed her sister back tightly and closed her eyes. A bit of tension eased from her shoulders. *She needed this*, he thought as he averted his eyes from the sisters to give them a little privacy in their moment.

"We need to talk. To everyone, actually. It's important," Lily said once they finally separated. It was then, finally, that Ivy's attention turned to Albert, like she had just realized he was there at all. Her eyes narrowed a little, but the rest of her face remained pleasant enough. All of the Everetts, save for Rose, seemed to be incapable of being anything less than cordial.

"Well, it's clearly not to tell us you're coming home. Mom and dad are in the kitchen; I'll get Rose and the rest. Meet you there in two minutes." With only a brief backward glance at Albert, Ivy climbed back up the stairs in search of her older sister.

Lily's hand wrapped once again around his own. "Well, this is going to suck. No pun intended. But let's do this." She tugged him toward the kitchen.

The kitchen was by far the heart of the Everett household. It was big, larger than even his spacious kitchen and probably magicked to be so, with a huge butcher block dining table crowded off to the side near the bay window. Mismatched chairs, clearly pulled from other sets to accommodate a large group, were all pushed neatly under the table and took up every inch of space around it. The Everetts were always prepared for guests.

Damien Everett, Lily's father and master of the kitchen, stood at the oven, eyeballing whatever was inside through the little window, while his wife, Hyacinth, fussed over a salad on the other side of the kitchen. They both turned to look as Lily and Albert entered the room.

Hyacinth dropped the knife she was using to chop vegetables and ran to her daughter in an instant, pulling her flush against her body in a bone-crushing hug. "My Lily, you're home. I was so worried about you. I thought... well, it doesn't matter what I thought. I'm just glad you're here." Lily's family was acting like she had just dropped in unexpectedly and like they thought they would never see her again, despite the fact that Lily had called her mother yesterday to say they would be around for dinner.

Albert watched as her father, Damien, rushed over and wrapped his daughter and wife in a long-armed embrace. "Oh Lilybelle, we missed you," was all he said, but Albert could see the man close his eyes as a few tears leaked out.

He felt every bit the intruder in the happy scene. Lily had a family who loved her so completely that even after a fight, they welcomed her home so boisterously. Albert didn't have that. These people didn't accept him; only Lily would ever greet him in such a way. Yes, he had a small group he could call friends, people he knew loved him in their own ways, but only Lily could he count as family now.

Maybe once upon a time he had that, a loving family. Not like the Everetts, of course, who were loud and proud with their familial affection. The Hsu family had been more subdued. Hugs and kisses on cheeks were not common in his childhood home. But love came in the form of small, special smiles and strokes of his hair from his mother whenever he did something good. Love was the approving pat on the shoulder from his father when he came home with exceptional grades. Love was the special treats and moon cakes his neinei made for him with secret promises not to tell his parents.

Now love came in the form of Lily, in all her glory.

A part of him, though, wished he had more, like the love from the Everetts.

But then, as Hyacinth and Damien drew away from their daughter, their eyes darted toward him, and while Damien's gaze turned wary, Hyacinth's turned downright hostile. "What is he doing here?" she spat, not taking her eyes off him. Like she expected him to attack at any moment and rip out their throats. He felt the crackle of magic build around her and knew he should be careful with anything he said around the older witch. She would do anything to protect her daughter, and that included blasting the hell out of him if it meant she was protecting Lily.

"I wanted him here. Because he's who I choose to be with. He's my partner. And if you have a problem with Albert, then you have a problem with me. Is that what you want?" She lifted her chin in challenge toward her parents. Lily loved her parents, respected them deeply, and Albert knew what a big moment this was, her standing up to them—standing up for him.

Her mother gave her a placating, sympathetic look. "Lily, honey, he's not safe. He's a vampire and you know what they are like. He'll hurt you, even if you think he won't."

"No offense, I'm sure you are a very lovely young man when you aren't sucking people dry," Damien added quickly, with a sheepish look at Albert. Backhanded as the compliment was, Albert couldn't help but like Damien. More than anything right now, he wished Damien liked him in return.

"Full offense taken," Albert muttered as he crossed his arms tightly over his chest, which earned him a stern frown from Hyacinth. Lily gave him another backhanded touch against his chest. He should play nice, but that didn't mean he had to take their insults. Albert wanted their approval, not to be their doormat.

"Not helping, Bertie," she hissed softly. He kept his arms crossed, but smoothed his features out into something neutral, something non-threatening. It did nothing to change the narrowed eyes and looks of distrust from Hyacinth. Damien just looked uncomfortable. Albert could tell he wasn't a man of confrontation, and maybe, just maybe, he didn't entirely want to go along with his wife's judgment of him.

Lily turned her attention back to her parents just as her sisters and their partners walked in. He watched as Ivy's boyfriend James thumbed off the hearing aids at his ears. From what Lily had told him, this was his norm, preferring to purposely ignore conflict happening around him. Ivy herself looked concerned, but Rose, unsurprisingly, glared daggers at Albert. No, more like wooden stakes, thousands of them, enough to penetrate his whole body to make sure there was nothing left of him once she was done.

"What's the bloodsucker doing here? I thought we made it pretty clear, Lily, that you were no longer allowed to see him," Rose sneered.

"Girls, please," Damien pleaded, but nobody acknowledged him.

"I don't need your permission to date anyone. I'm allowed to be with whomever I want, Rose. So maybe stop being such a bitch," Lily shot back, to the gasps of her mother and Ivy.

"Language, Lily," her mother chastised, as if that was the most offensive thing that had been said that evening.

Rose glared at her youngest sister, her frown so fierce it seemed to be permanently etched on her face. "I may be a bitch, Lily, but I'm not the one putting myself and the rest of the family in danger just to ride some cold vampire dick!"

"Girls, stop!" Hyacinth screeched, but neither Lily nor Rose paid attention to her. Their showdown had been a long time coming, and Albert knew Lily wasn't going to back down from her eldest sister, not this time.

"If you took even half a second to stop making moon eyes over that killer, your sight would show you that he is going to kill you soon. Why do you think we never said anything until now? There are plenty of vampires out there who don't kill because they are not animals. But he's not one of them. Unlike you, the sight showed me what he really is and what he will do to you," Rose yelled, her rage filled the whole kitchen as she pointed accusingly at Albert. He felt the magic crackle around Rose, just as it had with Hyacinth. But this felt more raw, less controlled. He wasn't totally certain that Rose wouldn't just snap and zap him before he had a chance to stop her.

Lily's eyes widened, and Albert heard her heartbeat quicken. He was so attuned to the beat of her heart that the sudden fluctuation concerned him. "What do you mean the sight showed you? You've had like five visions your whole life. The sight didn't show me anything."

"Granny didn't see anything either, and her sight is much stronger than yours, Rosie," Ivy said, though her voice was tentative as she tried to insert herself between her sisters.

From what Albert knew, Rose was the dominant one of the three sisters and browbeat the younger two into getting her way. So, to hear Ivy speak up against her sister was a surprise. Everyone turned toward Ivy, and her dark cheeks held a flush of red. She tilted her head down, letting her long braids swing down to obscure her face, like she was just as surprised as everyone else that she had spoken up.

Beside her, Rose seethed. Her brown skin was lighter than her sisters' and the red splotching on her skin, from her nose to the top of her close-cropped black hair, was much more noticeable. "Granny is a crazy old bat, out of touch with what the real sight shows her now. She just doesn't want to get involved with anything anymore. The sight showed me everything I needed to know. And I know he," and here she pointed accusingly at Albert again, "will kill our sister and us if we allow them to stay in this sham of a relationship."

Rose's voice had risen to a full shouting scream, and around them, the plates that had been set out for dinner rose into the air and smashed against the far wall. The shards rained down on the scrubbed hardwood floor. The room felt as if all the air had been sucked out, allowing the crackling magic to flare and prickle the skin even more. One single spark would ignite a fire around them all.

Hyacinth raised her hands, and with a flick of her bangled wrists, the room fell into silence—not a natural silence. No sound came from anyone in the room. Albert couldn't even hear the beating of their hearts. Rose and Lily tried to speak, but nothing came out. The only person who didn't seem to react was Jamie, but that was probably due to the fact he didn't notice the difference. It was a completely disconcerting sensation. With his powerful hearing, there was always noise in his ears. The complete lack of sound was almost more maddening than constant noise.

Without a word, Hyacinth flicked her wrists again, though no noise came from the bangles on her wrist this time; Albert just watched the jewelry swing there soundlessly. Everyone in the room, save for her, was suddenly lifted into the air, hovering a foot or so off the ground, and placed into chairs at the dinner table. Every member of her family was placed gently onto a chair, whereas Albert was nearly thrown into his. Though his ass stung a little from where it connected harshly with the wooden chair, he couldn't help but be impressed by Hyacinth's control over her magic.

Damien sat at the head of the table, looking exasperated, but unsurprised. This act was clearly something that happened often enough for no one to be taken off guard, except for Albert. The other partners, Jamie and Manu, both looked like they would rather be anywhere else, but each sat at the table anyway and waited.

Hyacinth stomped over and slammed her hands down on the butcher-block table top. As her hands connected with the solid wood, all noise returned and she began to address her family loudly. "I have had enough of this! You three fighting like teenagers when you are all grown adults. I expect better out of all three of you. And to insult my mother, Rose! I ought to beat your behind. You're not too old!"

The table remained silent, though they were able to speak again, until Hyacinth took her seat. She ran her hands down her dirt-covered khaki pants as if to smooth out the nonexistent wrinkles. "Now," she said, sitting up straighter and putting on what Albert assumed was her matriarch face. It was time for business. "For once, we are all going to talk this over like rational witches and adults and not like a bunch of emotional clowns. No more plate smashing and no magic at the table." She looked at each of her daughters in turn, then Manu, and finally, she used her hands to sign to Jamie, who nodded and then turned his hearing aids back on—no hiding from this one for anybody.

"That means you, too, dear." She looked over at her husband, who held up his hands in defense.

"I'm just the kitchen witch, here. So, unless you're concerned about me feeding people to death, you don't have to worry about me." He looked over at the food he had been preparing and flicked out a finger toward the oven, where the display switched from the temperature to a warming setting. "That's it, that's all I'm doing. I'm not going to let that casserole burn."

"Oh, for Goddess' sake, Damien. Just go get the casserole and we'll do this over dinner. No sense letting good food go to waste," Hyacinth said as she turned in her chair, crooked her finger, and summoned more plates from the cabinet. Plates flew across the room and settled at each place setting, Albert's included.

"Do you even eat real food, vampire, or is it just the blood of innocent women?" Rose sneered, the only tone she seemed to have for him, then quieted at the warning glare her mother shot her. Rose seemed to decide it was better for her to say nothing to Albert than face her mother's wrath.

Lily squeezed his knee under the table, and he placed his hand over hers. "I can eat, but it doesn't do much for me sustenance-wise. It's a shame, really, because I enjoy cooking." He was going to be pleasant in the face of the hostility. Rose would never like him, never trust him, but he could at least try to win over the rest of the Everetts. He would show them he loved Lily and would never harm her. And if it pissed Rose off to not rise to her instigation, well, that was just a bonus.

"Oh, you cook!" That got Damien's attention as he set the casserole on the table and then beckoned the salad to set itself down.

Albert took this as a good sign and nodded. "Yes, my neinei, my grandmother, taught me when I was young. She was an exceptional cook." If he wasn't mistaken, it looked like Damien and Hyacinth's eyes softened toward him, just a bit. Maybe if they saw him as more than a vampire, they would accept what he and Lily had—maybe.

Down the table, Rose scoffed again, "Did you kill her, too? Bet you drained your whole family when you became a bloodsucker."

Albert felt his whole body tense. A wave of sadness mixed with extreme anger coursed through him. But he had to maintain control of his emotions. Any lashing out would just set him back more in the eyes of the Everetts. "They all died in the earthquake of 1906 in San Francisco. I was still human." His hands clenched into fists under the table, but Lily's hand, still on his knee, grounded him. He was loved so fiercely by her. S

She knew his past and was there to help him through this. But it hurt. It hurt so much that his body felt actual pain at just the reminder of what he had lost.

As he sat around a family that was so close, so loving, even when they were fighting, he thought about how he would never have his family again.

Rose had the decency to look ashamed of her words. Albert didn't care about winning her over, but at the very least, she couldn't think the absolute worst of him. "We're so sorry for your loss. I'm sure even after all these years, it doesn't really take away the pain of losing them," Damien said, and he had a faraway look for a second.

He knows all about loss, Albert thought as he gazed at Damien. Albert knew that look; Damien knew what it was like to lose his family, to be left alone in the world. Maybe that's why he put so much effort into making everyone in his family safe and happy. Albert was surprised to find a kindred soul in Lily's father.

Damien shook off whatever pain he felt in that moment and grinned uneasily. "I take back the young man part; you are older than I am."

Hyacinth narrowed her eyes again. "Maybe too old to be dating my youngest daughter."

Lily sighed deeply. "You're one to talk, momma. You're like what, twenty-five years older than dad?"

"Twenty-five years is a lot closer than over a hundred," Hyacinth shot back, though there was no bite to her words. Witches lived far longer than humans, though they were not immortal like vampires. Hyacinth and Damien looked barely out of their forties, even with three grown daughters, one of which was approaching forty herself.

"Why don't we all eat something and we can continue this conversation? There will be a lot less hangry voices if we're all fed," Damien piped up, once again trying to diffuse the tense atmosphere.

They tucked into the casserole and for several long minutes, there was nothing but the sound of chewing. Lily held his hand under the table the whole time, easy to do since he was left-handed and she right.

"I want you all to know that I love Lily with all that I am, and I only want to keep her safe because my maker has returned," Albert suddenly blurted. Why had he said that? Sure, he had been thinking of it—thinking nonstop about it, actually. But he wasn't going to say it aloud. He wasn't going to involve the rest of the Everetts in his family business.

"You're a vampire; there's really no way you won't hurt her. My vision showed me you killed her. And now I see it over and over every time I sleep. I won't let anything happen to my baby sister, even if it means I have to save her from herself," Rose said with a raised voice across the table as she tossed her fork down. Her wife, Manu, put her hand on Rose's forearm to calm her.

"Rose, you're going overboard with this. Even though you said it wasn't entirely clear, you insist it's an absolute. I think they are very sweet together. Why can't you see how in love they are? I can read their emotions so clearly. He would die for her." Manu's voice grew in conviction. She was defending them against her wife?

Rose looked at Manu, surprised by the challenge. "Manu, he might not mean to hurt her. Obviously, they are in love, even I can see that. But it doesn't mean something couldn't happen by accident."

"Oh, just stop, Rose. I let you push me into trying to set her up with Cameron. But whether you like it or not, Lily has made her choice, and I don't think he's all that bad. He takes care of her, obviously," Ivy piped up, sparing a glance toward Lily and Albert. Jamie nodded next to her and actually smiled toward Albert.

They had all been so open with their emotions, something that was foreign to Albert. He was never so open with strangers, and he highly doubted Manu was one to be very vocal against her wife, from what Lily had told him. Something seemed odd about the whole interaction.

Lily seemed to have the same idea because she stood abruptly and dropped his hand. Her fork clattered against her plate. "Daddy, you didn't!"

She looked accusingly at her father, and Damien wouldn't meet her eye. In fact, he didn't meet anyone's gaze. "It was just to get us talking, honestly. No more beating around the bush. Truth is always the best course of action, and it was just enough to loosen tongues."

Albert looked up at Lily, and all eyes were on her. "What's going on?" He reached out and took her hand in his and pulled her back down onto her seat.

Lily pointed an accusatory finger toward her father. "Dad spiked the casserole with yarrow again." She turned toward Albert, the only non-witch, so he had no clue what that meant. "It's a truth-telling plant, and infused with dad's magic is basically a truth serum."

Around the table came outraged cries, all directed toward Damien. "Damien, we talked about this when the girls were younger. You can't just force everyone to tell the truth," Hyacinth chided her husband, though Albert could see the gratefulness in her eyes. She wanted the truth out as much as any of them did. She might not like Lily being with him, but Albert was starting to suspect it wasn't necessarily personal.

"Well, I'm done talking until this wears off." Rose grabbed her plate and left the table. Manu followed with her own plate.

"Where are you going? We're not done here." Hyacinth looked up at her eldest daughter with pleading eyes.

Rose and Manu moved toward the exit, carrying their dinner. "I'm probably going to tell my wife about all the sexy things I want to do with her once we're done eating. Because even if it's spiked, it's still really good, dad."

Damien looked like he was ready to crawl under the table from embarrassment. "Serves you right for putting truth spells on the casserole. Now you have to hear about your daughters' sex lives." Hyacinth laughed as Rose and Manu left the house to return to their own cottage on the property.

"I don't want to think about that!" Damien took his plate and left the table to sulk in the kitchen proper. Ivy and Jamie made an effort to keep their mouths shut as they, too, left with their plates.

Lily and Albert were left at the table with only Hyacinth, and Albert found it a challenge not to say anything. The yarrow's magic pushed him to spill his guts to this woman. She needed to know that her daughter came before all else in his life. That one of his favorite things in the world was to cook for her and see her smile as she ate the food he made. How he dreamed of their future, their wedding, and how he tried to push all thoughts of one day outliving her from his mind. Because Albert was sure that once his Lily died, so would he.

But he said none of these things, though he longed to make Hyacinth understand the depth of his love for Lily. It was still a struggle; he wanted, needed, the words to be said. They were so near to bursting from him that he had to constantly focus on holding them in. Now that he knew the magic was there, he could feel it urging him along, wanting him to speak his truth. It was an uncomfortable feeling now that he zeroed in on it.

Lily seemed to fare better and kept her mouth shut tight. This was not her first time fighting the effects of yarrow, he could tell.

When she stood, he followed her lead. "Well, Mom, this has been a not-at-all-illuminating night. Let's try it again when everyone isn't on the verge of spilling their guts to the whole family. I want to know more about Rose's vision."

Hyacinth only nodded as they took their plates to the kitchen. Lily's plate was clean and though Albert had finished half of his own food and enjoyed the flavors, it held no sustenance for him. Damien puttered around the kitchen sullenly, cleaning up the leftovers and wiping the counters.

"I'm sorry, Lilybelle. I was just trying to help," he said as Lily hugged him.

"I know, dad, but next time, don't." She gave him another big squeeze and then they left the farmhouse and the disaster the night had turned out to be. At least they had a large container of leftovers Damien had insisted they take, though Albert wasn't sure if eating it was the best idea. Maybe once they were alone in their own home, it would be safer to eat. The food was quite good, and it would be a shame to waste it.

"I love you. I'm still mad, but I also still love you. And you can sleep in our room again tonight," she said as they sped away from her family home.

He reached across the console after switching gears and grabbed her hand and brought it to his lips. "And I love you, my darling."

CHAPTER 12

"It was a total disaster! Nothing got resolved at all. We didn't even get to ask them about Simon. I can't believe my dad put yarrow in the casserole! He used to do that when my sisters were teenagers and sneaking out. But come on, we're all adults." Lily whined to Brie as she draped her head down on the shop counter.

"Hey, it's not that bad. At least you have a dad," Brie said with a straight face. Lily looked up, her eyes wide, feeling a bubble of guilt. Here she was whining about her family when not only had her friend lost her birth parents, but her adopted mom as well. But when Brie started laughing, Lily eased back onto the counter.

"You can have mine, then. Let him embarrass you for a change," she groaned.

Brie snorted out her laughter. "No thanks. I have my big brother around to embarrass me enough. Speak of the devil." The doorbell tinkled as Wes walked into the shop. He carried a large plastic bag, and Lily was greeted by the smell of something delicious.

"The devil has brought you lovely ladies some dinner, so be nice or I'm eating it all in front of you."

Wes set the bag of food on the counter and gave Lily's bent head a pat. "What's going on, Lils? Trouble in fanged paradise?"

Lily lifted her head again and stood up straight. She sighed. "Albert and I are just fine. It's the rest of my family that's giving me trouble."

Wes shrugged. "I mean, the guy's a dick. But I also sorta love him, so I don't know why the fam is suddenly dunking on him." He started taking out the various food containers and setting them next to Brie and Lily on the counter.

"Traitor," Brie mumbled. "Dude, take it to the Storage Room. It'll set up a nice table for us. You're not messing up my counter." She made Wes shove the containers back into the bag.

"You act like you own the place already. Last I checked, this was still Ezra's place, unless he's so stupidly love-struck that he just signed the place over. Actually, that wouldn't surprise me," Wes grumbled as he let his sister push him through the door into the Storage Room.

Brie chuckled. "Ezra owns the back, but the front of the shop is mine. I spend more time up here than he does, so I'm claiming squatter's rights."

Lily loved the Storage Room, had since she was a little girl and Ezra brought her back there to see the magic it could do. It always had something that could be used for any situation and was more than happy to accommodate.

As they walked into the magically spacious room, a beautifully carved table walked up to the small platform where they stood, followed by four chairs and four sets of plates and cutlery. "You've been way too influenced by Beauty and the Beast." Brie laughed, addressing the Storage Room like it could understand her, which Lily supposed it could. It wasn't alive exactly, but it definitely had a mind of its own.

"Oh, you brought out the fancy plates, like we were planning on using plates like adults. Honestly, Room, do you even know us?" Wes asked with a grin, addressing the table. A large stack of napkins appeared on the table near Wes's chair.

"I think the Storage Room is trying to say you're gross," Brie deadpanned as she grabbed the takeout containers and spread them around the table. She looked delightedly down at the cheeseburger in the container. "Lils, don't tell Ezra we had burgers tonight. He's trying to convince me and Wes that greens are good for you."

Lily smiled down at her own veggie burger, knowing full well neither St. James sibling would ever indulge in plant-based anything. For being grown adults, they ate like teenagers when Ezra wasn't forcing fruits and vegetables on them.

"So, where is Mr. Bitey this evening?" Wes asked as he polished off his food in record time before he started to eyeball his sister's fries.

Lily shrugged. "No idea. He was gone by the time I came in from the garden. He texted that he would meet me here, so I'm sure we'll see him soon." It wasn't untrue; she didn't know exactly where he was, only what he was doing. And it was something, as Albert stressed many times in their relationship, that was not for Lily to see.

But Brie at least already knew that, since he came by already. Albert had left for the shop before her, though it was still just light when he left to pick up the envelope he got every week from Ezra. It always had a name, an address, and a time.

A willing donor.

Someone for him to feed on without fear. Ezra had connections all over the city and was able to provide a safe way for Albert to feed without going into blood-lust, and it was more fulfilling than animal blood. Now he only fed on those who were ready to die, like cancer patients and the old, or those willing to give.

Lily had once told him his chosen way of feeding was a mercy. That he gave peace to those who needed it most. But Albert did not agree. Some part of him hated what he was, though how large that part was, Lily didn't know. In his eyes, he was still a monster preying on the vulnerable, only now they asked him to do it.

"Still with us, Lily?" Brie's voice punctured through her thoughts. She hadn't realized she had drifted out of the conversation. Her mind wanted to wander back to Albert, to what he was probably doing now. Feeding was one thing that Albert would never share with her. Albert thought his need to feed was savage, and he never wanted Lily to see him that way. So, she imagined him wrapping a fragile human in his arms while he pierced their neck with his fangs. Would they make a sound as he began to drink? Would they cling to him as he drained them of their life's blood? Or would they fight him, their fight-or-flight kicking in even as their body weakened? As much as her mind wanted to linger on the idea, she forced herself to remain present with her friends.

"Yeah, still here. Just tired. I didn't sleep well last night, for obvious reasons." She waved them off and turned her attention back to her food. She watched as Wes started to steal the fries from Brie's plate and as the two siblings bickered, her thoughts again wandered back to Albert.

He had held her so tight in the early morning, before the sun came out. Sleep had not come for him at all. Several times in the night, she had woken to him stroking her hair or back, looking at her with wide eyes—like he still couldn't believe she was there. Or like he thought she would disappear any moment.

Her thoughts were again interrupted by the sound of a bell tinkling from outside the Storage Room. "Shit, gotta customer. Don't leave a mess. The Storage Room will totally throw a tantrum if you leave it dirty." Brie jumped from her chair, gave her brother a pointed look, and headed for the only door, back into the front of the shop.

Lily and Wes had just started to clean up the containers when Brie's voice called through the open door. "Lily, you need to come here." There was an edge of unease in her voice.

The flatware and cutlery on the table disappeared instantly, and the table had already begun to move itself back to wherever it came from when Lily and Wes started for the door.

Brie stood just on the other side at the shop's counter. Lily's attention first went to her friend's face and then she noticed Brie's gaze was fixed on something on the counter. Her eyes moved down to see a single white lily tied to a shining red apple, both pure and pristine. A stark white card leaned against the apple. But Lily already knew what it would say as she picked it up.

To L

Love S

"Simon," she breathed, and the card fell from her fingers back onto the counter. Her whole body went cold. He knew where she was. The shop's protective magics hadn't stopped him from entering.

Was she shaking? Or was the room just moving? She couldn't tell. It suddenly became hard to breathe and her body felt like it was heating up now, but too much. Sweat began to bead on her forehead. She felt wild and frantic, her heart starting to beat faster and faster and faster. It felt like she was drowning, like there was no way to get enough air into her lungs.

"Nobody touch anything. I'm calling Ezra. Lily, call Albert; he'll want to know what's going on. Wes, leave that gossipy bitch Apollo out of this." Brie already had her shell phone in her hand but still gave her brother a long and pointed look. Wes held his mobile phone, fingers poised over the keys.

Lily pulled out her own phone to call Albert while Brie got Ezra on the shell phone. Her fingers were uncooperative as she tried to press his contact information. She could barely think, barely breathe, and somehow, she was supposed to function? Holding the phone to her ear was proving difficult as her hands continued to shake. Albert picked up after only a single ring. "Darling, is everything okay?" he asked by way of greeting.

Just hearing his voice was enough to soothe some of Lily's anxiety, just enough that she could finally speak. "It's Simon; he was here at the shop." Her voice came out too soft, too shaky.

She heard Albert hiss on the other end. "That bastard! Did he hurt you? Did he threaten you?" The anger in his voice quickly faded into fear. If Albert was afraid, she was terrified.

Lily shook her head, like Albert could see her, then she remembered to voice it aloud. "No, I didn't even see him. He just left me a few things. Can you please get here?"

It came off sounding more needy than she intended, but she didn't have it in her to care. Right now, she did need him, and to get far away from Simon's *gifts*.

"I'm on my way, darling. Just stay in the back and wait for me." Then the line went dead. Lily stood holding her phone still to her ear until Brie started to tug her hand away. She still had not stopped shaking, and if she had thought about it, Lily might have been surprised that the phone managed to stay in her hand.

"Come on. Let's get to the apartment. It has the most protective spells." Brie pulled Lily toward the door just as Ezra stepped through it. He let the women pass, and Brie hit the number three button on the panel beside the Storage Room door, the one that would open into Ezra's apartment.

Behind them, Wes and Ezra talked in hushed voices over the flower and fruit still sitting on the counter, then Ezra scooped them up and he and Wes followed the women through the open door.

Lily walked on autopilot, letting Brie lead her down the hallway and into the open living room. "Breathe, Lily. I need you to breathe, okay?" Brie's voice was soothing. Was she not breathing? No, she was. But it was too fast, way too fast. Not enough air was getting into her lungs and she was near gasping. Brie whispered soothing words to her while she led Lily through the apartment. It took effort, but Lily finally managed to corral her thoughts long enough to focus her breaths, to slow them down and let the air reach down into her lungs and ground her a little.

Gentle hands on her shoulders pushed her down onto the couch, and a moment later, a glass of amber liquid was placed in her hand. "Drink, Lily. It'll help." Ezra's voice broke through the fear and anxiety in her head. She sipped automatically and the bite of the whiskey was enough to draw her back to her surroundings.

She took another fortifying gulp before speaking. "Thank you," she choked out. The shaking had stopped and her body began to cool off again, but her mind absorbed all the activity her body was not.

Nobody spoke for a long time. Lily could tell they were all watching her, but she kept her head bowed and her eyes fixed on the floor. *I just want Albert. I need him.*

It was hours, or perhaps only minutes, when a knock came on Ezra's door. "That's Albert. Lily, can you move? There are wards up to keep out vampires, so Albert can't come in here." Ezra's voice was soothing, like he was trying to coax a wounded animal. And that's almost exactly what she felt like: wounded. Because Simon had struck at her in a place she thought was completely safe.

She nodded and made to stand. If it meant Albert was her destination, she would move wherever they needed her. Ezra gripped her arm for support as she wobbled on her feet once she finally stood to her full height; her body felt so heavy and all her energy had drained away. Brie and Wes looked as if they wanted to fuss over her, each taking a step, and Brie reached out a hand. But Ezra shook his head and Lily was grateful that he kept them from overwhelming her.

The second she stepped over the threshold of the apartment door, Albert was there, enveloping her in his arms, clutching her so tightly that she could scarcely breathe again because he was crushing her so. But she didn't mind. It was the kind of breathless she wanted; all that mattered was he was here. He was solid beneath her hands. Her heated body pressed against his chilled one.

He was her safe haven.

He was home.

He was her everything.

"Are you okay, darling? Did Simon hurt you?" Albert pulled her back just enough to look into her eyes. His hands moved to cup her face. Lily kept her arms latched tightly around his waist and refused to let him move too far from her reach. Holding onto him was like her lifeline, and she wasn't about to let him go.

Her head shook in his hands. "No, I didn't even see him. We were in the Storage Room having dinner."

Albert gazed into her eyes, searching for something, answers maybe.

Then his gaze turned accusingly toward Ezra. "You were supposed to keep her safe. How did he get in? I thought you had all this magic and wards up. What's the point of them if Simon can just walk right in?" He was practically shouting by the end, but Ezra didn't flinch, nor did his face change from his placid visage he usually wore when Lily looked back at him, tugging her face from Albert's hands. Beside Ezra, Brie looked positively murderous, eyes narrowed into burning slits at Albert.

"Don't you blame him! That vamp is your maker. You're the one bringing trouble to our door." Brie's agitation broke through as she sniped back.

"I seem to recall being dragged into your troubles just last year when we had to save your sorry human ass. And even then, you couldn't stop yourself from getting killed." Albert stepped away from Lily and moved toward Brie.

But Brie didn't back down, didn't move at all. "Fuck you, Albert. Nobody asked for your help and you didn't even do anything."

"Lily could have been killed trying to rescue you. Selfish human, you didn't even care if others got hurt." He took another step toward Brie. Lily wanted to reach out, wanted to pull him close and tell him it wasn't Brie's fault. But she couldn't form the words. Her body didn't want to cooperate and she just stood there. She wanted him to comfort her, not fight everyone.

But Brie was braver than she was. "Lily isn't a porcelain doll that will break. You, of all people, should know how strong she is, and instead, you want to wrap her in a bubble! Get your head out of your ass and be there when she needs you, but also let her take care of herself!"

Lily knew Albert loved her intensely, but to hear her friend stand up for her warmed her heart. "Albert," she finally managed to croak out as she reached for his arm.

But he didn't turn, didn't even acknowledge her touch. Lily stepped up to stand next to him and looked up into his face. There she could see it; his eyes were glowing a crimson color, one she had never seen before.

Bloodlust.

Ezra took a step in front of Brie and Wes put a hand on her shoulder, a protective stance from both men. "Watch yourself, Albert. Brie isn't saying anything untrue. The wards worked fine. Simon himself didn't enter the shop. He stayed outside while he had a human bring in his threat."

"And how do you know that? You told me no one was around," Albert snapped, his crimson eyes still burning.

But it was Brie who answered his question. She pointed up. Lily and Albert followed the direction of her finger. There above the Storage Room door was a spyglass with an eye looking out at the end. "Charles Vane's spyglass, it records everything. Like a creepy security camera." The eye blinked once, twice. Lily had never noticed it there, but she was sure it was a newer installation. *That's really creepy*, she thought, looking away from the spyglass.

"So, he can just do whatever he wants here so long as he uses a human to do it?" Lily asked as she grabbed Albert's hand to give her some stability. A quick glance up into his face assured Lily that the crimson was gone from his dark eyes. The bloodlust was fading.

Ezra looked thoughtful for a second. "It's possible. But now that we know he's using that tactic, I can see what we can do about putting further protective magics in place. I would suggest doing the same at your home."

"Can you get us what we need? Money isn't an object. Just get me the best protection magic you have." Albert's voice sounded like a plea to Lily's ears. She wrapped her arms around his middle again.

Ezra nodded. "I'll see what I can do. I'll text you when everything is ready."

"He texts?" Wes loudly whispered to his sister.

"Like a grandpa. Full sentences and punctuation," she snorted back. Despite the situation, Lily admired that Brie and Wes never seemed to lose their humor or let too much bother them. They were strong like that, having been through so much in their lives, having lost so much.

The tension in the room dissipated quickly. But now all Lily wanted was her bed. "Let's go home, Bertie. It's been a night." She tugged him away from the group. "Thank you all for helping me tonight. I really appreciate it," Lily said over her shoulder as they prepared to step out into the late summer night.

Just as they turned to go, the door to Spirit Antiques burst open, the bell tinkling wildly. There in the doorway, looking as if he had just run to get there, was a man that Lily could only describe as a golden god. An annoying golden god, with a supplicant of one, and that was himself.

Apollo bent double, hands on his knees as he breathed hard. "Oh my gods, what did I miss?!" He already had his mobile phone out, probably prepared to send out a group chat to everyone within a fifty-mile radius.

"I told you not to tell him!" Lily heard Brie shout at Wes as she and Albert continued on their way out of the shop and toward home.

CHAPTER 13

It was close to dawn, but Albert couldn't wait any longer. He stayed at the house until Lily was fast asleep. But the minute her breathing was deep and even he made his way to his car and took off into the night. Guilt gnawed at him as he drove. He shouldn't leave her vulnerable like that, alone, not even knowing he was gone. He was comforted only by the knowledge that Lily had placed several layers of protection wards on the house before they went to bed. There were plenty already, but she did as many as she could to completely lock the house down. Once they had Ezra's protective magics, no one would ever be able to get to her inside their house.

Now, though, he needed to find Simon, needed to take care of this once and for all, needed to get Simon and his family of vampires out of their lives for good. Albert would give them a deadline, then he would come up with a plan. Maybe he hadn't thought the confrontation through enough. But he couldn't just do nothing, not after Simon threatened Lily. There was no way he could let that slide and the longer he waited to confront Simon, the more Simon would torment them, knowing he could get away with it.

The single lily Simon left was a mocking gesture, but it was the apple that held the most threat. Apples, Lily had told him, were a symbol of death. A simple message then, that Lily would die and Simon could kill her so easily. Simon went through a lot of trouble sending a message in a form Lily loved so deeply. Because his maker knew Lily would interpret his message easily. Albert had to do something—anything to keep her safe.

Even if it meant killing Simon.

If he could kill Simon. His maker was old even by vampire standards; Albert didn't know how old. That wasn't something Simon ever discussed with the family, though Albert figured it must have been several centuries.

And assuming he could even touch Simon, there were strict rules about killing one's maker. Vampires did not take kindly to patricide. There may not be codified laws with vampires, but there was one that all vampires knew; it could get you killed. It was all dangerous territory. As one of the vampire representatives on the Council, he also had that code to adhere to. At the very least, it would put his seat into question. He would need to remain an exemplary member of the community if he were to be trusted to represent the vampires of New Britain.

But I would face it all for her. I will deal with Simon or die. I can deal with the Council if I do kill my maker. Every last obstacle I will face eagerly, if it means that at the end of it all, Lily is alive, safe, and happy.

It took no time at all for him to arrive at the Hotel Nosferat. He wouldn't need to ask for Simon; his maker would find him. Albert was not surprised when he entered the hotel and found Celia standing in the center of the lobby.

"Of course, he sends my most favorite person to greet me." Albert's words dripped with contempt. Celia's eyes flashed with malice, even as her smile was sickly sweet. *She would be beautiful if she wasn't such a vile creature,* he thought as he stopped a few feet from her.

"Charming as usual, Albert. He's been waiting for you. Honestly, it took you long enough. I thought you would be here the moment you found Simon's gift." She turned, flinging her long black hair over her shoulder dramatically, letting the waves cascade through the air just so.

He followed, glowering at the back of her head. "I had more important things to worry about, like making sure my partner was alright. You see, that's what you do for someone you love; you put their needs before things like vengeance."

Ahead of him, Celia laughed, a light musical tone that was at complete odds with her character. "Oh, Albert, how soft you've grown in your time away. We'll have a lot of work to do to get you back up to fighting form. But don't worry. Simon will stamp out that bit of humanity you've picked up and you will be good as new."

Albert didn't bother with a response. There wasn't a point in telling Celia he was not returning to the family. They all thought it was inevitable that he would. Simon had deluded them all into thinking they couldn't survive outside the family. Celia, most of all, would never leave Simon. She was too devoted to him—even more than she was to Aron. If Simon walked into the sun tomorrow, Celia would follow him without question. But Albert, out living his undead life, was proof of Simon's fallibility—though maybe not enough proof for Celia.

Celia led him to the elevator and up and up they went to reach the penthouse. For a hotel full of powerful and wealthy vampires, Simon's use of the penthouse was just another means to convey the message he was older, more powerful, and wealthier than the common lodger.

As he followed Celia through the door, the open space living room should have awed him. The view from the floor-to-ceiling windows was spectacular. Hotel Nosferat had the unique status of being in a desirable area but was completely cloaked from human view. And through decades of manipulation from the owners, no buildings were ever built around to obstruct the view.

But all Albert could focus on was the assembled vampires, lounging on the various pieces of elegant, dark wood furniture. And there, the focal point of the space, the commanding presence in the room, sat Simon, in a deep high-backed chair, looking for all the world like a king draped across his throne with his court assembled around him.

"There he is, my wayward child, my dear Albert. What took you so long, sweetheart? I expected you hours ago." His smile was saccharine, and he looked like the picture of nonchalance. But Albert knew that bubbling under the surface was something more sinister. Simon didn't like to be kept waiting and hated disappointment even more. Not rushing to him the minute his threat to Lily was discovered was indeed a disappointment to Simon.

Good, that meant he had Simon off kilter just enough, though it also meant that Simon was at his most dangerous. "I would say I'm sorry, but I'm really not. My priority was in caring for Lily and less on your bullshit games." He kept his tone cool, as if none of this bothered him. He would give nothing to his maker, give nothing to the group of blood-suckers.

Inside, though, Albert wanted to rage at Simon. If he could scream at him, it would bring him a small delight. There was a fire burning in the pit of his stomach and it urged him to end Simon now before he could do anything further to Lily.

But I can't. Not now. I won't be able to protect her if I'm dead.

Albert's attention caught on Celia as she took a seat next to Aron on the long, plush couch. He draped his arm over the back of the seat behind her head and began to idly play with a few strands of her dark hair.

At the other end of the couch sat Eiko, her feet curled up on the couch with a book in her hands. Albert couldn't fault her for her disinterest in the matter. She was still young and probably didn't understand all the resentment that had been building for decades between him and the rest of the family. Albert was probably to her what Rosalind and Robert Lutece were to him: a sad story, a cautionary tale told to young vampires about the risks of going off on your own.

It took Albert a moment to notice Sam. They stood at one of the windows, nearly blending into the shadows. Sam was very good at blending in, remaining unseen when necessary, making them the perfect spy for Simon. No doubt they were the one that tracked down Albert and Lily and reported back all they had found out. Probably tracked down the human to use in delivering Simon's message, too.

Albert drew his gaze back to Simon and he internally smiled when Simon glowered at him. There was some satisfaction in making his maker lose his easy coolness. But he couldn't gloat over it because while Simon would let him get away with small insults, he could easily snap and end Albert quickly.

"I hope your appearance tonight means you are ready to come home." Simon quickly regained his composure, his face melting back into his casual smirk. "Eiko, why don't you properly greet Albert? I imagine you two will be spending a lot of time together since you are now his responsibility."

Eiko sighed deeply and rolled her eyes but set down her book anyway and unfolded herself from the couch. She moved slowly toward Albert; she had at least mastered control over her speed. But the last thing he wanted was the young vampire near him. Like hell, she was going to be his responsibility. He hissed at her, baring his fangs in a clear warning of violence to come if she continued to move closer.

Eiko stopped in her tracks, and a brief flash of fear passed over her face. She was at least passed the age of feeling invincible as a vampire and recognized when there was real danger in front of her.

"Now, now, Albert, you're going to have to learn to play nice again. We can't have you frightening off poor Eiko. After all, not everyone can survive on their own like you. Well, if you can even call it surviving." He chuckled to himself, then motioned to Eiko to return to her seat. Her part was over for the night, and Simon would think nothing more of her for the time being.

Albert crossed his arms lazily, determined not to let Simon rattle him. "You misunderstand, Simon. I'm not returning. I'm here to tell you to leave. You will not bother me or Lily any further and will never step foot in New Britain again. Best probably to leave Connecticut altogether, actually."

From the couch, Celia laughed. It was loud and lacked all humor. "Oh Bertie, you have developed the ability to joke. How fun." Beside her, Aron snorted loudly.

Simon waved them off with a simple flick of his wrist, and when he spoke, it was no longer the smooth caress it had been. It was something harder, full of authority. "And who are you to command me, Albert? I made you. Should I choose to end you, I am able to easily." Faster than even Albert could see, Simon stood before him, so close that if he breathed, it would flutter Albert's hair. The elder vampire caressed Albert's neck, cool soft fingers against the vein, pressing lightly. Once, Albert would have submitted to this. Would have moved his head to expose his neck just a little more to his maker, a show of fealty. Because Simon was all about control. That's why he never let his family members leave. The only permanent escape from him was the sun.

But Albert had lived the last thirty years without Simon. Built a home, a community, and found love without his maker to dictate his immortal life. Never again would he bow to this vampire or any other.

Still, he surprised himself when he grabbed Simon's wrist and flung it away. The elder vampire looked stunned, and an eerie silence filled the room as Albert realized what he'd done. Before he could fully process his actions, Simon had him by the neck and had slammed him against the nearest wall.

In his eighty years with Simon, Albert had never been on the receiving end of his maker's ire. But now Simon bared his fangs, the blue of his irises bled into crimson, consuming the color and the whites as they bored into Albert's still-dark eyes. Simon's hand tightened further around Albert's throat as he let the blood-lust take over. Even without the need to breathe, the clamp around his throat was uncomfortable, like the bones of his neck were ready to crack and then shatter into pieces.

Without a doubt, Albert knew it would take very little effort for Simon to sever his head from his neck. *Why didn't I think this through? I never should have come alone again.* He thought of Lily. Of how she would react when she woke up and found his note, but then he never came home.

"I pulled you from the rubble of that crumbling city. I challenged death for you and gave you a new life in the wake of devastation, gave you a home and a new family. I could have left you to die with the rest. But I chose you. You owe me everything." He seethed in Albert's face, his cool demeanor long gone.

But then Simon withdrew his hand quickly with a hiss of pain. He stared at his hand as if it was the very thing that caused the injury. "What magic is this, Albert?" he growled out, still staring at his hand. There were no markings, no sign of damage at all on the flawless skin of his palm. Albert remembered then.

The Nazar.

He had worn it every day since Ezra had given it to him and he had completely forgotten about it. Seemed like the magic worked, after all. He would have to thank Ezra later, once he got out of this disaster.

The rest of the family had stood abruptly at Simon's exclamation, in offensive positions, ready to strike at Albert when Simon gave them leave. Simon, however, recovered quickly. Nothing ever phased his maker for long. Simon's laughter filled the room. Unlike Celia's cruel laughter, Simon's chuckle was melodic and sweet. By his very nature, Simon was designed to be appealing and enticing so that he could lure unsuspecting beings into his web. He was the perfect predator.

There was a time when Albert longed to be the cause of Simon's laughter, to be the one he smiled at whenever he did something to please his maker. Even now, that sound enticed Albert; he wanted more of it. Things hadn't been so bad with the family, not with Simon, anyway. But that's what Simon wanted; he wanted Albert to crave his laughter again, to crave his smiles, and attention—to crave him.

Distracted by the laugh, it took Albert a moment to remember Simon's question. Like hell he was going to tell him about the amulet hidden beneath his shirt. "I have friends with old magic. They look out for me." At least his head was clear enough to manage the words and hold something back.

Simon's face returned to its customary casual smirk, even as a thoughtful look crossed his features. The rest of the family, save for Sam, stood at the ready. Sam had quickly resumed their position against the window, though their eyes never left Albert. Celia's beautiful face had morphed into a hateful sneer. It fit more to match her black heart. The slightest prompting from Simon would have her ripping Albert's throat out in a second, of that, he had no doubt.

But Simon showed more amusement with the whole situation. "Run home to your little witch, Albert, and prepare your goodbyes. You have until the end of the month before we head to France. I know how much you love the French countryside at the end of summer."

He should have said something, should have rebuked Simon's words instantly, but instead, Albert made for the door without a glance back. He would let Simon have the last word for now.

"Oh, and Albert, if you choose to disobey me again, I won't just kill her. I will terrorize her. I will pass into her visions again, meet her in that space, and I will break her psyche down until it is a shattered mess with no pieces large enough to put back together. And only then will I let her die." Simon said it with such a large, fanged grin that Albert couldn't suppress the shudder that went through his whole body.

Albert rushed from the Hotel Nosferat and sped the whole way home, his foot barely letting off the acceleration until he was pulling into his driveway.

Lily was still asleep in their bed just as the sun started to peek over the horizon. Albert crumpled the note he had left and shoved it into the wastebasket. He quickly undressed and slid in next to her, wrapping his arms tightly around her, and listened to the rhythmic beat of her heart. It was the most precious sound in the world. Like hell he would let Simon take it away. He just didn't know how he was going to stop him.

CHAPTER 14

$\mathcal{A}$ knock came on the front door. Lily stopped in her tracks, carrying a basket of herbs from her latest harvest. She wasn't expecting anyone, and Albert was out for a few hours at the Council meeting. Not that he wanted to leave her, but as one of the vampire representatives, he had an obligation. And Lily absolutely hated Council meetings. So, she forced him to go with many promises that she would be perfectly safe. He left with much reluctance and tried to turn back several times before she threatened to hex him if he didn't get a move on.

While she appreciated his concern, and it really did make her feel safer knowing how seriously he took her wellbeing, it was starting to become a little overbearing. Not to mention, it did nothing to quell her own anxiety. Albert's ramped-up emotions were taking as much of a toll on her as they were on him.

Another knock on the door drew her to the matter at hand. The only people who visited the house were Brie and Wes, and Brie would be at the shop while Ezra was also at the Council meeting. None of her wards tripped to indicate anything malicious. And if the wards weren't triggered, it had to be someone she or Albert permitted in the house. She set the basket on the kitchen island and padded to the front door, pulling it open warily.

Standing on the large front porch was the last thing Lily ever expected to see at her house. Gathered in a huddled group were six Everett women, each loaded down with canvas bags and various potted plants—not only her sisters, but her mother, and her two sisters, and even her granny.

Lily didn't get a word in before they pushed their way inside with a loud jumble of chatter about the things they brought. They were clearly continuing on a conversation that started before Lily opened the door.

"Lily, dear, where can we set these bags? I have mugwort, witch hazel, and some of my mixed berry jam. Do vampires eat jam? Doesn't matter—everyone loves my mixed berry jam. Perfect headache cure." Her Auntie Petunia swept past, already heading for the kitchen like she owned the place, her chatter endless as she went.

"Oh, please, Tunie, it's a hangover cure. We all know that's why you made it, you damn lush." Auntie Daisy snorted from behind her sister. Hyacinth kissed her daughter on the cheek as she swept past, barely pausing long enough to do so, leaving Lily wide-eyed and open-mouthed, staring, still holding the door open.

"Here, take this," Rose gruffly said, thrusting a large wreath made of dill. Lily looked down at the wreath in her hands. It was well crafted; she could clearly see that Rose had taken great care in weaving her magic into it—dill to ward off evil spirits and welcome prosperity into the home. It was thoughtful and kind—so very unlike Rose. Their mom probably made her do it, but Rose was known for her magical arrangements. How someone with such a horrible attitude most of the time made things so lovely and delicate never ceased to amaze Lily.

"Thank yo–" Lily began, but Rose kept walking and ignored her. Lily looked down again at the wreath in her hands. It really was exceptionally crafted; Rose was truly gifted. When she looked up again, her sister Ivy came up to the door with her own canvas bag.

"Don't mind Rose. She and Manu had a huge fight, and she's been in a mood for days. She'll get over it. We've got bigger things to worry about." But before Lily could question her further, Ivy had already followed the rest of their family into the kitchen.

Last came her granny. Lily wrapped the diminutive woman up in a strong embrace. "Nice place you have here, child. Your fanger has good taste." She gave Lily's cheek an affectionate pat as she pulled away from the hug.

"Granny, what's going on? Why are you all here?" Lily didn't want to sound ungrateful. She really was happy to see her family, especially since her last several encounters with them hadn't exactly gone well.

Her granny took her hand and led her toward the rest of the group. "You should offer your granny a drink first. I know your mother taught you how to treat guests."

Lily could only nod and the eldest and youngest Everett witches made their way into the spacious kitchen. Not that Lily needed to offer much hospitality since her family had already taken over the space. The Everetts took "making yourself at home" quite literally on every occasion.

The kettle was already on a stove burner, next to a cast-iron pot stirring itself filled with what smelled like her dad's vegetable stew. Auntie Daisy flicked her wrist, the oven door opened, and she slid in a pie pan.

At the island, her mother and Auntie Petunia sliced vegetables and fruit for a salad. Granny took a seat at one of the island stools and filched pieces of sliced veggies from the pile while she waited for her drink. Ivy started to pull containers of tea out of one of the bags she had brought while Rose riffled through the cabinets.

"Where are your teacups?" Rose asked gruffly, not bothering to turn around.

"Last cabinet on the left." Lily sounded bewildered to her own ears. Here were the women in her family bustling about her kitchen as if they did this all the time, instead of it being their first visit.

The sight of them all gathered here, just like it had been at the farm, warmed her heart. She hadn't realized how much she had missed the simple bustle of her family being around—the easy camaraderie among the women, the seamless dance around the kitchen, like they all knew the steps perfectly. As much as she wanted to question their coming, for just a moment, she wanted to savor the scene around her and pretend that everything was normal with them. The prickle of tears started, seeing them all in their element, and she longed to step into that dance and forget all her problems.

Questions needed to be answered, though, so she broke into the bustle. "What are you all doing here? Mom, don't you have the Council meeting tonight? Like right now. Or are you blowing off your representative duties?"

The women barely paused to acknowledge her words. Hyacinth waved her hand, and the knife she was holding began to chop on its own. "Your father is filling in for me as my proxy this evening. We thought it was more important to see you while Albert is away."

Lily tried not to panic, to not think the worst of the situation. But now she realized it made sense that they would come when they knew Albert was out of the house—to isolate her from him and talk her into leaving him and moving home again.

This was an ambush, not a social visit.

There had still been no explanation of what Rose saw in her vision that convinced the family Albert would kill her or do even worse. There had been so little communication since then that Lily didn't know what to think.

Breathe, she commanded herself. She was getting ahead of herself, thinking the worst of the situation. It would only cause her anxiety to spike and then her mother would fuss even more and nothing would be resolved.

While Lily worked to calm herself, the teakettle whistled loudly, and Ivy went to retrieve it. Her sisters worked in tandem to put together a tea spread until there was a steaming cup for each woman. "Do you have a bit of something stronger for the tea? My cold bones could use the boost," her granny said, feigning a weakness Lily knew she didn't have.

Auntie Daisy snorted. "It's summer, Ma. You're just a boozehound. It's where Tunie gets it."

The elder Everett woman sniffed. "Having three daughters such as you would drive anyone to drink. Besides, a bit of whiskey in my tea is the secret to a long life." There was indeed a small liquor cart in the kitchen and Lily pointed her finger toward it, then with a beckoning gesture, she magically coaxed a bottle of whiskey from the assembled alcohol. The bottle sailed across the room, loosened the cap, and poured a generous amount into Granny's still-steaming tea. Then, with a flick of her wrist, the bottle capped itself and returned to its place on the liquor cart.

"I see ma is the only one who gets the good stuff," Auntie Petunia mumbled as she sipped her own tea, though she didn't actually make a move toward the cart. Despite the teasing from her sisters, Auntie Petunia only drank during holidays anymore. But her youthful alcohol-induced exploits were the stuff of legends in family lore.

The Everett women assembled around the kitchen island with their tea, all of them looking toward Hyacinth expectantly. She pretended not to notice as she continued to sip her beverage for several more seconds. "Oh, for Goddess' sake. Fine, let's get to business then," she finally huffed as she set down her teacup and focused her attention on Lily. "Lily, dear, we love you. I know things haven't been ... good since you moved out." Hyacinth shot a sharp look toward

Rose, who looked as if she was going to say something, but she quickly shut her mouth again.

It was a total understatement, but Lily decided splitting hairs when they are all cozy now was not the best idea. But before she could respond in what she hoped was encouragement, Granny let out a loud cackle.

"Not good, Hyacinth? Well, that's just hilarious. You've had your phone strapped to your hand for weeks, ready for Lily to call. Pacing around like bad news will arrive any second. That one," she pointed to Rose, "has scowled at everyone for everything, and it's a wonder her wife hasn't thrown her out. Always waiting at a moment's notice to go off and slay the monster that doesn't exist. And you," this time she turned to Ivy and pointed a finger, "know perfectly well how things really are and do nothing but try to placate everyone with pats on the back and there theres. All of you have gone off half-cocked over one blurry vision from someone who isn't strong in the Sight. Some might think you have some prejudice against Albert just because he's a fanger."

To say the table was stunned was an understatement. Granny rarely involved herself in family drama, or any issues in the magical community, despite being an elder. But here she was, standing up to her daughters and granddaughters for Lily and Albert. If it was possible for a heart to overflow with love, Lily's was doing just that. All her life, she had a special bond with her granny. She taught Lily how to use her sight, helped her interpret her visions when she was too young to understand. They were too alike, the elder witch would always say.

The moment was quickly broken by Rose's angry voice. "I don't need to be strong with the sight to know what I saw. He'll kill her because that's what he is: a killer."

"He's not!" Lily found herself yelling back before Rose could continue her tirade. Raising her voice was so unlike her, especially when it came to her family. Lately, though, she had been doing just that a lot. Frankly, she was tired of Rose's bullshit. "Yes, in the past, he was, but that's not him now. Not once since I've known him has he ever bitten me. Or, for that matter, anyone who Ezra didn't arrange for him. And you all trust Ezra, right?" She looked around the table as every head nodded. They had all grown up going to Ezra's shop, save for granny, who started going the minute Ezra set up shop in New Britain over a hundred years ago.

"So, trust in me and Ezra. We know Albert. I know Albert. He's the twin to my soul, and he would walk into the sun if it meant sparing me even an ounce of pain. What I don't understand is why it took one vision from her," she pointed accusingly at Rose, "to make you all forget that you like Albert. He's been to every Samhain celebration for years. In the last year, he's been to every solstice and equinox celebration without issue. Mama, you've even gone out of your way on many occasions to make sure we've had something for him to eat. So why now?"

Lily looked at each person in turn, but every one of the Everett women, save for Granny, shifted their gazes away from her. The tension and guilt were palpable. *Good,* she thought; she wanted them to feel guilty.

"Oh, look at that. The stew is ready." Auntie Daisy hopped away from the island and removed the stew from the burner.

"Leave it, Daisy dear. You come back here and we sort this out," Granny said, using her own magic to bring bowls and spoons out from the cabinet and drawer. The pot of stew and a loaf of bread sitting on the counter flew to the island. Granny turned her attention back on her daughters and granddaughters, completely ignoring the magic that ladled out heaping helpings of stew and sliced bread.

"Now, I think it's best that we all see what vision the Sight has given Rose. Why you haven't done this before just proves I've raised a bunch of idiots. Join hands, ladies, and Rose, focus your Sight." The assembled women followed their matriarch's lead and, around the island, they reached for each other's hands. With eyes shut tight in focus, Granny started the chant.

"Your mind with my mind, your Sight with my Sight." It was a simple enough spell, one every witch with the Sight learned at a young age when they were too young to understand their visions and needed the aid of an elder witch.

Lily took up the chant next, then Rose, her eyes shut, brow furrowed as she called to the vision. The rest of them joined in, voices low, squeezing hands tightly.

And there it was, a sudden brightness of color in Lily's mind.

The images appeared suddenly, taking shape, two people, a man and a woman, but they were blurry; she couldn't quite see their faces or features. It was like they were out of focus in dim light, seen through foggy glass. There was no sound, no voices or breathing, which wasn't unusual for some visions, especially since Rose was not strong with the Sight.

But what was clear was that the two figures were in a heated argument. In seconds, though, faster than they could perceive, the man was behind the woman and sinking fangs into her neck. She struggled, flailed in his arms, to no avail. Her movements began to slow and then ceased altogether until she hung limply in his arms. Lily expected him to drop her body to the ground, but he didn't. Instead, he held her in his arms and gently lowered her until she laid serenely at his feet. And when he dropped to his knees, he bent over her body and his shoulders began to shake. He appeared to be weeping, though no sound came from him.

For a moment, just one blink, the vision seemed to focus just enough that Lily could see the details of the scene before her. A flash of gold in the man's hair, the dark skin of the woman before him. And then the vision ended and their hands dropped.

"Now you can see, like I've been telling you, that fucking bloodsucker is going to kill her. Sure, he's going to feel bad about it, but that doesn't change his nature," Rose said, a hint of triumph in her voice.

All was quiet around the kitchen island. Something caught in Lily's mind, though. Something in that one instant where the vision was clear. "That's not me. And that's not Albert."

Rose scoffed. "You would say that. It was clear enough, Lily. Just because you don't want to believe doesn't make it true."

"No, didn't you see? Right as the vision was about to end, everything was clear for just a split second. That vampire was blond and she was darker than me. I know Albert, and that's not him. Not unless he can somehow turn himself into a blonde-haired white man." It almost looked like it could be Simon, though Lily couldn't be sure since she had only seen him the one time.

"I saw that, too," Auntie Petunia said, and beside her, Auntie Daisy nodded as well. "There's no way that was Albert. He's too sweet of a boy to do anything like that."

"Weren't you just saying on the way over that you'd like to drop him off in the middle of the desert in the summer?" Ivy prompted, a wry grin on her face.

"Child, I have never said anything about wishing violence on anyone in my life," Auntie Petunia retorted, but Lily saw her mother roll her eyes.

"Lily's right. Your vision wasn't of Albert. But there has to be a connection then. Otherwise, why would you receive this vision?" Hyacinth addressed her comments toward Rose. Lily's eldest sister couldn't hide the conflict on her features. Rose didn't like to be wrong or to show any weakness in her magic. And here both happened. Despite her confidence, the Sight rarely came to Rose, and when it did, it was always vague and blurry. There was no chance she would be able to convince two witches, especially adept with the Sight, that her vision was absolute. No visions really were, by nature, absolute; the future was too unpredictable for even magic to determine. Rose's certainty in her vision had been greatly misplaced.

Lily felt sympathy for her sister. Sure, Rose had never liked Albert, and maybe that disdain clouded her interpretation of the vision, but she knew Rose's heart was in the right place. She just wanted to look out for her little sister. But that didn't wash away all the hurt and betrayal that Rose had caused over the last weeks, not just to Lily, but to Albert as well.

"Start eating, ladies, and let me tell you a story," Granny said as she tucked into her stew.

"Ma, I don't think we need stories right now. We need answers," Hyacinth started, but at the look her mother threw her, she quieted instantly. It was a well-practiced glare that Granny used to command rooms.

"Hush all of you and listen. This is not often told in our family anymore, but with our lineage and time, plenty of stories fall through the cracks. I had all but forgotten it. But I'll tell it as my mother told me." Granny's eyes took on a faraway look as her words began to weave the magic. Above the kitchen island, a dense cloud started to form, white and nearly opaque. From within the cloud, figures began to take shape. At first, they were little more than grey smudges, but as Granny began to speak, their forms had more solidity and detail.

This was the power Granny was most known for, story weaving—a way to manifest a tale into images that were acted out in real-time. She could pull from the past or invent stories of her own. It delighted children, and for the adults, it was a reminder to keep the old traditions alive.

"Our ancestor, Juniper Everett, was a witch powerful with the Sight. She was renowned throughout the West Indies for her visions. People traveled from afar to have their fortunes read and to find the name of their sweetheart; even the white folks went to her for all manner of things. She was beautiful and bold, and vowed to let no man bring her low." One of the grey images solidified into the image of a beautiful young woman. Her skin was so dark it was nearly black, her brown-black hair was in several long braids down her back. The family resemblance between the image of Juniper and the women around the kitchen was noticeable.

"Mama Juniper had a life full of powerful magic, a man to love, and children of her own." The image changed to show Juniper, with three young daughters and one son. Daughters always came in threes for Everetts, but the son looked to be the same age as one of the daughters, both of them barely more than newborns. Twins, most likely, as twins ran in their family. And next to Juniper, with his arms wrapped around her, stood a handsome man with close-cropped hair and light golden-brown skin. They all looked so happy together.

"She was happy with her family. But then tragedy struck. Juniper's beloved husband died, and she was left with a broken heart and her young children were left without their father." The image of the man faded, and Juniper's brilliant smile turned to sorrow. Lily's heart ached for her ancestor. She tried to imagine losing Albert, and the thought hurt too much to even consider.

Granny continued with her story weaving, unaware of the crying hearts around her. "A few years passed, and our Juniper continued to work her magic for all who came to her. The stories of her gifts reached a vampire who took a special interest in her magic. He wanted to know his future, and so he sought her out on her island home." A new figure appeared in the cloud above the island and Lily gasped when she saw his face materialize through the fog. Blonde hair and sun-kissed skin, impeccably dressed, though not showy. There were no rings on his fingers like there were now. But Lily would never forget those pale blue eyes, never forget the feel of his cool fingers against her head as he snapped her neck.

"Simon."

It took her a moment to realize everyone had turned to look at her. She had said his name aloud without meaning to.

"You know this vampire?" Hyacinth asked.

Lily nodded. "He's Albert's maker. The one he ran away from." She felt the need to add the last bit so they would know he had no connection left to Simon.

"Shit," Auntie Petunia gasped.

"Yeah, what she said," Auntie Daisy looked stricken.

Granny cleared her throat to continue. "Everything is connected, it seems. Mama Juniper read the fortune of this vampire once. Then he came back and asked again, and again she told him his fortune. That began a pattern. He would show and she would read. For weeks, this continued. And what sparked was a passionate love affair between vampire and witch. In those days, our kinds mingled frequently, though we were not so friendly with other creatures. Rules in the magical world were stricter then."

The images in the cloud changed to show Juniper and Simon smiling as they wrapped around each other in a loving embrace. Simon's smile was wide and genuine, his fangs on full display, his eyes soft as he looked upon Juniper. There was nothing terrifying about his face in the story weave, not like in her vision. It was a face of a man in love. A moment later, the children reappeared, a little older, one attached to Simon's leg with the biggest smile on her face and the boy holding onto the vampire's hand. They were a family, and clearly, a happy one, judging by all the smiles.

"But then the humans came and tore their lives apart. They came to kill Simon for what he was, believing he was a blight on their crops and enterprises. Simon killed them all, as a vampire is able." The images showed torches and stakes advancing on Simon, then cut to a field of dead humans and Simon covered in their blood.

Once again, the image changed, and the scene took on a familiar tone. Juniper and Simon stood together, arguing like in the vision Rose showed them. "The vampire believed it was Juniper who sold him out to the humans in an attempt to save her own life from their human superstitions. And in that moment of perceived betrayal and bloodlust, he killed her." The image, now in full detail, was of Simon drinking from Juniper. Then he laid her reverently on the ground and wept so violently his whole body shook from it. When his tears subsided, he looked down at his lover with such sadness Lily felt her heart go out to him. Simon reached for something hanging around Juniper's neck—a simple necklace with a long piece of black tourmaline in a rough silver setting, a pendant for mind, body, and energy protection. He slipped it around his own neck and then the scene faded. Lily recalled seeing the same necklace on Simon in her vision. Now she knew the significance of it and somehow that made it that much worse to think about.

"The vampire brought her to the home they had shared for many years and fled into the night, leaving the body of Mama Juniper for her family to find. From then on, our family has avoided the vampires. Until now." Granny's story weaving came to an end, and her focus returned to her family around her. The cloud above the kitchen island dissipated, though the images were imprinted on Lily's brain. The looks of love shared between Juniper and Simon and their children, and then the terrible sorrow Simon faced once he realized what he had done.

There was quiet all around; nobody touched their food or said a word. Their gazes averted from each other, but the tension was too much for Lily to bear.

"Albert is not Simon. And I'm not Juniper," she whispered, though they could all hear her.

"We know that, baby, but that doesn't mean history won't repeat itself. Albert is one of Simon's, after all," her mother said, eyes pitying. If she was closer, Hyacinth would surely pat Lily's arm, but Lily didn't want patronizing.

"No!" Lily shouted. "Simon may have made Albert what he is, but Albert is not Simon. He left the family decades ago because he is not like them. He has worked hard to be better than that. To take only what he needs from people willing to give it. You all are ready to punish Albert for the sins of his maker."

"And any vampire is able to go into bloodlust and kill without meaning to," Rose shouted back as she slapped her hands down on the counter. The sound was ear-splitting in the mostly silent kitchen. The aunts flinched away from the sound, as did Ivy. But Lily wouldn't let herself flinch, wouldn't let Rose's outburst get to her.

"So can a witch! Plenty of witches have lost control of their powers and the devastation has been huge. We are not so blameless, either." Lily felt the crackle of magic beneath her skin, just as she felt Rose's rise within her. Never in their lives, despite plenty of fights, had Lily or Rose used their magic against each other out of malice. But any of them were capable of losing control when their emotions got the better of them.

Ivy, ever the diffuser of conflict between Lily and Rose, spoke up. "I don't think Albert would ever hurt Lily. Even if he thought she'd betray him, he would kill himself first. Lils is right. Albert is not Simon."

The aunties nodded in agreement. Hyacinth looked less sure, but still nodded. "I want to believe so, too."

Rose scoffed again. "You're all idiots," she spat and threw down her spoon and stormed out of the room. Lily heard the front door slam and a heavy weight fell to the pit of her stomach. She didn't expect to win over Rose, but she expected something, at least.

"She'll come around, eventually. Now, why don't we have you and Albert for dinner this weekend, and we can start anew and welcome him to our family properly since he's going to be around a long time," Hyacinth said, a tentative smile on her face.

Lily smiled at her mother. She was unsure about what would happen at another family dinner that involved Albert and Rose in the same room. This would all go like every other family disagreement, though. Everything would be swept under the rug and the family's earlier dislike of Albert would be forgotten and never acknowledged again. Knowing that would happen, she was hopeful that her family was willing to make an effort to bring Albert into their loud, chaotic fold. If they could see the good in him and love him like she always hoped they would, it wouldn't matter how things started out, and they could rug sweep all they liked.

Lily should have told Albert everything that happened that evening when he got back from the Council meeting. But he looked so tired and annoyed that instead, she took him straight to their bed, where they took turns bringing each other to orgasm again and again, forgetting everything else.

But now, as the day turned from soft morning light to glaring afternoon sun and heat, forcing her out of the garden, Lily knew she had to tell him what had happened with her family. She found him in his study, working at his desk. There were stacks of papers in front of him, and he sat slightly hunched, his focus completely on the document before him.

Albert had the luxury of having too much money. He didn't have a traditional job, more like his job was keeping track of and moving the wealth he had amassed over the last century, and looking after the several businesses he owned but was not part of actively running. He was absolutely meticulous about his bookkeeping, and that kept him busy enough.

She knocked on the threshold to get his attention, though he already knew she was there. "Am I interrupting?" She felt a twinge of guilt drawing him out of his work, but he had been working for hours and could use the break.

Albert looked up and smiled softly. "Never. What's on your mind, darling?" Leaning back in his chair, he relaxed into the leather. Lily had seen him like this several times; it was probably his favorite chair in the whole house. He looked so at ease for the first time in weeks, Lily hated the thought of breaking it.

"Something happened last night while you were at the Council meeting. Nothing bad," she added quickly as she saw him start to tense. Of course, his first thought would go to something with Simon. She continued quickly, "My family came over. Just my mom, sisters, aunties, and granny. They brought a few things and food. They wanted to talk about what Rose saw in her vision."

Albert settled back in the chair only slightly, but it was enough for Lily to feel okay with continuing on. "Rose shared the vision with all of us, but it wasn't nearly as clear as she made it sound. It was a vampire killing someone who vaguely resembled me. But it wasn't us. It was my ancestor and her lover." Lily took a deep breath before continuing because what she said next would be a lot for Albert to handle. "It was... it was Simon." Her voice came out more of a whisper than she had intended, but Albert heard her all the same.

She let that hang between them for a long moment, feeling her heart pound in her chest in the silence.

"You know this for certain?" His voice was soft, tentative, as he closed his eyes and dropped his chin to his chest.

"Yes, completely sure," she breathed. They were both practically whispering at each other, like speaking too loudly would make it all too real. Lily found it a struggle to keep her breathing even. As well as she knew Albert, she really didn't know what to expect from him at this revelation.

Finally, Albert broke the silence. "I knew Simon had a witch paramour centuries ago. But I never would have thought it was an Everett witch. That's why he came back. He found out about us, probably from Sam, if I had to guess, and the last thing he would want for one of his children would be to be with an Everett witch. I don't doubt that Simon would like to wipe out all the Everetts if he had the power."

Lily crinkled her nose in thought. "I'm not sure about that. Granny showed us with her story weaving. He looked in pain, like he killed a part of himself when he killed her." Lily suddenly had a thought. "What if... well, what if Simon doesn't want history to repeat itself? Maybe he's worried that another Everett will betray a vampire, and you'll live with the guilt of killing me, like he has?"

Albert shook his head and pinched the bridge of his nose. "Maybe. I don't know. He's threatened to hurt you, to kill you. If he was so worried about history repeating itself, why would he do that? Why would he want to kill a descendant of his lover?"

A valid question. Wish I knew, she thought and slumped against the door frame.

"I could use the Sight again to find him. If I could only talk to him, understand –" she started, but Albert cut her off, his eyes were hard.

"No! Absolutely not. Lily, last time he killed you in the vision. I know it affected you. I still see you rub your neck like it's just been snapped. I won't let you take that risk again." He slapped his hands down on his desk. Lily jumped at the loud sound of flesh hitting hard wood.

Albert immediately looked apologetic. "I'm sorry, darling. I'm just worried. He could hold you in the vision, do unspeakably cruel things to you without killing you. I don't want you to go through that again. I don't know what he's capable of in that space."

Lily placed her hands on her hips, exasperated. "I control the vision, not Simon. I'm prepared this time. If I don't, what then? Do we just wait for him to kill me for real? Do you go with him at the end of the month? We need a plan, Albert. We can't just keep avoiding this!"

Because we are avoiding it. Even when we talk about it, we're not talking about how to fix the problems. The realization hit her with such clarity that she was surprised she hadn't thought of it before. They had spent so much time and energy over the last several weeks focused on the issue between her family and then Simon's reappearance, but the only thing they had done was try to talk to each side individually. There was no solution, no plan for when talking failed. With the month deadline Simon imposed approaching faster than she would like, she had no idea what they were going to do. It wasn't like they could avoid it, blow off Simon's threats, and carry on with life.

Her family would be more accepting now that Rose's vision turned out to be about Simon and Juniper and not Albert and Lily. Well, everyone but Rose would start to accept them. But that didn't solve the problem with Simon. Because Lily knew that Albert would go with the family at the end of the month if it meant saving her. He would readily give over to the misery he experienced with them just so she could live a normal life. They would destroy the man he had become, and he would let them.

It felt like her heart dropped to her stomach at the revelation. "You're just going to go back to them at the end of the month, aren't you?" She didn't mean for her voice to sound so defeated. *But that's how I feel. Like there's nothing I can do to fix this.*

Albert looked away, dropping his gaze back to the papers on his desk. Tears pricked at her eyes, but she wouldn't let herself cry. "I don't see another way. If I don't go, it won't be Simon who'll come for you. It will be Celia. And Celia is the cruelest vampire I know. She won't just make it hurt; she'll have you begging for death and still deny you that release for as long as possible. She'll make me watch as she tears you apart. If I go, at least I'll know you'll be safe." He didn't once lift his gaze. Instead, he talked to his desk like he couldn't stand to face her.

Now the tears came and there was nothing Lily could do to stop them. "So that's it, then. Were you going to tell me, or were you just going to disappear one day?" Her voice was accusing between the tears.

Some part of her took a measure of satisfaction when she watched him flinch away from her words.

"I was going to tell you once everything was settled. I wanted to make sure you were taken care of; that's what I'm working on now. The house, a few of my bank accounts... I'm putting them in your name. You'll be set for life. Do whatever you want with the house. Stay or sell it. It's yours to do with as you want once I'm gone." His little speech made her want to throw something, to scream like she never had in her life.

"I don't want your fucking house! I want you!" she yelled. But he only shook his head, and that angered her more.

"This is the only thing that will keep you safe. I don't want this, Lily. I want to spend the rest of our lives together. But I won't see you hurt. I won't let them kill you for my own selfishness." He turned his gaze up toward her finally, and she could see the pain behind his eyes. But he didn't deserve to feel that pain, not when he was the one breaking her heart.

"You're an idiot, Albert Hsu." With tears streaming down her face, Lily fled the room, slamming the door behind her.

She ran to their bedroom and shut and locked the door behind her. Part of her wanted to collapse on the bed and continue to cry. *But what will that solve? I just need to get out of here.*

Near bursting with anger and sadness, she stalked to the closet and pulled out a suitcase. She started to throw clothes in; most were identical pairs of overalls, the only variation was the color. She went to the bathroom and gathered up her toiletries and shoved them into the suitcase as well.

Lily zipped the whole thing up, but then stopped and put her hands on the top of the suitcase. *What am I doing? Where am I going?* She wasn't second-guessing her decision to put some space between her and Albert; she just needed to figure out where to go. The instinctual choice was to go home, back to the farm. But her family would see it as her moving home for good and leaving Albert behind. She wasn't. She just needed the time to cool off and come up with a plan for them since Albert had resigned himself to his fate.

No, she couldn't go home. There were Brie and Ezra, but she didn't want to impose on them any more than she already had. They only had the one room, and she would be up in their business if she slept in the living room. Lily took out her phone and pulled up her text conversation with Brie. A quick text exchange and she had a place to stay for at least the night. Longer if she needed it.

In minutes, she was out the door and in her car. Albert stayed in his office; he didn't even try to stop her from leaving. Lily was thankful for that. If he did come out, one look at his face would have kept her at the house, and she wouldn't get the chance to work through her complicated emotions. They would just lapse back into a cycle of not talking about the issues they were facing, and Lily would be stuck counting down the days until Albert left her for good.

Later, she would talk to him and let him know where she was staying. But for now, she concentrated on driving to the apartment Brie shared with Wes. Not that Brie spent much time there anymore, which is why she offered it to Lily.

"You look like shit, Lils," Wes said as he pulled the door open and stepped aside to let her through. Once the door was shut, Wes pulled her into a tight hug.

"Just what every girl wants to hear, Wesley," she mumbled against his shoulder. The hug was exactly what she needed, just to melt against another person and let their solidity comfort her. Wes hugged like he was trying to keep all her pieces together, to keep her whole.

After a few moments of the two of them embracing without words, Wes pulled back. "So, do I need to kick his ass or stake him? If I need to stake him, just remember you've seen me fight, and I'm kind of the worst." He chuckled and Lily let that sound ease some of her tension.

He's right. He's the worst, she managed to laugh to herself.

There would be no way Wes would even get a hit in before Albert would stop him. But what Wes lacked in fighting skills, he made up for in bravery and determination. Or maybe it was stupidity and stubbornness, a trait both St. James siblings seemed to share. "That won't be necessary. I'm mad at him, but not in the stabby kind of way. We just need some space tonight until he stops being stupid."

"Well, then, you won't be waiting long. Not that he's not a total idiot, but he's also stupidly devoted to you and will do whatever you say. Come on, let's get you some wine. Brie is on her way over; she was on campus when you texted. Then you can spill on what's happening between you and your fanged man."

Brie arrived at the apartment a few minutes later, out of breath. "I got here as soon as I could. Fuck, I'm out of shape." She bent double over her knees, taking big gulps of air. "You'd think I would have gotten myself together after what went down last year and the importance of cardio or whatever, but ugh..." She finally straightened after a few seconds and her breath evened out. "What did I miss?"

Lily gave her friend a watery smile. This was what she needed: two people who cared for her but who wouldn't pressure her into anything. She loved her family, but they could be too much at times. Lily didn't have many friends outside of her family and coven. Not because she didn't want them; there just never seemed to be time, especially during the harvest.

"Nothing much. Just some wine and threats against Albert's undead life." Lily laughed. Though her eyes still felt puffy from crying, the tears had stopped.

Brie threw herself onto the couch next to Lily. "Oh good, something I can get behind. Do we ride at dawn?"

Lily snorted. "No, we don't. We're just having a dumb fight. He's giving up and thinks it's better for him to return to Simon rather than risk me dying. He's trying to be the noble white knight, and he won't listen to reason."

"Can we at least smack him around? Knock some sense into him or something like that. I volunteer to do it," Brie said, taking the glass of wine Wes offered her.

Wes topped off his and Lily's glasses before settling back against the couch. "What we need is to come up with a plan to get rid of Simon and keep the lovebirds together. And then tell Bert he has to follow Lils' lead and shut the hell up with his whiny savior complex," Wes said as he pulled out his phone.

"Don't text Apollo. It's none of his damn business. He'll tell everyone he's ever met what's going on, and then we'll lose the element of surprise," Brie warned, making a swipe over Lily to take the phone from Wes's hand.

He moved easily out of reach, but stopped texting. "Fine, fine. Though, there's really not an element of surprise. Simon is like ancient. I'm sure he's aware that an Everett witch isn't going to just take it lying down."

Lily sighed. "He would know about that pretty intimately." She told them about the vision and the story of Simon and Juniper. It was easier this time since the siblings weren't tied to anyone in the narrative.

"Why does this feel a little incestuous? It's not really, but vampire families and witch families are really entwined." Wes swirled the remains of his wine.

"Stop making it weird, Wes. Besides, this was all centuries ago." Brie shot her brother a look that clearly meant for him to shut up.

Lily laughed as the two siblings went back and forth. She truly loved her friends. *It doesn't feel like it now, but I know things are going to be okay.* She sipped her wine while Brie and Wes went back and forth. They would figure something out together and then she was going to hold on to Albert with every fiber of her being. Whether he liked it or not.

It was hours later, after too much Chinese takeout, that Lily's phone finally rang. Of course, it was Albert. She was surprised it took him so long to finally call. She held up her phone to the siblings. Brie made a face, but Wes directed her to his room so she could have privacy.

"Hi, Bertie," she said once she shut the door behind her.

"Are you okay, darling? It's been hours. I thought... I hoped you would come home soon." He sounded absolutely miserable and guilt bubbled up hot within her. "Lily? Darling? Are you still there?" he asked when she didn't respond.

I have nothing to feel guilty over. He's the one giving up. With her mind cleared, she spoke. "Are you finished with your sacrificial lamb bullshit? Or do you still plan to just leave with Simon at the end of the month?" Her voice was hard and even; she would not let her emotions get the better of her.

She could hear him suck in a breath over the line. "Lily, I... I don't want to go back to him, to the family, but if the choice is between keeping you safe or losing you, then you know my decision."

The pain felt like her heart was physically cracking inside her chest. It was too much. Lily sat on Wes's bed and doubled over so her face was near her knees. "I love you, Bertie. But until you get your head out of your ass, I'm not coming home. Take this time to think about what we can do instead. Bye, Albert." Before he could say anything else, she ended the call, and then she dropped the phone on the bed and cried into her knees.

Lily couldn't remember a time in her life where she had ever cried so much. There were few hardships in her life to compare. Not that it was much of a comparison. Teenage love and dramas were nothing compared to the thought of losing the love of her life.

Magic crackled through her body, reacting to her emotions. She wasn't like Rose; she didn't lose control so easily and let things fly and crash around the room. But that was only because when Lily let her magic take control, she was pelted with visions. Full-bodied visions that scared her because they felt too real, too hard to escape. There was always the fear that she would be stuck there, her mind trapped in the vision, unable to discern what was real and what was not.

They were there, floating at the back of her mind now. She kept her head pressed tight to her knees as the tears kept coming, and the vision crept closer, ready to swallow her whole.

It slammed into her all at once, and her breath caught in her chest by the force of it. The laughter was the first thing she heard, and she knew immediately that it was Simon.

"Back again, Everett witch? I thought our last talk would be enough to keep you away, yet here you are." His tone was mocking. In the vision, he was lounging in a chair, his back against the armrest, his feet draped over the other side. He made no move from the chair, but Lily knew he could be across the space before she could blink. She assumed her vision self looked exactly like how she was in the real world: a mess. For a moment, she thought she saw Simon's gaze turn soft, but it was gone in a blink and his eyes hardened and his features turned mocking again. "Ah, I see. Breaking your heart, is he? That's the way of it. He breaks your heart, you break his, and then he'll kill you. I know this dance well. Which is why it's best for all of us if he just comes home. You want to live a long life, don't you, Everett witch?"

Lily wiped at her eyes; she wasn't going to keep crying in front of Simon. "It doesn't have to be that way. He's not you. And I'm not Juniper." She tried to put strength in her words, though she felt very little strength in the rest of her body. She felt like a hollow shell.

Simon was out of his chair in an instant. His hand was around her throat before she could take a breath. "Don't you dare speak of her!" he hissed in Lily's face. His grip wasn't tight. It was a threat, not an attempt to kill her. But he wanted her to know that he had the ability to kill her at any moment. *Not like I don't already know that.*

"She is my ancestor. I'll speak of her all I like. Because that's what you see when you see me and Albert. You see her. You see what you had and what you did to her." She tried to swallow, but his hand clamped a little tighter around her throat. It didn't matter if he killed her in the vision. It would hurt and scare her, but this was her chance to speak to him, and she wasn't going to let her fear take control.

"And what about what she did to me?" He brought his face close to hers and bared his fangs. "She betrayed me! She destroyed our family. And you'll do the same one day to Albert. I won't let the same fate befall one of my children. He is mine and I will tear apart this city to keep my children safe from witches like you." Cold fingers tightened against her throat, and this time, he did cut off her airway.

It was worse than when he snapped her neck. She tried to breathe, but nothing came through. Lily grabbed for his hand, desperately trying to pull it away, to get him to break his hold. Scratching at his hands did nothing, kicking produced no results. In moments, her vision started to darken on the edges. Simon said nothing, just stared at her with a gaze filled with conflict. He wasn't entirely committed to killing her, but not enough to loosen his grip.

With her consciousness fading, she briefly wondered if he saw the moment he killed Juniper in his mind as he killed Lily. The flicker in his eyes betrayed that the act was causing him distress. But then Lily stopped fighting for air, her body went limp, and all was dark.

The knock on the door drew her out of the vision. She must have been in the vision longer than she had thought. "Lils, can I come in?" Brie asked, her voice soft.

Lily could barely speak through her tears and the pain in her throat, but she managed to croak out a yes. It was enough of an invitation for Brie, who slowly opened the door and poked her head in. One look at Lily had her throwing open the door and rushing to her friend's side. Brie sat down on the bed and threw her arms around Lily and pulled her close. Lily nestled close and let herself be held while Brie wrapped her up tight in her embrace and rested her chin on the top of Lily's head.

Neither of them said anything. Brie rubbed her hand up and down Lily's heavily tattooed arm while she hummed tunelessly into Lily's hair. Lily was glad she thought to put her hair into two thick braids this morning, or else her friend would be face first in a mass of curled, untamed hair. An odd thing to think about at the moment, but her mind was frazzled and all over the place. She realized her tears were soaking Brie's shirt, but her friend didn't seem to care or just didn't notice.

Lily's hands remained clasped tightly in her lap to keep her from touching her neck. She wanted to reach up and feel where Simon choked the life from her, but she didn't want to worry Brie further. So, she just kept her hands away and let Brie hold her while the tears kept coming.

It was several minutes before the two women broke apart. Lily's tears had stopped again, and she felt drained. Brie looked at her with concern, but then her eyes snagged on something under Lily's chin.

"What the hell happened to your throat?" she gasped.

Lily's hands shot up to touch where Simon's hands had been. It was tender and it hurt. She got up off the bed and walked to a small mirror hung up near Wes's desk.

A set of bruises in the shape of fingers could be clearly seen around her neck, exactly where Simon had choked the life from her.

Her eyes remained on the mirror as she spoke. "It was Simon. I saw him in a vision. He killed me. Again. I don't know what we're going to do. But whatever it is, we need to do it soon. He thinks he's protecting Albert from me, or from himself, and I don't know what he'll do to keep Albert safe."

"You don't think this is just about getting back what he thinks is his?" Brie asked, standing from the bed.

Lily shook her head. "Maybe, but I don't think it's the main reason. Simon may be a monster, but his family means everything to him. Albert leaving must have really messed him up."

"Great, so let's deal with the vamp fam and keep you from dying in the Matrix and real life." Brie pulled out her shell phone to call Ezra. A planning session was about to go down.

"We're watching the Matrix?" Wes asked, confused, as he appeared in the doorway.

"No, dork, we're making war plans," Brie said, then turned her attention to the shell phone to tell Ezra she wouldn't be coming into the shop.

Lily turned back to the mirror and ran her hand over the bruise again. She would find a way to make this work. She wasn't giving Albert up without a fight.

Never.

CHAPTER 16

He couldn't work, couldn't do anything. How could he when she wasn't near? Albert never thought their relationship was perfect, but small disagreements always ended up with one or the other apologizing. Now she wasn't here, and he didn't know when she would come back, and it was agony. Worse, he was the one that drove her off.

It had only been a day and Albert now knew that when he left with Simon, it would kill him. He didn't try to sleep in their bed because it was empty. He didn't bother to sleep at all. He felt no hunger for blood. There was no way to get his mind to focus on anything but her. Without her, he was empty.

I would rather die than live without her. When did I become so melodramatic? he thought, staring unseeing at the papers on his desk.

But that was exactly what he planned to do. Albert was going to leave. He would go off with Simon and the family to save her. Albert wasn't even sure if it would save her. Simon would keep his word; he wouldn't touch Lily if Albert left.

Celia was another matter. She would happily kill Lily and make Albert watch while she did. Of course, Simon would punish her to keep the rest of the family in line, but it wouldn't be severe; she would be fine. She wouldn't even lose her position as second. Simon would just call it a youthful indiscretion and nothing further would be said.

So, what am I doing? Why am I doing this if it changes nothing?

If leaving might not save Lily, and staying put her at risk, what could he do? He was so sure giving up would be best for Lily, for her family. Thinking it through, he realized that he didn't just have Simon to worry about. The family would make sure there was nothing for Albert to go back to.

When did everything get so complicated?

This time last year, he was still pining over Lily. He had moved his usual day at the shop in the hopes of crossing paths with her. She made him feel handsome and interesting, and yet he turned into a babbling idiot when she was around. There had always been that allure about her. When they had finally kissed at Samhain last year, he had never felt so happy in his life. It was better than his first taste of human blood— better than even the most tender moments with Simon or any other partner. That was the moment he knew his undead heart was hers forever.

Every decision he had made in his life since becoming a vampire had led up to the moment when their lips met next to a bonfire to celebrate the Witches' New Year. There was no way Albert could just let that go. He had waited for her, pined after her for too long to just give up what they had so soon. Lily was his everything, and he was tired of running away.

Thirty years ago, he ran and it saved him, but he had always looked over his shoulder, waiting for Simon to find him. He sought refuge in New Britain because it was as far away from the family as he could get. And while he was expected to exist in the dark underworld of the magical community, he felt himself longing for the light of those who lived in peace within the city. Ezra saved him from continuing the hunt for humans, saved him from himself and the damage Simon had done to him. He owed Ezra everything, just as much as he owed Lily his love and devotion.

Because it wouldn't be just Lily he would leave behind. There was Ezra, the only friend he had ever had outside of the family. There was a whole magical community that he helped to represent in the Council. Other vampires looked up to him enough to want him to speak for them. The people whose suffering he eased at hospices and homes not only nourished him, but he brought peace to them and their families. Everyone wanted to die with dignity, Ezra had told him when he first started giving over names to Albert.

His life was in New Britain. Lily was in New Britain. His friends, his community, his home, everything he had built for himself over the last three decades, was right here. Simon wasn't going to take that from him. Simon was not going to make him walk away from everything he loved just for his own sick, twisted idea of family and control.

Because it was always about control.

Maybe that was the problem. Maybe Simon was losing control over the family. After all, one family member left and seemed to thrive, so why couldn't the others? And even before Albert was made, the Lutece twins walked into the sun without Simon's leave. It was just a theory, but there wasn't a better explanation for Simon's sudden appearance after thirty years. But who would want to leave? If he had to guess, it was Sam. They were Simon's shadow, his spymaster. But the problem with living in the shadows is that you never get to walk in the light. Metaphorically speaking, of course. Sam was always the black sheep of the family because that's what Simon wanted them to be. Simon would hate to lose his favorite spy.

Until he knew for sure, he had other things to focus on. He needed Lily. Well, first, he needed to grovel and beg her for forgiveness because she was right—he was giving up too easily. He had been conditioned to jump when Simon said so, and it seemed he had not yet broken out of that conditioning. Albert would spend the rest of his immortal life making up for every moment he had made Lily doubt his love for her.

The mobile phone was in his hand in an instant. He thought first to call her, but then thought better of it. There was a good chance she wouldn't answer after their last conversation. It was time to grit his teeth and do the absolute last thing he wanted. He dialed Bridget St. James's number and waited for her to answer.

"The fuck do you want, asshole?" Her charming greeting came after the third ring.

Albert sighed. *Maybe I would have been better off just calling Lily.* "Bridget, charming as ever. I..." He broke off, and tried to force the words out. "I need your help."

Brie responded with a derisive laugh. "No shit. You really messed her up. I shouldn't let you anywhere near her."

The thought alone terrified him. "Is she with you?" He believed Lily would go to her family. After the Everetts visited their house, he was sure things were on the mend between them all. Did she not want to risk him showing up at the farm?

A moment of silence, then she answered, "Yes, she's here. We're taking care of her."

At least she was somewhere safe. Ezra had put up enough wards at both his place and the apartment the St. James siblings shared. "I'm coming over to the shop now. I need to speak with her. Tell her she was right. I am an idiot."

"Oh, I will absolutely tell her." Brie sounded delighted and he wanted to dislike her more, but he deserved it all right now.

"Give me ten minutes," he said and then disconnected the call. The less time he had to spend on the phone with Bridget, the better. He wasted no time in leaving the house. Traffic laws be damned as he sped across town to Spirit Antiques. He was lucky the sun had already set; otherwise, it would have been a very uncomfortable ride. One he would have done without a second thought, despite the risk.

The car was barely parked before he jumped out and ran to the door of the antique shop. The little bell tinkled overhead. It was pure luck that the place was empty. His entrance would have scared anyone standing nearby. Behind the counter stood Ezra, flipping through an ancient ledger.

The angel looked up as Albert approached slowly, and a tentative smile graced his lips. "Albert, I wasn't expecting you today. I don't have anything prepared, but I can get it for you, if you like."

"No, that's quite alright. I'm here to see Lily." His eyes darted around the room, behind Ezra, toward the Storage Room door. She wasn't in the main part of the shop, so chances were good Brie had taken her to the staff room or maybe Ezra's apartment.

Albert's attention was drawn to Ezra's face and the confused expression there. "Lily isn't here. She hasn't been here in days. She's been with Brie and Wes at their apartment. Brie called yesterday to say Lily was staying over, so she couldn't come into the shop."

Of course she did, the tricky human. Though she had never said they were at the shop, only that they were together.

As if summoned by her name, the Storage Room door opened and Brie walked through, leaving the door open a crack behind her. Beyond that door was Lily, he knew it. But it would take Brie less than a second to close the door behind her, and he didn't know which button on the panel led to her apartment. No doubt there were several protective magics that would keep him from going through the door, anyway. He would have to wait for now.

"Are you prepared to grovel and be yelled at? Because Lily is going to hand you your ass for this stunt." Brie crossed her arms and smirked at him.

Actually, everything about her demeanor was smug. To think he helped save her from that awful warlock last year. *Help might be a strong word.* He was there, at least. That counted for something, and here she was, keeping guard between him and Lily.

"What's going on, sweetheart?" Ezra asked. Brie must not have tipped him off to what happened earlier with Lily. At least the meddling human didn't go off telling all their secrets.

Brie looked up at her paramour. "Albert is planning to leave with Simon. Just give up Lily and pack it up. Naturally, she didn't take him being a coward very well."

A coward! She called him a coward, the child. He had faced down horrors she couldn't begin to fathom, and she called him a coward. He wanted to do the most noble thing he was capable of, and break the heart of the woman he loved just to keep her safe, and the human dared to call him a coward. The red began to leak through his eyes; bloodlust brewed within him. But no, he had to hold it back. For as close as they were, Ezra wouldn't hesitate to end him if he threatened his girlfriend.

So instead, Albert clenched his fists and bared his fangs at her. For now, he would have to be all bark and no bite.

Ezra drew himself up to an even more impressive height. Like puffing up his chest when he sensed danger. Albert knew he had to calm down. Ezra was level-headed, but Albert's actions were threatening. Albert schooled his face into neutrality and tried to clear his head of the bloodlust pounding at the back of his mind. *No threatening the human.*

Ezra must have sensed Albert was calm enough to continue. "You really are an idiot," he said, folding his arms across his chest to match Brie. The two of them stared him down, twin pillars of judgment. "Lily is the kindest, gentlest person I know, and you want to break her heart so you can take the easy way out?"

"There's nothing easy about leaving her. I don't want her to die. You don't know what Simon will do, what the family will do to her if I don't go." It was pointless trying to defend his actions now. He wasn't going to leave her; he just didn't know how he could stay. First, though, he would have to deal with being chastised by his friend, and eventually, Lily.

"You don't think I know what it's like, Albert? Are you fucking with me?" Ezra's stern voice cut through him. Because, of course, Ezra knew exactly what it was like for his past to threaten the woman he loved. Worse, Ezra held her in his arms as she died.

He sighed deeply. "I know I'm an idiot," he mumbled as he cast his gaze down at the floor, defeated. The look of judgment on Ezra's face was too much. Albert knew better. He wasn't the only one to have ever been haunted by the ghosts of his past.

"At least you admit it." Lily's voice came from behind the door. Albert's head snapped up, and he watched as his lover walked out from behind the Storage Room door. Her eyes were still puffy, and she was in the same clothes she had left in yesterday. Even looking a mess, she was still beautiful. It took every last bit of willpower not to dash across the room and wrap her in his arms. But she might not want that right now. Things were tenuous between them for the moment, and it was best for him to keep his distance. For now.

His eyes caught on the dark marks at her throat. They looked very much like a set of fingers had been pressed into her skin. She had been bruised. As if she could feel his eyes on that part of her skin, Lily brought one hand up to rub at her neck over the bruises. "A gift from Simon. We met in a vision again." Her voice was nonchalant, but Albert could see the fear in her eyes. Simon had killed her again in the vision space. He was certain of that. Lily kept putting herself in dangerous situations when it came to Simon. He had to stop her.

"You have to stop meeting him in your visions. One of these times, it will kill you for real." Did he even have a right to say anything to her? It wasn't like he hadn't put himself in harm's way with Simon. He had gone to see the family on two occasions now without her, and Simon had physically threatened him last time. If he kept at it, chances were Simon would finally snap.

"It wasn't intentional. He found me, which is why we need to take care of him sooner rather than later. Together." Lily responded with a pointed stare at him at the last word. They should have already been working the problem through together. Should have been finding ways to get Simon and the family to leave the city, or banish them completely. Instead, he had wasted time and energy feeling sorry for himself and thinking he was doing the right thing by leaving her.

The counter was still between them, yet he wanted to throw himself at her feet and apologize for everything. They still had an audience, though, and he didn't see Brie or Ezra leaving any time soon. *Those two thrive on drama*, he thought, and he didn't want to give either of them more fuel to ridicule him.

"So, what do you plan to do, Bertie?" Lily's voice cut through the chatter in his mind. *What is my plan? Do I even have one?* He decided that, no, he didn't actually have a plan. All he could think about over the last day was Lily and keeping her in his life. Solutions to get Simon and the family out and to keep Lily and her family safe were practically nonexistent.

"I'm staying with you. We're staying in our home. We'll figure out the rest from there." He kept his voice gentle, his volume low. He wanted her to trust him, to want to be with him. And for that to happen, he would have to humble himself in front of her and prove to her she could trust him.

One step at a time, Lily rounded the counter and made her way to Albert. She didn't rush, and the wait made Albert want to sprint those last few feet and take her into his arms. It would be so easy. But he wanted her to come to him, so he would let her make the first moves and follow her lead. She would set the pace for how this would go.

"I'm going to keep you, Bertie. Lucky for you, I didn't spend all of the last day pouting. We have an idea that might work and would keep everyone alive. Come on." She pulled his hand into hers and dragged him back toward where Ezra and Brie stood.

"Ugh, he's coming to my apartment? Really?" Brie groaned. Albert would rather not enter the human's place, either, but he would let Lily lead him anywhere.

"I thought we could just grab Wes and head up to Ezra's place. If that's okay with you, Ezra? You have better drinks." Lily gave Ezra a tentative smile, probably the best she could come up with considering her emotional state.

Ezra nodded, and Lily stuck her head through the still cracked-door and called for Wes. A few seconds passed before Wes stepped through the Storage Room door and shut it behind him. Now the door no longer opened on Brie and Wes's apartment.

Brie approached the door next and pushed the number three button on the side panel. A small noise indicated the door had changed successfully, and Brie opened the door to reveal a darkened hallway.

"I'll have to rework a ward to let you in, Albert. And, obviously, invite you inside," Ezra said as a pure white light illuminated his hands to work the divine magic. Albert didn't take offense at being barred from his friend's home, so he waited patiently for Ezra to finish.

Albert didn't want to let go of Lily's hand, so he gripped it even tighter, like he thought she might run away at any moment. When Ezra finished, they filed through the door. Just as Ezra passed the threshold, he half-turned and verbally invited Albert inside. Lily went through before him, and as Albert stepped through the portal, the door swung shut behind him.

Ezra's apartment was meant to look like a forest, a living one right in the main room with a breeze and swaying leaves. In all the years they had known each other, Albert had only been inside one other time, and that was recently. Ezra had removed the wards as a one-time thing. Up until then, the place had been warded against him and his kind. It was a protection for Bridget's sake and now Lily's. Maybe the wards would let Albert pass from now on.

It's called trust. He trusts you.

Brie threw herself onto the couch, perfectly at home, which Albert supposed she was since she was with Ezra. Lily let go of his hand and sat down next to Brie, and Wes took the spot on Lily's other side, flanking her. *So that's how it's going to be.*

For now, they wouldn't let him near Lily for too long, and judging by the look in Lily's eyes, she was a little grateful for it. That one look broke his heart a little more, but it was his own fault she felt that way.

He sat on one of the chairs instead while Ezra headed toward the kitchen. Nobody said anything until Ezra returned with glasses and a bottle of wine balanced on a tray. Once they each held a glass of the red wine, Albert spoke. "You've all thought of a plan, then?"

"Yes. George Brown," Brie responded, like that told him everything he needed to know. It didn't.

"I don't follow," he replied with confusion.

Brie rolled her eyes. "George Brown was the father of Mercy Brown. She was suspected of being a vampire after her death, so he had her body exhumed and removed her heart and liver. She wasn't, as far as anyone knows, an actual vampire. But the power of fear and unyielding faith is quite potent. The Storage Room has one of his crosses. It's like a talisman now, imbued with the power to destroy a vampire's heart, well, and its liver, but I think the heart would do it."

"I don't want to kill Simon. I just want him to leave us alone." Albert was aghast. For as much as he wanted to distance himself from Simon and the family, he couldn't imagine a world where Simon didn't exist in it. There would always be a small part of him that loved Simon. He was Albert's maker; that was a bond that would never go away. While he loathed most of his vampire siblings, he didn't want them to die, either. *Celia might be the exception.*

"We won't actually kill him. A threat can work just as well." Lily looked at him with a sympathetic gaze. There was something else there. Not malice, no, that wasn't Lily. Determination, maybe, like she wasn't afraid to hurt someone for him. He had seen her battle-magic before, choking vines that could wrap and entangle and kill when she was threatened. It was as beautiful as it was terrifying.

Albert kept his eyes on her while he asked, "How do you know it works?"

Brie scoffed, and his attention turned back to her. "Care to test it yourself?" *She would love that. It isn't exactly a secret that she can't stand me. Not that I have ever given her a reason to like me.* Theirs was a mutual dislike.

"I'd rather not, since the whole point of this is to keep both Lily and *me* alive," he said sharply.

"Shame," Brie replied before Lily elbowed her gently in the ribs. "Whatever. Anyway, I think it would be best to get Simon here at the shop. Keep him on our ground. We can lower the necessary wards on the front of the shop, and if things go to shit, we have the wards in the Storage Room and here." Her eyes darted to Ezra, seeking his approval.

Ezra sat thoughtfully. He rubbed his chin with a finger and held the wine in his free hand. "I don't relish the idea of lowering the wards, but if the rest stay up, we could make it work. But if he destroys anything in my shop, I'm using the talisman on him myself. There's valuable stuff out there among the junk still."

The rest of them nodded in agreement, though Albert refrained. Even the remote chance that they would use the George Brown talisman against Simon seemed appalling to him.

Does Ezra value his shop over another's life?

Of course he does. Albert had seen all of them, except Wes, kill someone. They all had the capability for ruthlessness if the situation called for it, including himself. And Albert couldn't fault Ezra, couldn't fault any of them. This was his past catching up, his problem that was affecting all of them. This was their home, and they had every right to defend it from his problem. So, he would have to face the reality that, at the end of all of this, Simon might have to die—for real, this time.

But all Albert felt was overwhelming dread.

CHAPTER 17

A week had passed since what was dubbed the war meeting in Ezra's apartment. Lily went home with Albert that night, but even a week later, things were still tense. Lily hated the feeling, and Albert was doing everything he could to shower her with affection and remind her how much he loved her. It just felt like with the threat of Simon hanging over them, even with the plan, Lily couldn't really settle back into their usual routine. She was on edge all the time. She didn't want to feel too close to Albert because the fear of losing him was too much. But at the same time, she didn't want him far away if their time was limited. In a constant state of conflict with herself, she was tired.

What she needed was extra assurance that things would not go completely wrong—that she would not lose Albert or her life when they finally confronted Simon for good.

You're an idiot. You come from a family of powerful witches, and you didn't think to go to them? She could kick herself. Things were getting a little better after the surprise visit with her family. Well, they weren't as awkward, at least. Lily always felt she could go to her family with any problem, and they would be there to help her. So why not now?

This was one of the biggest problems she had ever faced in her life, and even after everything that had happened over the last few weeks, her family would help. Even if they didn't fully approve of Albert. Even if they now knew he wasn't just a passing fling. They would still help them both because Lily knew her family just wanted her to be happy and safe. And Simon was a threat to both.

"Do you want to go to dinner at the farm?" she asked Albert as she walked in from her garden. It was spur of the moment; they hadn't discussed seeing her family in some time. But with the clock ticking, only days to go before Simon's deadline, it was as good a time as any.

"If I say not really, will we still go?" He tried to put some humor behind his question, but it didn't meet his eyes.

"Yeah, we'll still go, but I thought I would ask first. We could use their help. They could boost our protections against Simon. We don't have to go into the meeting with him with the wards down and no other means of repelling him. What we need is a fail-safe. Just in case he calls our bluff with the talisman. I don't really want to use that thing." She gave him a smile at first, then her face looked thoughtful.

"You have a point. It would be good to have something else. Something that will keep all of us safe. The idea of exploding a heart and liver inside of anyone sounds gruesome. Will Rose be there?" He meant it as a joke, but he was also secretly hoping Lily's eldest sister would not grace them with her presence. If he could avoid Rose forever, it would be best for everyone. The rest of the Everetts would come around to him eventually, but Rose never would.

Lily laughed, and this time it did reach her eyes. "Yes, of course she will be. She lives on the farm. Package deal, remember. You want to be with me, you deal with the whole family, sisters and cousins included."

Albert groaned dramatically, just to add to the levity of the moment. They hadn't had this kind of ease between them in a week, and he was going to enjoy every second of it.

"I'll call my mom and let her know we're coming. Dad will need to know that he needs to make extra." She started to walk through the house with her phone out, first to contact her mom and then shower.

"Bring our food containers for leftovers. We don't need any more mystery butter containers," Albert called as she crossed the room.

"Don't know what you mean." Lily laughed as she texted her mom.

"It's a gamble grabbing a butter container, whether you will actually get butter and not whatever your dad made." Albert pointed to the refrigerator to make a point. Lily just laughed again as she left the room. It was nice to laugh together. Now she just hoped her family behaved tonight.

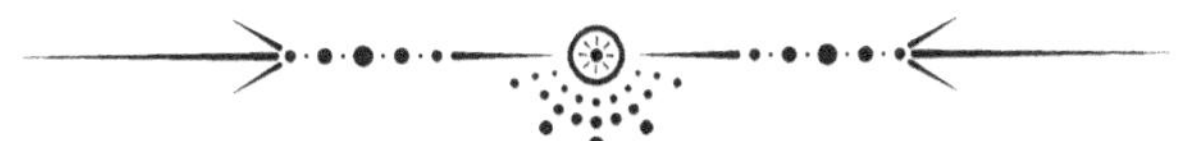

"Did you have to bring the bloodsucker?" Rose asked from her spot on the porch rocking chair, though it lacked her usual bite.

Does she just wait out here every time I come home?

"Yeah, I did. Nobody bothers you about having Manu around," Lily snapped back.

"Because Manu is my wife and a witch, not a leech," Rose responded, her voice hard.

"Get over yourself, Rosie. He's my partner, and you can just get over it." Lily didn't spare a second glance at her sister as she walked through the door, leaving Rose to huff angrily on the porch.

"Warm welcome," Albert grumbled from behind her as he shut the door. There was noise coming from the kitchen. Her dad would be finishing up soon.

Lily led them toward the noise, but then a voice called out, "Lily, Albert, we're in the living room. Come join us." Her mother's voice cut over the bangs of the kitchen. So Lily steered them in the opposite direction, farther into the house. Assembled in the living room were her mother, Granny and Pawpaw, Ivy, Jamie, and Manu, with her daughter Violet stretched out on the floor with a book. Pawpaw had his head tilted back and was snoring softly; Granny dosed on his shoulder.

"Sit down, both of you. Want something to drink? Your dad kicked me out of the kitchen, so I have to keep everyone entertained while he works his magic." Her mom seemed overeager, likely trying to make up for the last few times they had been to the farm and what they all thought Albert was going to do to her. Leave it to Hyacinth Everett to overcompensate for being a bad host.

"We're good, mom. We already got the warm welcome from Rose," Lily said as she sat down on one of the couches. Albert chose to awkwardly perch on the armrest beside her and kept his mouth shut. Probably for the best, for now, until they could get a read on how her family was feeling.

Hyacinth made a dismissive noise. "Ignore her. She's going to be Rose, and there's no changing that. Look at Manu. She does it all the time." A small laugh went through the group, but Lily could detect the undercurrent of nervousness. This is where the rug sweeping would begin. Her mother wouldn't directly mention what had happened before or how they had wanted her to leave Albert. It would be skirted around, and Albert would be welcomed in like nothing had happened. Lily shouldn't have been surprised.

"So, Lily dear, what made you decide to join us tonight? Not that we don't love seeing you and Albert. We just weren't expecting it." Hyacinth took a sip of the white wine she had been holding.

"They need help. A magical backup plan for when they face the vampire. The mean vampire." All eyes fell to the floor, where Violet flipped a page of her book but didn't look up at the grownups as she spoke.

"Violet is showing an affinity for divining magic. We're very proud of her," Manu said brightly as she smiled down at her daughter. Lily never understood how Rose and Manu worked. Manu was one of the sweetest people she had ever met. And Rose was, well, Rose. But somehow, they clicked, and Lily knew they both loved their daughter fiercely. Violet was a bright kid with a good head for green magic. But Lily would be lying if she wasn't excited to have another diviner in the family. Granny was the family diviner, and Violet was lucky she was still around to show her the ways.

"Well, Vi, you totally nailed it. That's the main reason we're here. That, and I just wanted to see you all, especially since you're not taking over my kitchen." Lily smiled down at her niece and laughed with the rest of the group.

"What would you have us do? If we're a backup, I assume you have a plan to deal with Simon," Hyacinth said, curiosity coloring her tone.

"We do. Ezra has provided us with an object that we hope will be enough of a deterrent to convince Simon and the family to leave. But I know Simon, and I worry that it might not be enough to keep him away for good." Albert kept his eyes on Hyacinth while his voice remained even, almost monotone. Lily felt a tinge of pride that he was speaking up, being a part of the conversation with her family.

Her mother made a humming noise in acknowledgment.

Across the room, Jamie's hands started to flash quickly. He directed his speech toward Ivy first. "Jamie has an idea if you're open to it," she said for him. Lily and Albert nodded together.

Jamie's hands started to sign again in earnest as he detailed what he thought would work. Lily translated aloud to Albert, "He suggests summoning Juniper. Confront Simon with his past."

"How would we do that?" Lily signed back while speaking aloud for Albert's benefit. Summoning took a lot of time and energy. Time and energy they likely wouldn't have when confronted with Simon. It could also be dangerous because some spirits didn't take well to the idea of being dead and would try to possess the summoner.

Once again, Jamie signed his explanation to the room, and Lily translated for Albert. "We could summon her before and ask that she allow us to store her spirit until she's needed. She would have to agree, of course. We can't just trap her in an object." She signed back to Jamie, "We would need something powerful enough to store a witch spirit. Ezra might have something."

"Actually, I think we might have something. Spirit storing was in fashion back in the spiritualist age. Ask your granny about it sometime. We can check in the attic. I'm sure it's in one of the boxes up there," Hyacinth signed and spoke to benefit all in the room.

"After dinner," Damien said from the doorway. A dishtowel was thrown over his shoulder, and his apron had flecks of some kind of sauce. "Food's ready, so get moving to the dining room now." He disappeared back the way he came, and the rest of the family followed him. Lily grabbed Albert's hand as they stood and followed the group into the kitchen.

Granny and Pawpaw still slept on the couch; nobody bothered to wake them. It was best to let them sleep. Pawpaw tended to be really grumpy when he was woken from his nap too soon. Lily gave her sleeping grandparents a parting look before leaving the room.

The dining table was nearly groaning from the feast placed on it. Damien had gone all out for the meal, like he was feeding twice as many people as were assembled. It looked like Thanksgiving in summer. There were several roasted chickens, green beans, baked macaroni, spiced apples, mashed potatoes with gravy, and steamed broccoli covered in cheese for Violet since she wouldn't touch green beans.

"Got enough carbs there, Dad?" Ivy laughed as they took their seats.

Damien scoffed. "As if there is such a thing. You all eat up and leave your Tupperware on the counters after so I can get rid of the rest."

"There's barely enough room left in the fridge as is, so please take it all," Hyacinth grumbled as she started to pile food on her plate.

Nothing more was said for several minutes while they passed dishes around the table. Lily was pleased to see Albert take a bit of everything. Though the food did nothing to actually nourish him, the man still enjoyed the act of eating and the flavors. She could easily see Albert and her dad exchanging recipes. Maybe one day they would get there.

"You really went all out, Dad. Seriously, one of your best. There're no magic truth spells in this one, are there?" Lily asked, though she was only half joking. She wouldn't put it past her dad to pull the same trick twice.

"If you want to call love magic, then sure. But no, we've all had enough truth out there for a while." Her dad grinned and then took a big bite of chicken.

They lapsed back into silence to eat some more, the only sounds those of chewing and grunts of appreciation. A few minutes into the meal, Rose appeared and sat down heavily next to her wife and daughter.

She fixed her plate and said nothing, nor did she make eye contact with anyone.

Lily did her best to ignore her sister and focus on the food before her. She hadn't realized how ravenous she had been. The last few days, she had been so focused on her garden to keep her mind off everything else that she had skipped lunch more than a few times, much to Albert's displeasure. It just made the family meal that much more special. She had missed this, the easy feeling of being surrounded by love. Meal times were always a big event in the Everett household. Their lives revolved around the magic of their gardens and food. Growing up, they never missed a meal. It was family time, her dad always said. No phones, no arguing, no rushing off until everyone was finished. It was a time to be together and just enjoy being a family.

Lily knew how lucky she was to have them all. And while they might not completely accept Albert now, things would get better. Because Albert was not going to kill her. Albert was going to fight for her, and they would live a long, happy life together until either they decided to go their separate ways or she died.

"What exactly are we looking for with the spirit-storing thing?" Lily asked once she had cleaned her plate. There were probably any number of magical trinkets in the attic. Generations of Everetts living in the house had accumulated a lot of junk that was just thrown up there. Lily wouldn't be surprised if the room was magically expanded to accommodate it all.

"It's a box; I'm pretty sure. I remember your great-grandma showing it to me once, decades ago. If memory serves, it's a plain wooden box with a serpent wrapped around a cornucopia on the top." Hyacinth had a look of deep concentration on her face as she tried to recall the item.

"The symbols of Hades? Fitting," Albert said, setting his fork down.

"You know your mythology." Hyacinth sounded delighted. Her mother had an interest in mythology, any culture's mythology. She said there were truths in all of them, and she enjoyed tracing what was real by what existed now in the magical world.

Albert shrugged. "Greek and Latin were requirements in school back in my day. Didn't have much choice."

"Don't you think you're a little old for my sister, then? I mean, you're older than our parents. Probably closer to Granny's age. It's kind of gross." Rose's disgust was palpable. *Great, now that she can't pin my murder on him, she's going for the age gap,* Lily thought as she stared down her sister. Rose was just determined to find any reason to hate Albert.

Albert picked up his fork again. "Maybe," was all he said, which only seemed to infuriate Rose. She needed someone to fight with her, and when they didn't, she had no way to vent her anger. Lily hid the smile as best she could, lest Rose blew up on her.

"Well, we should get up to the attic if we hope to find anything," Lily said, standing from her chair. She snapped her fingers and the containers she had brought from home lifted out of the tote bag she had left near her chair and set themselves on the counter. Albert collected their plates and placed them in the sink as Damien instructed. Just as Albert walked away, the water started to flow, and the dishes left on the counters set themselves inside the filling sink. A sponge lifted from its place and started to scrub away the remains of the food.

Lily grabbed Albert's hand and led him out of the kitchen, the conversation continuing behind them. "When I was little and got in trouble, Dad would make me wash the dishes after dinner by hand. No magic allowed." Lily laughed at the memory of her pruny hands and splashes of soap when she was really angry. Though she only had herself to blame for the chore.

"With a family as big as yours, I imagine it wasn't particularly fun." Albert smiled from her side. They reached the stairs, and he dropped her hand to walk behind her.

"I hated every minute of it. But it was great motivation to keep me out of trouble. My parents made sure my sisters and I never took our magic for granted. So doing stuff the human way was a go-to punishment." She led him up and up until she pulled open the creaky attic door and revealed a steep set of wooden stairs. A flip of the light switch at the bottom of the stairs illuminated the slightly treacherous climb. At the top of the stairs, the room still looked dark and just a little foreboding.

"You do realize this attic is a movie cliché, and I feel our chances of being murdered by something up here have increased," Albert said, his face serious. If it weren't for the sparkle of mischief in his eyes, Lily would have almost believed he was serious.

"Well then, do the gentlemanly thing and go first. That way, if a murderer does pop out, I have a chance to get away." She gestured for him to go and shuffled off to the side.

"Ah, I see how it is. Well, here I go, prepared to die for love." He reached over, gave her hand a squeeze, and then walked up the steps. Every single one of the wooden boards creaked. "If the murderer didn't know I was coming yet, they do now." He chuckled. Lily followed behind him, trying to hold in her laughter.

Their humor lasted just until they reached the top of the stairs, and then the realization of their task lay before them.

There were so many boxes. A ridiculous number of boxes. Lily wasn't sure if there were actually walls or windows up here because she couldn't see any. The space might just be made of boxes by the look of it. The attic ran the whole space of the house, and every inch of space was taken up with boxes with narrow pathways woven throughout. Some of the boxes were just that: typical square cardboard boxes. Then there were hulking worn trunks, hat boxes without lids, suitcases with patterns from decades ago, plain plastic bins with airtight lids. "Is that ... an Ikea bag?" Lily pointed to a gigantic blue bag with recognizable yellow lettering on the handles. It was filled to the point of nearly spilling over with junk.

"Darling, I'm starting to believe you come from a long line of hoarders," Albert quipped, turning his head to examine the room further. "Is there perhaps a spell you could use to find the box?"

"Maybe a locator spell. But I doubt it's the only magical thing up here, so there will probably be a lot of interference. Best I can hope for is a general area.

Maybe within a few boxes. Let's find out." She closed her eyes to concentrate. First, she pictured the box in her mind, or at least a close approximation based on her mother's information. The magic flared under her skin, sending tingles through her body, and wove around her as she called to the box to reveal itself. A small tug began in her stomach. It was a comfortable sensation, almost like the magic was telling her gently to follow. Lily opened her eyes, and a faint trail of golden light wove its way through the boxes.

"This way," she said as she headed into the maze of boxes. The tugging in her stomach matched the direction the light was heading, and Lily hoped it would get them to the right box in one go, however unlikely that was. The whole room radiated magic, so she would take what she could get from the spell. She followed the tug and light deeper into the attic, Albert close on her heels. Too quickly, though, the light faded against a wall of boxes and the tugging ceased in her stomach. At least it was narrowed down to a smaller wall of boxes stacked one on top of the other and perhaps a few deep. It wasn't great, but it was better than wading through every box in the attic. She said as much to Albert, who nodded in agreement, though he eyed the wall and sighed.

Lily pulled a box from the space and started to open it. The first one was a regular cardboard box. "Just grab one, and let's get looking. I get the feeling this is going to be a long night." She kneeled on the floor and started to pull things from the box. Albert grabbed one of his own and mirrored her actions.

There was absolutely no organization whatsoever in the box. Some books, broken amulets, a mix of feathers from various birds, like things were just tossed in until the box was full.

"I don't think it's in this one," Albert said hesitantly. He quickly set the box off to the side, ensuring it was closed again.

Lily gave him a confused glance. "Stuff was just thrown in. It's probably a good idea to look through the whole thing."

Albert shook his head. "No need with that one. It's all ... uh, vintage intimates. If you get what I mean." He looked thoroughly embarrassed, and he wouldn't meet her eye.

Lily laughed so loudly and for so long that her stomach started to ache, and tears pricked her eyes. Albert sat beside her with a pinched look on his face. When she finally caught her breath again, she said, "Are you saying that's a box full of my ancestors' lingerie?"

Albert dropped his head into his hands. "Let's never speak of this again. In fact, I'm going to do my best to block the memory of having my hands all over my girlfriend's great-grandma's panties."

Lily let out a fresh wave of giggles, her whole body shaking with her mirth. "Please don't say panties. It makes it so much worse," she struggled to say between laughs.

"You can do this on your own, you know," Albert huffed as he picked up another box and started to sift through the contents carefully, like he was afraid to discover more underthings. Lily returned to her own box, letting her giggles peter out as she focused on the task at hand.

An hour into searching with still nothing to show for it, a silver tea tray found them. A pot and two mismatched cups and saucers sat along with small containers of cream and sugar. "Kids, you still up here?" Damien's voice sounded through the attic.

Lily half collapsed into the opaque tub she was sifting through. "Yeah, we're over here," she yelled, though the tub muffled her voice slightly. It took a few minutes and more calling out before Damien finally found them. By then, Albert was already pouring the tea for them. Lily watched him. He was always so delicate when serving tea, reverent almost.

"Any luck?" Damien asked as he settled on the floor next to them. Lily tossed the item she'd been holding, what looked like a cup and ball toy that had no string, back into the tub and pushed it away.

"Not really. I narrowed it down to these boxes, but knowing our luck, it'll be the last box in the stack." Lily took the cup offered by Albert and let the warm tea soothe her. It was starting to feel like a fruitless effort, and she debated just giving up and heading to Ezra's shop to see if he had something. Though Ezra was currently going through inventory, so there was a good chance he would have no idea where one was, if he even had one.

"Don't give up, Lilybelle. I brought you something that might help." Damien pulled an object from his pocket and held it out to her. It was small and was shaped like a beetle. Lily took it and examined it. It wasn't alive, but was clearly packed with magical energy. "It's a Hide and Seeker, good for finding hidden or lost objects. Your granddad Jones had an affinity for tinkering and made this for me when I was younger. I lost everything all the time; your grandma was convinced the house was stealing my stuff because we never found anything again. Until your granddad made this. Nothing ever stayed lost for long after that. It's a pretty useful gizmo."

"And where was this an hour ago? Would have saved us a lot of time sorting through a bunch of family junk." There didn't seem to be a mechanism to turn it on, so Lily waited until her dad gave her further instruction.

Damien chuckled. "I actually forgot about it. How funny is that? I haven't used it in so long. It's just been in one of the kitchen drawers for a while. Just hold it in your hand, think of what you're looking for, then tell it to find. But be sure to use the Swahili word."

Lily looked at the little beetle in her hand and thought of the box with the symbols of Hades on it. She lowered down to the ground with the Hide and Seeker cupped in her hand and said, "Kupata." The beetle leaped from her hand and scurried forward toward the boxes.

"I didn't know you spoke Swahili." Albert sipped his tea on the floor, his legs crossed over each other.

Lily sat back on her heels. "Oh, I don't. I know a few words that Dad taught me, but that's about it. My grandparents were from Uganda." She grabbed the tea still sitting on the floor and took a sip. "So how will we know if this thing finds—" A flash of light and a whistle sounded at the same time from the mass of boxes. It wasn't too far back, and Lily could see that it originated from a small brown cardboard box two back from the one she had been searching through.

"That's how you know," Damien said with a huge white-toothed grin.

Lily rolled her eyes and set down the cup. "Thanks, Dad." She crawled over to the box and pulled it out. The Hide and Seeker crawled out of the box and up Lily's hand and arm until it found its way into the pocket of her dress.

She gave the pocket a pat, then turned her attention to the box. It was definitely much smaller than any of the others she had gone through. When she flipped the flaps of the box up, she saw it. Sitting right on top of what looked like a mound of scarves was the spirit box. She pulled it out with two hands and studied it. The box itself was rectangular but rather small and made of teak. The image of a snake wrapped around a cornucopia sat in raised relief on the lid. Lily made to open the lid, but halted. "Do you think it's occupied right now?" she asked her dad.

"No idea, you'll have to ask your mom." Damien slowly rose from the floor and the other two followed his lead. "Let's go ask her and then you two can either get on home or stay here for the night."

The three of them headed down the stairs, Damien carrying the tea tray ahead of them while Lily and Albert walked a few paces behind. "What if there's someone already in there?" Albert asked, his voice light.

Lily stared at the box as they walked down the stairs. "I feel like that would be weird. Like, 'Oh, hey, sorry to disturb you, but we need to shove another soul in here, so could you please leave?' Are there rules of etiquette for this sort of thing?"

Albert shrugged as they made it to the landing. "Maybe? Probably. It seems everything runs on decorum when it comes to the dead."

"You would know," Lily said flippantly, but then the full weight of her words hit her, and she suddenly felt like an idiot. "Sorry, I didn't mean it like that."

Albert hooked an arm around her waist and pulled her to his side. "You're fine, darling. I know what you meant." He kissed the top of her head, and the two awkwardly walked down to the ground floor side by side.

When they were back in the living room, everyone else was gone save for Hyacinth, who was lounging on the couch reading. "Did you find it?" she asked when they entered the room, setting her book aside.

"We got it," Lily said, holding the box up in one hand. "But we wanted to check to make sure no one's in there. How do we know?"

Hyacinth straightened up on the couch and reached out a hand to take the box. Lily crossed the room and put it in her mother's hand. Hyacinth studied the box for half a second and handed it back. "Not occupied. It's ready to be used."

"How do you know?" Lily asked, looking back down at the box in her hand.

Her mother tapped the snake with her fingernail. "The snake's eyes. If there's a soul inside, the eyes will open and glow. Now they are closed and there's no light, so there's a vacancy."

Lily kept her attention on the box. "Great, well, then we need to prepare a summoning."

225

CHAPTER 18

Albert had been to his share of seances, especially in the early years after he was turned. It was still the height of spiritualism then, but nearly all were frauds and scams. He was familiar with the covered circular table, a medium draped in shawls with an exotic but fake accent, and even crystal balls. They were always full of people telling sob stories to each other about the people they wanted to reach or about the celebrities they wanted to contact. In short, they were prime pickings for a family of vampires.

Simon had once taken the family to a seance that was interrupted and debunked by Harry Houdini. That one was probably Albert's favorite. Simon had insisted that nobody could drink from the famed magician, which Aron had seemed greatly disappointed by. The oaf thought Houdini's magic was real and that he would get his powers if he drank from the magician. That is to say, Albert had witnessed table raps, ghostly music, and supposed phantoms more times than he could recall.

But what Albert had never witnessed was an actual seance. If you could call what was happening in the Everett family's living room a seance.

Five days after they found the spirit box, Hyacinth arranged for the whole family to help call the spirit of Juniper Everett. Lily invited Ezra, Bridget, and Wes to join them, though Albert didn't see the point of having the two humans there. Wes had some power since he was a guardian, but Brie was otherwise useless now that the spirit of the Morrigan no longer resided in her. But Albert didn't say anything to Lily. He supposed the humans were there for moral support rather than magical support. The house was packed full of people, as all of Lily's aunts, uncles, and cousins also were in attendance. It was part family reunion, part actual seance.

The kitchen overflowed with food since everyone had brought something. The dining table was packed and dishes covered every spare inch of counter space in the kitchen. The younger Everett cousins darted in and out of the house with loud squeals, while the older ones poured wine or passed around flasks.

Albert had been to plenty of Samhain celebrations at the farm over the years, and this was comparable. It was loud and claustrophobic. Everyone wanted to talk to Lily and him to ask about their relationship—when they were getting married, if they were going to adopt children since, obviously, they couldn't have any of their own. Albert lost count of how many times one of Lily's relations told them they better get married soon because her mother wasn't getting any younger.

Lily gracefully ducked all inquiries about anything to do with their future, which suited Albert just fine since they hadn't discussed anything themselves. With everything that had happened since she had moved in, there had never been a time to just talk about what would happen now that they had taken a more serious step.

Overall, the whole thing felt like a party. "This isn't what I expected when you said you were having a seance," Bridget said before taking a swig from the flask offered by one of Lily's cousins. Albert couldn't remember his name; it was Sequoia or Oak or something tree related, the Everett men all had tree names and the women all had plant names. It was only the ones who married into the family that created any disturbance in the tradition.

"Are you kidding? This is subdued by Everett standards. Everybody is being really chill to get ready for some power channeling." Lily grabbed the offered flask from Bridget and took a large drink before passing it over to Albert.

"If they invite me to Christmas this year, can I get out of it?" Albert winced as the cheap rum hit his tongue, but swallowed it dutifully before passing it on.

"Bertie, even if I wanted to help you, I couldn't. My mom would personally drag your ass here now that she has accepted you as part of the family." Lily laughed.

"I think I liked it better when they all hated me," he grumbled, his words nearly lost in the cacophony of the room. Lily gave his chest a playful backhanded tap.

"No, you didn't." She smiled up at him. She was right, of course. Lily's family believing he would kill her was too much for her to handle. Neither one of them minded that Rose didn't approve, but it was important to Albert that her parents approved of him.

If his family were alive, though, they likely would not have approved of Lily. The fact that she wasn't Taiwanese would have been their biggest grievance. It was good that he met Lily when he did, and not when he was human. Their relationship wouldn't even have been legal in his time. But there was no one left of his human family to judge them or force them apart because she wasn't the right culture. Now it was just his vampire family that disapproved for completely different reasons.

"*MasterChef* is on at eight, so let's get a move on!" Lily's aunt Petunia yelled out above the chatter. That was enough to draw everyone into the main room, which still wasn't large enough to accommodate everyone. Everett relations spilled into the adjoining room and hallway.

The center of the living room did, in fact, have a circular table with the wood spirit box in the center, flanked by two white candles. It was decided that Lily, Albert, Hyacinth, and Granny would call the corners since it was Lily and Albert asking the spirit and then the two most powerful witches in the family.

"Alright, you all know the drill; make sure everyone is touching somebody, so we're all connected and channeling. Our ancestor was a powerful witch, and we're going to need the juice to hold her spirit. You gotta sneeze or cough, do it now because if any of you breaks the circle, I'm coming for your butt," Hyacinth announced, taking her place at the north end of the table.

Lily took east, Albert south, and Granny west. They joined hands around the table, and one by one, the Everetts and their friends placed hands on each other's shoulders and formed the connection. The hum of power was overwhelming, electrifying the air, and made Albert's ears buzz.

"Juniper Everett, Mother of us all, hear our call. Join your children here in our hour of need." Hyacinth's voice rose with each word. She closed her eyes in concentration, and the others at the table did the same.

There were no more words spoken; the rest of the ritual was in the magical intent Lily had told him. Magic channeled through the family members, concentrating on the circle in the middle.

It was as if all the air had suddenly been sucked out of the room. Hearts beat loudly in Albert's head in a maddening cadence. Just as it all reached a crest, it felt like a tear had happened in the world, and air rushed back into the room in waves. There was a presence there that hadn't been there before.

Albert slowly opened his eyes; every single person's attention was on the apparition at the center of the round table.

He didn't know what he expected from this kind of ritual—a floating specter, most likely something ethereal, translucent. But the spirit standing above him was solid and looked just as real as any of them in the room.

She looked as Lily had described her, dark skin, just a few shades from black, black hair wrapped in long braids, though wisps of curls escaped, deep brown eyes wide as she stared around the room. Her dress was a simple linen shift, worn, but well made.

"Where am I?" Juniper Everett asked in a thick accent that Albert couldn't place. She turned in a circle atop the table, taking in the assembled people—her descendants.

"Connecticut, many centuries from your time. We've called you here to ask for your help." Hyacinth kept her hands tightly grasped in her mother's and her daughter's hands.

Juniper stared down; her attention focused on Hyacinth. "And who are you to call upon the dead?"

Hyacinth looked up into the face of her ancestor with bright eyes. "We are your blood. The children of your children's children. We are your legacy."

The spirit's eyes widened, then her brow furrowed as she studied Hyacinth. Once again, Juniper turned in a circle, taking in the faces in the room. She seemed to look into the eyes of every single face assembled, judging them, learning them. Tears slowly began to roll down her face. "I see it. I see them in your faces. There are so many of you!" She brought her hands to her mouth and choked back a sob.

Albert couldn't imagine what it must be like to see generations of your family spread around you—to see the legacy of your life in a room overflowing with people. It would be overwhelming for anyone. Several people chuckled quietly, and smiles spread around the room. It wasn't every day you got to meet your long-dead ancestor.

Hyacinth grinned up at Juniper as the spirit turned back to her. "There are, and we add more every year, it seems. But we have called you here to ask for your help, Mama Juniper. My Lily," she indicated Lily with a head nod, and Juniper turned to face the younger woman, "is mated with a vampire. He is the child of the vampire who killed you."

Juniper's hand flew to her heart. "Simon." Her voice hitched on the name.

"Mama Juniper, we don't want to kill him. But he's threatened my life, threatened to take Albert back by force. I know it's asking a lot, but we need your help to keep Simon away from us, from our family." Lily addressed Juniper this time, with an encouraging nod from her mother.

"Maybe this would give him peace as well, facing you. He made me over a hundred years ago, and in all that time, he has mourned you, hated you. He is my maker, and he is in pain. I want to be free from him, but I also want to see him freed from his own pain." Albert didn't know what had compelled him to speak, but it felt like it needed to be out there.

Juniper turned to him next, her face unreadable now. "He killed me for something I did not do. I only ever loved him, despite what we were. I hope his suffering has been long and that he remembers every day that he destroyed the only love he will ever know." There was no malice in her voice, just sorrow.

Albert couldn't imagine the pain she felt, even after all this time, to have been killed by the one person she loved the most and for something she didn't do. *Will that happen to Lily if I can't control my bloodlust one time?*

The thought alone was almost too much to bear. Lily could betray him a thousand times over, and he would never think once to harm her. Not that she ever would; Lily was simply too good a person to ever do something so heinous to someone she cared about. *Just like I can't kill Simon or let him die.* It might make their lives easier if Simon was just gone, but despite all that Simon had put him through, put them through, he cared too much to see his maker dead.

So as Juniper stared down at him with eyes that melted into unending sadness, Albert thought of Simon and the true pain he must suffer knowing the woman he loved had died by his own hands. Either that, or Simon had never really loved Juniper, and her death meant no more than a vendetta to him. But, somehow, Albert knew with certainty that wasn't the case.

"He would suffer more seeing you. At least, then he would have to face his own guilt. I know this is selfish, Mama Juniper, but Albert and I want to just live our life together without the threat of Simon hanging over us and our family. Please, help us." Lily's eyes shone with unshed tears as both Albert's and Juniper's attention turned toward her. Albert squeezed her hand just a little tighter, conveying through that touch alone how much he loved her.

The rest of the room was silent beyond them, though Albert could still feel the magic being channeled through him. All eyes were fixed on the circle.

Juniper kept her eyes on Lily as she crouched down on the table so their eyes were level. "Child, love is full of wonders. But it is also full of pain. I will help you, for love is the one thing that is worth all, even after all I have suffered for it. You and your mate will be safe. This I promise you, blood of my blood." She reached out and cupped Lily's cheek. Lily did not flinch away from the touch, though Albert wondered what it must feel like to be touched by a solid spirit.

"But you must do something for me." She kept her hand on Lily's cheek and kept her eyes locked on the younger witch.

"Anything," Lily breathed, her gaze caught on that of her ancestor's. Albert caressed the back of her hand with his thumb, but she didn't respond, didn't even acknowledge his touch.

Juniper's hand pressed a little harder into Lily's cheek, the indents of her fingers just visible. "You must carry my curse. To any vampire who harms one of my own, they shall know the true death." Several people gasped, but Lily was silent. Albert knew a little about curses, but not what it meant to carry one. *Will it be dangerous for her?* He wanted to ask aloud, but his instincts told him this was not the time to interrupt. Juniper agreed to help them but only for something in return. Lily wouldn't put herself in danger just for a spirit's vengeance. At least, he hoped she wouldn't.

Lily nodded her head against Juniper's hand. "I will. In exchange for your help." She sounded like she was swearing an oath, and that thought made Albert uneasy.

The smile Juniper gave Lily was small and still held hints of sorrow. "Good," she said, then her hand slipped from Lily's face so she could rest her palm above Lily's heart. Juniper's hand began to glow a brilliant white against Lily's chest, but the white color quickly turned crimson and pushed itself into Lily's chest, where it stayed there, glowing for several seconds. The look on Lily's face flashed with pain for just a moment, and Albert almost dropped Granny's hand to dash to her. But the old woman on his other side seemed to sense his intention and tightened her grip with surprising strength. Albert could not stop himself from flashing his teeth in warning. Neither Juniper nor Lily paid attention to his reaction.

Just as quickly as the magic and pained look came, it was gone again. The hand on Lily's chest dropped, and Juniper stood once again. Lily remained unmoving, her grip a little loose against Albert's, though not enough to drop his hand.

Juniper looked out again at the gathered people—her family. Taking them in for what would hopefully be the last time. Twin tears rolled down her dark cheeks as a small smile tugged up her mouth.

Then she stepped back and vanished. The spirit box, which until that moment, Albert had completely forgotten about, snapped shut, the sound filling the room like a thunderclap. It emanated a faint light for a few seconds and grew dim, with only the eyes of the snake faintly glowing red, indicating that a spirit was in residence.

"It is done," Hyacinth whispered, and in the quiet room, her voice carried. As one, the Everetts all dropped their hands from each other's shoulders, and the magic slowly began to dissipate. Granny's grip finally loosened on Albert's fingers, and he immediately dropped the old woman's hand to rush to Lily.

He tugged on the hand, still clamped tight to his, and pulled Lily close to him. He cupped her cheek with his free hand and raised her face so he could look into her eyes. "Darling, are you okay? She didn't hurt you?" If he sounded frantic, he didn't care; all that mattered was that Lily was well.

Lily leaned forward without a word and kissed him sweetly. There was no fiery need like many of her kisses; it was just a gentle melding of their lips, like she needed that moment of grounding. The hand he had rested against her cheek slipped down so he could wrap his arm around her waist and pull her close.

Somewhere in the crowd, someone whistled while another yelled, "Get a room!" Lily pulled away from Albert, laughing, and his heart sang at the sound.

Lily turned her head over her shoulder. "It's more action than you'll ever see, Ash," she called loudly. The room filled with laughter, and all the tension of the seance drifted away with the rest of the magic.

"Well, that was all super weird," Brie said, coming up from behind them, flanked by Ezra and Wes.

"Which part? Talking to my centuries-dead relative or being appointed harbinger of a killing curse?" Lily wrapped an arm around Albert's waist from behind as she moved to stand next to him.

"Both? All of it? Yeah, all of it. Guess that means no BDSM for you two. Can't imagine it would be very sexy if Albert died in the middle of a spanking." Wes laughed.

Brie punched him hard on the arm. "Stop being gross! Seriously, you've been talking to Apollo too much lately." Wes rubbed his arm where his sister punched him but said nothing else. The mischievous glint in his eye, though, indicated he had more to say. Albert didn't want to hear it. Didn't want to hear the siblings bicker or joke, either. He just wanted to get Lily home, where they could be alone and talk.

It took longer than Albert had hoped for that to actually happen. Just after Lily grabbed the spirit box, they were swept away by the crowd of family members. Hours passed, and Albert was still unsure how they ended up with plates full of food, watching *The Bachelor* on the living room floor, surrounded by Everett cousins.

"We're about to face down a powerful vampire and his murderous children, and rather than preparing for that, we're sitting at your parents' house watching television with literally all of your relatives." Albert leaned back against the couch as he set his half-finished plate next to him on the floor.

Lily leaned her head against his shoulder. "Can't think of a better way to spend my night. We could either be home worrying, or we can be here, watching that asshole," her attention was on the screen now, and she raised her voice, "make the wrong choice!" There were grumbles of agreement among her relations. She twined their fingers together. "Don't worry. Everything is going to be okay."

"How are you so calm about this?" he whispered into her hair. Lily turned to look up at him. Her eyes were wide, and she searched his face for something.

"I'm not. Not entirely. When Juniper gave me that curse, I saw something. The future wasn't clear, not really. But I knew we were happy and we were safe. Simon isn't going to hurt us." Lily kissed him sweetly on the lips. "I also took like double my normal dose of meds before the whole ritual, so nothing is going to bother me for a few more hours." She laughed lightly. Then she pulled back and settled against his side and continued to watch the show.

Albert could tell she was worried, despite her words and the abundance of anti-anxiety medication in her system. And if being around her family to watch some competition show eased that worry even a little, Albert trusted it was the best place for them. That, however, did nothing to assuage his own worry. That wasn't the right word for how he felt, though. *It's terror. I'm terrified I'm going to lose her.*

The last time Albert felt that level of fear was in 1906, as his world literally crumbled down around him. This fear was much the same, only it was the fear that his life was about to crumble down around him. Lately, he felt like Lily was doing all the emotional work to keep them together. He had resigned himself to walking away from their life, to return to Simon, all to keep her safe. It would have been easier. But it wouldn't save him from the heartache.

Maybe I am a coward.

He stared at the screen but saw nothing. The only thing he was aware of was the warmth of Lily's body pressed up against his chilled one. She had summoned the dead for him. She was prepared to dredge up a centuries-old issue for them. Hells, the rest of her family and their friends were all willing to do the same.

And they all did it so that Lily would be happy.

So many people, himself included, cared so much about her happiness. He would go to the ends of the earth to find the one thing that would make her happy. But he was slowly starting to realize that he didn't have to travel that far because it was all right here, in this house. Her family. Her friends. Him. Even the gardens she had spent her whole life cultivating and honing her craft.

They were going to live a long, happy life together. And nothing, especially not Simon and his vampire family, was going to take that away from them.

CHAPTER 19

Lily sat in her garden, the late summer sun warming her skin as she stared down at the plants before her. Her roses were perfect, which wasn't surprising considering how much extra help she gave them since it was their first year in the garden. If it were a normal day, she would be preening over them, letting them know how beautiful they were. She would sink her hands deep into the soil and give the roots of all the plants a boost. The living things in the ground would respond to her touch and help to feed the new life growing in her garden. The glorious sun would touch her through the leaves as they soaked in every last ray.

But there was no feeling of warmth within her today—no joy at feeling the earth and the green things pushing through the dirt. She felt heavy, like a lead ball sat in the pit of her stomach and dragged her down. All the happiness that her garden brought her could not be tapped into; she was beyond the reach of such simple luxuries.

Dread filled her completely. She spent the night tossing and turning, unable to sleep. Even when Albert wrapped her up in his arms, probably more to still her than anything, she felt restless. At one point, she thought to enter her visions, to see if there was any indication of how the evening would go. But she couldn't bring herself to do it. Since it would involve thinking of Simon, she didn't want to run the risk of summoning him again in that barren vision space. That thought alone caused whole body shudders to take control and her hand to come up to her neck again to rub against her smooth skin. The bruises had faded quickly, but it was like she could still feel his hands there, snapping her neck or choking the life out of her. Even if it wasn't real, the imitation of dying was haunting.

No, for once in her life, Lily's visions would not be helpful in navigating a problem. Instead, they were a hindrance, making her fear more than she wanted. There would be no comfort in her visions now, not until Simon was dealt with, however that may be.

Which was doing wonders for her anxiety. She had already had to call in a refill for her medication; it had been really fun trying to explain to her doctor why she had run out so quickly. Luckily, her doctor was a satori. He may look like a monkey, but his mind-reading ability made it easy to convey what she needed without trying to formulate the whole story. He merely wrote her another ninety-day script and told her it was dangerous to fraternize with vampires beyond her mate.

But she needed to put on a brave face for Albert. He didn't hide his own anxiety well at all. Ever since the séance, he had constantly been finding ways to touch her, to keep her in sight at all times. Last night, he held her so tightly she worried he would break her rib.

Lily could see him now, standing in the kitchen, watching her from far enough back that he wouldn't risk being in the sunlight. His eyes were guarded, and she contemplated running into the house to grab his hand and assure him they would be fine. But knowing Albert, he would keep her inside, drag her up to their room, and try to assuage his worry by making love to her and forgetting all their problems.

On second thought, that sounded like the perfect idea. Albert would hold her, please her, but she was also sure he would make it feel like it was their last time together. She didn't want that tainted by the threat of Simon lingering over them. Didn't want him to hold her like it was all going to end in a moment.

I want him to know it's not our last. I want him to be completely in the moment with me. She brushed her hair back from her face and struggled to pull it back in a hair tie as best she could.

Should have had Ivy braid it for me.

It would have been easier to deal with a murderous vampire without having to worry about her curls flying in her face. Too late now. They were facing Simon soon, and it would take hours to care for her hair, even with Ivy's quick work.

Finally, she stood up and brushed the dirt off her overalls and hands. She was too in her own head to get any more work done in the garden. She had a few remedies and potions to fix up for a few customers. Albert would hover around her in the kitchen while she worked, but at least they could talk, and that would be enough to keep her from thinking about all that could go wrong.

"Done already, darling?" Albert asked, as she shut the door behind her. He held up a mug toward her, and the scent of coffee was intoxicating. Lily took it gratefully and sipped, letting it soothe her, and nodded.

"I have some other stuff to finish before tonight. Where are we meeting the vamp fam?" She tried to keep her voice light; she didn't want to show any hint of fear to Albert.

But of course, he wasn't fooled. He crossed to her and wrapped her in his arms, careful to avoid the coffee in her hand. "The hotel. I sent a message asking to meet at Ezra's shop, but Simon rejected the idea. He doesn't want us to have the high ground by having our own location."

It wasn't unexpected. Simon clearly liked holding all the cards, and if he thought he had them by the balls, all the better for when they released Juniper. Because now Lily knew any Plan A they had wasn't going to work with Simon. But Juniper would. Nobody wanted to be confronted by their past, especially when she knew Simon still loved Juniper and still hurt every day from the perceived betrayal. *Funny how much you can glean from a person who is just about to kill you.*

"Didn't expect your vamp daddy to let us choose. But I'm going to start working on these orders. I need something to do with my hands." Lily squeezed him around the middle once and then let go.

He pulled her back against his chest. "I can think of something you can do with your hands," he whispered seductively in her ear as his hands traced down her sides.

She let herself lean back into him for just a moment, and then pulled away again, giving him a playful slap on the chest. "Later, lover boy, once we get through this. I'm not letting you out of bed. Now, I'm going to get to work, and you are going to talk to me about literally anything but vampires."

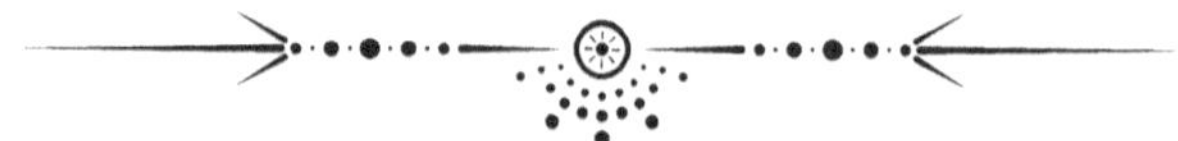

"Are you sure this is a good idea? Maybe you can push again to make him come here. We can protect you ... and Albert, I guess, if you're in the shop." Brie handed over a sachet of nettle to Lily. It would do little good against a group of vampires, but there was something to be said about the protective power of love. Brie had grown the nettle herself and made the sachet specifically for Lily.

Lily took it and put it in the back pocket of her jeans. "No, it's definitely not a good idea. But Simon seems like a guy who wants to be in control of everything, so I don't think pushing is going to do much. Besides, we have George Brown's cross, which I super don't want to use. And then we have Juniper, and I think we are better off calling on her first. Giving Simon the true death is not something I want on my conscience." She had killed once before, at least she assumed she had killed him, a starved, mad werewolf when they were saving Brie from Moloc. In the moment, it had made her feel powerful. But regret took its place soon after she was home and the adrenaline of the night had worn off. She still thought about it sometimes, even though she knew it would have killed her in an instant and without thought.

The last thing she wanted was to kill Simon. Not just so she didn't add another black mark to her conscience, but more because of what it would do to Albert. He may understand her reasoning if she killed Simon, but a part of him would never forgive her. Lily knew without a doubt that Albert loved her and that things with Simon were long in the past, but there was still that love between them that was deeply rooted, and nothing could change it. The bond between maker and child was an ancient magic that Lily couldn't even imagine breaking.

The shop was the right place to be before they met with Simon and the family. It was like preparing for battle at their own camp. Ezra had offered them a variety of protection charms, though not many were as potent against vampires as George Brown's cross.

"I still don't understand why all this is necessary. I mean, Ezra's an angel who literally brought Brie back from the dead. Why can't he handle them?" Wes asked from where he sat on the counter. Brie glared at her brother and made a hand motion to indicate he should get off the counter. He sighed and slipped down.

"And do what, exactly, Wesley? Blind them with divine light or pull out my flaming sword? I thought the point was not to kill any of them." Ezra crossed his arms and rolled his eyes. *Brie is totally rubbing off on him.* Lily laughed to herself. The grumpy angel she had known her whole life had mellowed but had also gotten much snarkier since Brie found him. They really were perfect for each other.

"I liked you better when you were stoic," Wes grumbled, leaning against the counter instead.

Next to Lily, Albert checked his watch. "It's almost eleven. We should get going."

Lily sighed deeply. She wasn't exactly eager to confront Simon and the family, but they needed to get it over with. They had done everything they could to prepare.

But will it be enough?

Or was she going to wind up dead and drained, with her boyfriend kidnapped by his vampire family, and the spirit of her dead ancestor still trapped in a box? What if Simon took Juniper's box? What if they didn't kill her and just took Albert and Juniper?

Lily felt herself spiraling. Her nerves were frayed, and she really couldn't take any more of her meds. They hadn't even left the shop yet, and she felt like she could barely breathe. Simon would see right through her and realize he could just walk away with Albert, and all Lily could do was crumple into a useless heap of anxiety on the floor.

I'm a fucking garden witch! I can't stop an ancient vampire from getting what he wants! She couldn't stop yelling at herself, couldn't pull her thoughts away from the ever-growing dread. What chance did she have against a vampire when she was basically a child in his eyes?

Last year, when she had helped Ezra find Brie, it had been easier than this. Probably because when they did that, it was all half-cocked and really stupid. The only thought put into that had been finding where Brie was being held and then charging in with literally empty brains and no regard for safety at all.

But this? Simon's threat had hung over them for weeks, always there. And in that time, they had schemed and planned and even pleaded to keep Albert from Simon. There were plans in place for tonight. Not just one, but backups as well. Which just left so much more time to think about everything that could go wrong and all the horrible ways each piece of their plan would fall apart. And goddess damn it, there was only so much medical science could do for anxiety.

"Lily? Are you ready? Do you want to stay here instead?" Albert's voice finally cut through the buzz of panic. It took her a moment to realize he was staring down at her, his hands on her arms. Concern clouded his features, and all she could do was stare into his gorgeous dark eyes and wish she could erase that look from his face.

"No, I'm ready. Let's go," she said after taking a deep breath. She would just have to work on her breathing on the way over; there wasn't time for much else. Albert didn't move; instead, his eyes never left hers. No doubt he could see it all on her face. Albert could read her like no one else, and even without saying anything, he knew just how deep her anxiety ran. She wouldn't even need to say anything. He would let her stay safe in the shop with Brie, Ezra, and Wes, and go alone to Simon, and he wouldn't fault her for it, or even make her ask.

But if he went alone, there was a strong chance that Simon would get the better of him, and she would never see Albert again, never get to have a proper goodbye. No, she was going with him, and she would just have to power through the panic in her mind as best she could and try to be brave for him. They were a united front, and she needed to act like it.

"Let's go, Bertie. We need to get this over with. After tonight, I don't want Simon in our lives, and our best chance of getting rid of him is right now." Straightening her spine, she lifted her tote bag, which held the spirit box containing Juniper, as well as a few random items to disguise it.

Brie and Wes pulled her in for a hug, one on either side of her. The warmth from their embrace gave her strength, and while she didn't relax, her heartbeat started to slow ever so slightly. Ezra stooped to give her a hug as well, something he had only done a few times since she was a child. "Be safe, and be strong, Lily. Take care of him," Ezra whispered into her ear before he straightened again.

Ezra pulled in Albert for a hug next, though it was brief and not nearly as sweet. Wes gave them double finger guns. "Knock 'em dead, you two," he said with a wink.

Brie kept her face neutral when she addressed Albert. "Anything happens to her, and I'll fucking kill you myself." Then she surprised everyone by pulling Albert into a tight hug, though they both quickly pushed away from each other, visibly uncomfortable with the embrace.

Albert took the tote from Lily's arm and grabbed her hand tightly. "You don't frighten me, Bridget. I could snap your neck easily." Brie retorted by flipping him off and then crossed her arms sullenly.

Lily wanted to laugh; they were never going to be civil with each other. But before the sound could bubble out, the laughter caught in her throat, and that feeling of breathlessness returned. She squeezed Albert's hand tightly and let him lead her out of the shop and to his car.

The ride to the Hotel Nosferat was silent. Lily tried her breathing exercises, but what good were breathing exercises when your whole world was teetering on collapse? Her hands clutched at the straps of the tote bag. She could feel the magic of Juniper's spirit radiating from the box, and it worked to calm her enough that she didn't fidget in her seat during the rest of the drive.

Lily was jittery and anxious and felt more emotions than she could possibly name. At the back of her mind, her visions were growing more demanding. With her nerves so frazzled and frayed, there was the possibility of her magic overwhelming her, of dragging her down into a vision and leaving her stuck in a world that wasn't real. It felt like she was standing on the edge of a cliff, her toes peaking over the edge, where shifting her weight just a little could send her tumbling over the edge and into the visionscape. And if that happened, the only thing that would be left of her would be madness trapped in a shell of a body.

Then Albert wouldn't have to worry about leaving me. I'll just be a mindless husk. The thought caused her heart to race faster, and her fingers gripped the side of the door harder than usual. Fingers numb against the metal, Lily looked over at her vampire.

Albert kept his gaze fixed on the road. His speed was subdued and closer to the actual limit than usual.

Neither of them, it seemed, was in a particular rush to meet their fate.

A thought crossed Lily's mind, and despite herself, she started to laugh. It started as a small giggle but quickly turned into a completely unhinged cackle. Her fingers finally released the side of the car, and the tension in her body eased. Albert stared at her out of the corner of his eye while still trying to watch the road. He looked ready to pull over. "Okay, I'm taking you back to Ezra's. I can face this on my own," he said and put on his signal to turn down a road that would circle back to the antique shop. Clearly, he thought she had finally cracked under the stress of it all. Maybe he was right.

She brought her hand up to rest on his arm. "Don't. We do this together. I'm sorry; it's just this whole thing is so stupid. I'm acting like we're going into battle, or like, to our funeral, and all we have to do really is let this guy's ex yell at him, and he'll probably go away. It's just..." She took a deep breath as she considered her words.

"It's just absurd that I'm feeling like the world is about to end, and it really isn't. Life will move on tomorrow, and we're freaking out about something that really doesn't matter." She flung her head back against the headrest and closed her eyes, letting her hand drop from his arm. Maybe she sounded a bit unhinged, but it was either laugh out loud at the ridiculous situation or stay inside her own head and let defeat take root.

Albert didn't laugh with her, but he kept driving straight to the hotel rather than turning back toward the shop. Bloodless knuckles clutched the steering wheel tighter. Albert wasn't thrilled about his decision to continue on with her, but at least he didn't say anything. After a few more seconds, Lily's laughter died away, and they lapsed back into silence.

"You're right. It is absurd," Albert said finally, cutting through the quiet of the car. He didn't look at her, but she could see his shoulders relax a little at his own words. "I've thought about this so often over the last three decades, and now it's happening, and it just feels silly. Simon spent all that time I was away showing he didn't care enough. It was once I was with you that he decided it was time for me to return home. He is jealous and fickle, and all of this worrying is because he can't stand someone saying no to him. He's a petulant child, and he needs to face up to his own failures. He's not the center of the universe like he wants to believe."

Lily nodded along with his words; Albert knew best about Simon's character. Though in her brief meetings with Simon, before he killed her in the vision space, she saw that he needed control. Beneath that surface of casual arrogance was someone who was cracked and broken. Someone who never recovered from heartbreak. It was obvious after their last encounter, and Lily was confident in her assumption that Simon never got over the guilt of killing Juniper.

This was going to work because one thing Lily was certain of was that Simon would crumble when faced with his great love. Would crumble in the face of his greatest mistake. Lily hoped it would eat him alive for the rest of his long days.

Too soon, they were pulling up to Hotel Nosferat; the valet opened the door to let Lily slide out. Albert rounded the car in a blur of speed and grabbed her hand tightly in his own. They locked eyes for a long moment. "Let's do this. And then, when all this is over, I'm not letting you out of bed for a long time," Albert whispered, flashing a fanged grin that didn't quite meet his eyes.

"Promises, promises," she responded, trying to keep her voice from shaking. She turned back to the hotel and pulled him along inside. *We can get through this if we believe in our tomorrow*, though it didn't sound all that convincing.

A rail-thin vampire in a smart black pencil skirt and maroon blouse greeted them as they entered the lobby, "Mr. Hsu, Ms. Everett, you are expected. Please follow me to the Crimson Room." Her accent was thick, Russian, by the sound of it. She turned sharply on her stiletto heels and strode away, not looking back to see if Lily and Albert followed.

They walked after her, still clutching tightly to each other's hand. "He's going to make this as dramatic as possible, isn't he?" Lily turned her chin toward Albert.

"Without a doubt. He really took the 'all the world's a stage' bit to heart." Albert's smile was barely there, but it was enough to ease the twist of fear in the pit of Lily's stomach.

The rest of the walk to the Crimson Room was quiet, with the click of the concierge vampire's heels echoing down the halls as the sole noise. She stopped before a set of doors that were indeed painted crimson with a black plate with gold lettering identifying it as the Crimson Room on the door.

"Do you require any refreshments? We have a lovely thirty-year on tap. I could have her sent over. And we do have an assortment of beverages for our human guests," the concierge vampire said in her clearest hospitality voice. Lily expected condescension toward her from the vampire staff, what with her whole not undead thing going on. *Guess I should examine my biases.*

"We're good, thank you," Albert said, his focus solely on the door in front of them.

The concierge gave them a polite nod and walked away, her high heels clicking on the floor until she turned a corner and was gone. Lily and Albert stood in front of the painted entrance for several long moments. The last thing Lily wanted to do was pull open the door and face Simon, but that's exactly what they were going to have to do. So instead, she waited for Albert to lead the way, but he remained rooted to the spot and did not reach out to pull the door open.

Before either of them could make a move, one of the doors burst open, swinging out toward them. Celia's arm held the door open. "For fuck's sake, stop standing there and get in."

Her arm fell from the door, and Albert caught it before it could shut. With great reluctance, they followed after Celia into the dark crimson covered room.

CHAPTER 20

$\mathcal{A}$lbert wasn't ready for this. No matter how much he had told himself over the last several days that he was. No matter how often he had checked in with Lily to assure her that all would be well, he wasn't ready. Not to face Simon. Not to face the family. Not to face the uncertainty of it all.

And yet his feet followed obediently behind Celia, his hand grasping Lily's tightly, just shy of crushing her fingers. "Were you planning to just stand there all night? Immortality really is wasted on you, Albert." Celia sounded bored. She was, of course, impeccably dressed in a long, flowing black gown with a slit up to mid-thigh. It clung to her body like it was molded to it. Her long black hair hung in waves around her. The diamond necklace at her throat was just large enough to be eye-catching without being garish. Albert wished he could choke her with it.

"I can practically feel your desire for murder, my dear Albert. You and Celia will have to work out that sibling rivalry if we're going to be a happy family again." Simon's silky voice echoed in the room.

He was the centerpiece of the Crimson Room. Reclined in a plush gold chair, he had his legs spread wide, ring-covered hands resting on the arms—the picture of arrogant decadence.

The rest of the family lounged about on the scattered furniture in the room, which was all covered in crimson-colored fabrics and dark wooden frames. An electric fireplace burned against one wall, casting dancing shadows around the space and causing the faces of the vampires to take on the visage of demons. There was little else in the room. The space was small enough to feel intimate, but not so tiny as to feel claustrophobic. Albert realized it must be one of the feeding rooms the hotel offered for private parties. Which, he supposed, this was a private party, of a sort, anyway. Not one he actually wanted to be in attendance of.

Albert pulled Lily to a stop several feet away from Simon. He didn't want them too close; he didn't know what type of mood Simon was in. It was best to keep their distance. Simon leveled his gaze on them, a faint smile on his lips and amusement in his eyes. "Aron, please take our guests' things." Simon motioned toward Lily's bag, the one that held Juniper's box. As Aron approached with a predatory smile, Lily gripped the strap tighter. But she took it from her shoulder and handed it over before Aron got too close—better for her to give it over now than fight for it. They couldn't do anything with the box, anyway; it wasn't time. And thanks to a few extra charms from Hyacinth, nobody but Lily or Albert could open the box. Lily had filled the bag full of other useless magical trinkets, little things that would make the box less conspicuous, as well as her wallet and keys and whatever else she normally kept in one of her tote bags.

Aron made short work of sifting through the contents, but the stupid asshole clearly didn't know what he was looking for. He held up each item for half a second and then tossed it back in. Even with Simon watching, Aron didn't waste time on any of the objects; nothing caught his attention.

"So, I take it that you have come to join us again, to say goodbye to your witch paramour and return to what you are truly meant to be." Simon's smile was nothing like Aron's. It was inviting with a flash of fang, but the look in his eye promised so much more. Promised bloodlust and pain. Triumph and debauchery. It promised unending pleasure and love in exchange for absolute fealty. But Albert didn't want that anymore. His future was with Lily. His life was with Lily. And there was nothing Simon could promise him that would be better than being with her.

"You're mistaken. We've come to tell you, once again, it's time for you to leave. You and the family. You're not wanted here." Albert kept his eyes trained on Simon and didn't allow himself to be distracted by the other family members. He held firmly to Lily's hand, letting the feel of her warm palm give him strength. "I don't want you here." The words were harder to say than he had imagined. Facing Simon after all these years and telling him exactly what he felt was more difficult than he could ever have imagined.

Simon's smile slipped just a fraction, but he quickly recovered, and that arrogant grin returned in a blink. He remained in his lounging position, ever keeping the air of boredom. "My dear Albert, you come here with no weapons, none of your powerful friends, and you bring the very woman you're trying to protect from me. Clearly, you didn't think this through. Did you really believe your words would be enough to send me off? To see the error of my ways and leave you and your witch alone? I thought you knew better than that. I thought I made you better than that. I must say, I'm disappointed."

Albert had to stop himself from clutching at his chest because hearing Simon say he was disappointed was a hard blow. He had been conditioned since his making to always please Simon. But even before he had met the vampire, there was the pressure to bring honor and respect to his family name. If he disappointed his parents even once, he would feel the shame of it forever. He cursed himself—over a hundred years old and he was still afraid of disappointing the important people in his life.

And Simon is important to me, whether I like it or not. He made me what I am. He cursed himself a thousand times over for the unholy bond between his maker and himself. There would always be that pull whenever Simon was close.

Celia sat on one of the chaises and crossed her ankles. "Oh, come on, Simon, you don't think that bag is full of useless trinkets? They aren't that stupid." The look she gave them, especially Albert, said she thought they were indeed that stupid.

"What are they going to do? Throw some stones at our heads?" Aron chuckled as he took a few crystals out of the bag. A few were for protection, but they were mostly for show, the magic in them too weak to do much good against a room full of vampires, according to Wes, but general protection never hurt. Wes would have weighed them both down with shiny rocks, given time.

"Your head is full of enough rocks," Albert replied blandly. Aron's face scrunched up in anger, and he balled his fists with the crystals still in his hands, letting the dust from the crushed stone slip between his fingers. He looked ready to attack, but Celia tugged on his arm and pulled him down onto the chaise she was sitting on.

"Now, now, love, don't let him get to you. He's just bitter and mean," Celia cooed toward her lover. Aron eased back and rested against her; the bag remained at his side.

She treats him like a child. Albert couldn't help feeling pity for him. Celia had been leading Aron on for centuries, breaking his heart over and over, and like a kicked puppy, he always came back to her.

Across from them sat Sam on one of the couches. They had their arms crossed tightly, one ankle resting on the opposite knee. It was unusual for Sam to be sitting. They liked to be ready to move at a moment's notice. Not that they couldn't move with incredible speed from any position. If anything, Sam was the fastest one in the whole family. Albert had long suspected that Sam just didn't feel comfortable without an exit strategy. Whatever happened in their human life had damaged them enough to always need a way out. So, for them to be sitting meant they felt comfortable enough to ease their guard. That was not a good sign for him and Lily.

"Oh, I have no doubt there is something of interest in the witch's bag, but it won't do them any good, especially since they no longer have it. But more than that, there is very little left in this world that can do me harm. Albert doesn't have the mental strength to hurt me or any of us. Do you, my dear Albert?" Simon's face was smug, like he already knew the answer. And damn him for being right: Albert didn't have the strength to hurt Simon. Didn't have the strength to hurt any of them, even Celia. So, he said nothing, refusing to make any indication to answer Simon's question.

Simon gestured to one of the open couches. "Sit, both of you." Albert didn't miss the way Simon stared at him, not once even acknowledging Lily. The arrogant bastard truly believed that this was Albert coming home. It wouldn't surprise him if Simon thought he brought Lily for them to share.

"Eiko, why don't you get our guests something to eat?" Simon lazily flicked his wrist toward where Eiko sat, legs crisscrossed on a couch. She stood with more grace than a human could accomplish and flashed a white smile. Eager to please, just as they all were when they first came to Simon.

"That won't be necessary. We don't plan to stay long," Albert said, holding up his hand to stop the young vampire. Eiko stopped in her tracks and turned to Simon for further direction. He just waved her off, and she resumed her seat on the couch; her smile wavered only for a split second before she recovered.

Simon kept his eyes locked on Albert. They had yet to leave his face, even when he was commanding Eiko and Aron. "Is this to be a quick parting between you and your witch? Or do you really plan to break my heart again, Albert?" Simon's smirk remained plastered on his face. Though he seemed at ease, a king surrounded by his adoring subjects, Albert could feel the tension in the air. Maybe Simon wasn't as confident about getting what he wanted this time. *Good*, thought Albert, because if Simon wasn't confident, Albert was.

"As I have said before, Simon, I'm not coming back. My life is here now, and the family can't give me the happiness I want. So, I will ask again that you leave New Britain and leave us alone." Albert was pleased that his voice remained even and calm because he really felt like shouting at Simon, at all of them—to scream at them all to leave him alone. But that would get him nowhere.

"Your life belongs to our master. He made you, and it's by his grace that you continue to walk the earth," Eiko said loudly from where she had curled back up on the couch. Her voice was soft with what sounded like a Manhattan accent. And that young, naïve devotion to Simon was the only reason she spoke out of turn at all.

That was me once. Only I would have ripped the throat out of anyone who spoke against Simon. I would have done it without a second thought. Maybe Eiko was a better person than he was and had managed to tame the emotional outbursts that came with the newly turned.

All eyes snapped to her, a good indicator, at least to Albert, that she did not contribute much to conversations within the family. "Eiko, you sweet dear. So devoted and so loyal," Simon purred at her, and she preened under his praise. The sight of it made Albert want to vomit. He really had been that way once, ready to spout whatever drivel would please Simon the most. There was nothing Albert wouldn't have done if it had meant pleasing Simon, even for half a second. He could see it so clearly in Eiko's face, in the way she stared at Simon like he had created the world and all the creatures in it. She was still so new to their world, and Simon ensured that the family members he brought in were completely enthralled by him. Attachments outside of the family were forbidden so that no one would question Simon.

How did I let myself be manipulated like that? Let him control me for so long?

Because it had always been about control with Simon. He never wanted any of them to believe they could handle life outside the family. That was why he was here now, because not only had Albert survived leaving, he had thrived. He had his life, his partner, his friends, a whole world that didn't revolve around Simon. And, as Albert now knew, most makers didn't hold on to their progeny for long. Most vampires were solitary creatures. They turned humans, spent a few years teaching them the ways of their kind, and then set them loose on the world, crossing paths through the centuries sporadically, whereas Simon hoarded his progeny like a twisted family, a constant band to validate himself. A stand-in for the family he lost with Juniper.

Albert focused on Eiko and spoke to directly to her, "My life belongs to me. Simon may have made me what I am, but he doesn't own me. He doesn't own any of you. And leaving him..." Albert slowly turned his gaze back to Simon, who still lounged in his chair, though he wasn't smiling any longer. "Leaving you was the best decision I ever made." Albert stared unblinking, lifting his chin a little in challenge. It was enough to make Simon frown. A wrinkle appeared between his eyes as he narrowed them, the only flaw in his perfect skin.

The whole time Lily had been silent, but she gripped Albert's hand between their chairs. She was letting him lead, though he could tell it took all her willpower not to lash out at everyone in the room. He was grateful for her trust in him.

"You're selfish, then!" Eiko shrieked. Albert turned to her again and instantly realized the danger. Her eyes were crimson, her teeth bared, ready to be consumed by the bloodlust. They could all hear it, the rushing of Lily's blood through her veins, the pounding of her heart. To a young vampire, riled up by what she saw as an attack on the most important person in her life, it would undoubtedly drive her mad at the prospect of blood. "She is food, like all mortals. You disgrace the gift Simon has given us by fucking her. We should just kill the witch now and leave." In a blur of speed, Eiko was there, yanking Lily up out of the chair by her throat.

Albert was on his feet for less than half a second before Celia was pushing him back in his chair. She was stronger than he was, older, and she held him back with a firm hand against his chest.

Eiko's fangs descended into Lily's neck, and she began to pull greedily from the vein while Lily struggled in her arms. He saw magic crackle at Lily's fingertips, but she couldn't seem to call anything more than a few sparks. Eiko was draining her quickly, with the force and lack of control only a youngling had. It wouldn't be a drawn-out feeding as if one of the older vampires drained her. This would be over in seconds if he couldn't do something.

A primal scream filled the room suddenly, and it took a moment for Albert to realize it was coming from his own throat. Tears stung his eye while he watched helplessly as Lily tried to fight off the young vampire attached to her neck, to no avail.

Albert's eyes flashed around the room, futilely hoping one of them would stop it, to Celia's smirk in front of him, to Aron's laughing face, to the startled look on Sam's. And finally, he stared at Simon, who just looked sad. Defeated even. Like this was the last thing he had wanted to happen.

But then the scream filling the room wasn't his own anymore. Eiko ripped her fangs from Lily and tossed the witch roughly away as the vampire screamed in pain. Blood dribbled down her chin, but she didn't notice, didn't wipe it away. Eiko's hand grabbed at her chest like she was trying to claw at something. "Simon, what's happening to me?" she cried out, eyes roving for her maker. Tears of blood began to leak down her face. A red glow appeared at her chest, where her heart lay dormant. Albert recognized the glow immediately. It was the same one he saw at the seance, when Juniper had given Lily the curse to carry. He had forgotten all about it after that night.

A curse for her descendants to carry to protect them against vampires.

"Simon, do something!" Sam cried out, standing from their spot. They looked on helplessly as Eiko crumpled to the ground, still screaming and holding her chest, unable to stand any longer. More blood poured from her eyes and streaked down her cheeks.

But there was nothing Simon could do, because then the screaming stopped suddenly, and from the glowing spot on Eiko's chest, flames appeared, and in half a second, Eiko was completely consumed by magical fire and had burnt to dust. The whole thing took less than a minute.

Albert quickly shifted his gaze to Lily, who had huddled up on the floor after Eiko dropped her. One hand covered the bite on her neck, putting pressure on the wound while she stared at the spot where Eiko had once been. Her beautiful face was several shades lighter, her eyes sunken, like some of her life had been leached out of her. He didn't know how much blood she had lost, but it was too much already. Any blood drained from her was too much.

The hand on his chest loosened enough for him to slip past Celia and fling himself down next to Lily on the floor. He gathered her up in his arms and held her tightly. The smell of her blood was potent, but he pushed through the temptation and held her while she clung to his shirt like it was a lifeline. "I'm okay, I'm okay, I'm okay," she frantically whispered into his chest, though he wasn't sure if she was trying to convince him or herself. He didn't know how much time they would have before the shock of everything wore off. They were in a really shitty position now. Would the family attack them right away? Would they continue to talk? There was no way of knowing. This wasn't part of the plan. It was all supposed to be simple, and nobody was supposed to get hurt, let alone die. All he could do now was hold Lily close and continue to kiss the top of her head repeatedly while they waited for what was to come.

It didn't take long for long fingers to grab him by the throat from behind and hoist him up, tearing him away from Lily. Simon's fingers dug in and he threw Albert across the room onto a waiting couch. Albert sprawled there, disoriented, as he looked out at the room sideways. Simon stalked over to Albert, not sparing any attention to Lily despite what had just happened. There was a fire in his eyes, burning in a way Albert had never seen before. And damn him, but he was terrified.

Simon crouched down next to the couch until his face was level with Albert's. There were no snarls, no baring of fangs; he didn't even look angry, even as his eyes still burned with that intensity. Once again, his hand reached out and held Albert's throat. "Now, here we were having a pleasant talk and it's all gone to hell. My poor Eiko, so young and vibrant... her death is on your hands now, Albert. Yours and that little witch's. She was only a child." He sounded mournful. Albert couldn't face the reality that Simon did care for his progeny, did indeed see them as his family. *Did he mourn for me like this when I left?* He had never considered it.

"She was going to kill Lily. It's not my fault you didn't train her to calm her bloodlust." Albert's retort was barely a whisper. Simon flung him back against the couch in disgust, like he couldn't bear to touch him anymore.

"Who has the time to train these children anymore? It was for her to figure out, and she failed. I expect better from my children." Simon turned his back on Albert and took his seat in his chair once again. Though Simon tried to put on airs again, to adopt his cool demeanor, the effect didn't hold. The sorrow in his eyes, the forced uptick of his lips, was not convincing. He was rattled by what had happened. But then again, so were they all, Albert included.

"So, what are we going to do about her?" Celia nodded toward Lily, who was still sitting on the floor in a heap. Celia had returned to her chaise and kept a firm hand on Aron as he looked like he was seconds away from tearing Lily apart, his own eyes flickering to crimson and back again to their normal color. Over on the other side of the room, Sam remained standing, staring at the spot where Eiko had burned away, but their face was stoic, their mask was up, and body tense and ready to spring.

"What indeed," Simon drawled, settling into his casual air, tense as it was now. None of the family made a move toward either Albert or Lily. Albert lifted himself from the couch and refrained from touching his now aching throat. The pain would fade soon enough, as would the bruises. His focus was solely on

Lily, who was trying to rise to her feet on shaky legs. Beautiful, strong Lily, still so powerful even after being attacked. He moved to her side quickly, before anyone could react. Not that they did. The rest of the family remained exactly as they were.

"Darling, are you okay?" It was a stupid question; of course she wasn't okay. He held onto her arm and was grateful when she put her weight on him. A crackling of magic, barely noticeable, appeared on the hand holding her neck. *She's healing herself. Good girl.*

Lily turned a brittle smile toward him. "I'll be okay. But I really want to go home now. Can we wrap this up and get out of here?"

Albert pulled her into his arms and kissed the top of her head. "Of course." They turned their attention to Simon, blocking the rest of the family out.

The smirk had completely vanished from Simon's face. Now he was all harsh lines and his mouth was set in a firm line, sending a clear message that a quick and easy exit was not happening. Even seeing Eiko turn to ash in front of him did not deter him from what he wanted. Control was what he craved, and he would have it, even when it seemed like the situation was beyond his expectations.

"My dear Albert, you know I can't just let you leave. As much as I want you to come home with us willingly, I'm afraid if I have to take you by force, I will. After all, look at what became of you after you left us; cavorting with an Everett witch, drinking from the half-dead like a leech, or worse, animal blood. You spend so much time now trying to blend in with the rest of the creatures of this world rather than your own kind that you have forgotten what you are. How far you have fallen, my darling predator." Simon sat up and drew his hands together. In less than a second, he stood before Albert, one bejeweled finger running down Albert's cheek in a soft caress.

Albert flinched back only a little and drew Lily behind him. "Lily, I think it's time we called for her," he said, though he kept his eyes on Simon.

He heard Lily mutter behind him, then Aron squawked loudly. Though he didn't tear his gaze from Simon, Albert knew Aron was reacting to the spirit box moving from its place in the bag. Albert reached back and grabbed Lily, taking a step away from Simon, putting distance between them.

"What is this?" Simon asked with curiosity in his voice while he stared at the spirit box now in Lily's hands.

As Lily opened the spirit box, the room was bathed in a blindingly brilliant light. Albert heard the hisses of the assembled vampires, and he shielded his own eyes from the light with his arm. In truth, the light burned, but what waited inside was worth the temporary pain.

When he finally lowered his arm and opened his eyes, Juniper was there, standing tall, her shoulders back, looking every bit like a witch queen. She stared ahead toward Simon; her face an unreadable mask as she took him in for the first time in centuries. Albert's attention moved to Simon, who stood in stunned awe, a mix of terror, sadness, and rage warring on his features. Hundreds of years of suppressed emotions raging forth, and Albert could not even begin to imagine how that felt.

"Juniper," Simon finally breathed out, his eyes wide. Albert had never seen his maker so undone, so raw. Simon raised a hand as if to reach for his former lover, but then he stopped and drew back. It was clear he couldn't decide how to feel. At their final parting, he had killed her, but the pain of that had plagued him for longer than Albert had known him.

"Simon," Juniper responded, her voice hard as stone, her eyes flinty.

"Who's this bitch?" Celia asked loudly, with accusing eyes narrowed at Albert. He only glared back at her. Celia wasn't his problem, and at least for now, she wouldn't do anything until Simon gave her permission.

"Fuck off, Celia." Simon's voice was barely there, the arrogant lilt gone, the easy drawl vanished. Now he was only a man confronted by a ghost. "How are you here, Juniper?" was all he was able to ask, though his voice trembled at the question.

Albert turned toward the witch, but his eyes flicked to where Lily stood still, holding the now empty box. She looked at him and gave him the barest hint of a smile. It was enough to reassure him. Their part was done. Now all they had to do was let this all play out between Juniper and Simon.

Juniper's expression didn't change as she responded to Simon. "My descendent had need of me. It seems you are out to ruin my family's lives. Again. You just cannot help yourself, can you, Simon?"

Simon's features turned defensive; anger appeared to win out in his swirl of emotions. "Help myself? You betrayed me, remember? You were going to let those humans destroy me. And for what? So, you could continue being the precious witch queen of that pathetic island? They were never going to allow you to live, anyway. You know how humans are. They turn on you just as much as they heap praise on you."

"I never betrayed you, fool. I said nothing of what you were. I tried to protect you. I tried to protect our family." Juniper's retort lacked Simon's biting tone. Neither of them raised their voices, though their faces were both warped in anger. It was a standoff that was centuries in the making.

Simon scoffed loudly, the noise cutting through the room and ringing harshly. "Well, you did a wonderful job of protecting me, Juniper. Were it not for my friends, I would have been ash. I had to flee the island, leave our family behind. Do you know I never saw them again? I ... couldn't." His voice faltered at that last; the flash of pain was there and gone again from his eyes as Simon let his anger continue to fuel him.

Albert reached for Lily's hand and pulled her back, letting Simon and Juniper have their arena. If he could have, Albert would have drawn Lily out of the room and escaped back to the antique shop. But Lily would need to release Juniper's spirit. They had to stay until it was all over.

Simon advanced on Juniper, but she held her ground, glaring daggers into him. "Do you expect me to pity you? You did not become ash, but I did. I never saw our family again because I was dead—because of you. Shall we compare plights, then? Since you have spent these many long years still alive and enjoying all that life has to offer. And it seems you had no issue replacing our family." Juniper's eyes swept around the room, taking in all the vampires assembled around them. They could only stare back at her with uncertainty. Juniper turned her head back toward Simon. "I would say my fate was much worse."

This time, she stepped close to him, and rather than meet her, Simon took a step back. Never in his time with Simon had Albert seen his maker back down from anything. Nobody cowed him. Simon was always the commanding force in the room.

But right now, Juniper was that force, and Simon's reckoning had finally come.

CHAPTER 21

The tingle of magic flowed through Lily's body as her ancestor faced down the vampire who had been haunting them all for weeks. All the energy her family gave toward holding Juniper's spirit channeled through her. The longer Juniper remained out of the spirit box, the more energy it would take to sustain her physical form. Her granny had warned her before she left the farm to be mindful of the energy pull. It wouldn't kill her, but it would leave her drained, and then there would be no way to stop Simon from taking Albert. No way to stop them from finishing her off in her weakest moment. Lily wasn't sure what would happen to Juniper without properly releasing her spirit. Would she return to whatever afterlife she came from? Or would she be stuck in this world, only diminished, unable to hold her form without the power being channeled into her? Lily didn't want to find out.

A spike of fear rippled through her. *What if I'm not strong enough to maintain this? What if I fail and wake up to find Albert gone? Or I don't wake up at all?* She tried to push the thoughts away and focus on the energy. Now wasn't the time to let anxiety tear her focus away from what she needed to do.

But that was easier said than done. She could feel her thoughts, her fears spiraling deeper into pure anxiety and panic. It wasn't like she could put a pause on whatever was happening between Juniper and Simon so she could go take one of her pills. Powering through the anxiety wasn't much of an option either since her hold on her emotions had been slipping for weeks now and was tenuous at best.

Albert's cold fingers slipped between her own, rallying her attention to a singular point to where their hands met. As he threaded his fingers with hers, she could feel the swirl of emotions inside her start to settle, if only a little. The magical energy was still there, still flowing strong as Albert pulled her close, grounding her in the moment. His presence by her side gave her strength.

Across the room, Simon and Juniper stood nearly nose to nose, though Simon was clearly on the defense even with the height he had on Juniper. "I spent years making excuses for your daily absences, and not once did I complain because we had a good life. I would have gladly walked onto the pyre myself if it meant keeping you from harm. And yet, without any proof, you destroyed my life, our life." Simon actually shrank away from the witch, wilting under her accusing stare. *It's a wonder he hasn't burst into flames,* Lily thought as she clung to Albert, unable to look away from the scene in front of them.

Their plan was working. She didn't expect that Juniper and Simon would get proper closure from this, but after weeks of being terrorized by the vampire, Lily could admit to feeling some satisfaction as Juniper put him in his place.

It was clear to her now that Juniper had truly loved Simon. Had built a life with him and had thought they would have decades together. She sounded like she had all the faith in the world that their love would have endured. But it seemed Simon had lacked that faith. And here he was now, facing the reality of that lack of faith in his love.

"You say nothing to me. Now is your time to justify your actions, Simon. Tell me, was it worth destroying my life? Destroying all that we had together?" She advanced on him again, and again, he stepped away from her, keeping just enough distance between them. The arrogance that had seemed to radiate off him before was completely gone. Simon looked no more imposing than a simple man faced with the consequences of his actions.

"You cared more about saving your own witching business. You gladly gave me up to the humans to save yourself," Simon managed to spit out, though there was no conviction behind his words, as if he didn't even believe them himself. Juniper stopped short, her eyes wide in horror.

"That is what you think of me? That I would be so selfish to save my business that I would betray the one man I truly loved? That I would destroy the lives of our children and bring ruin upon our home? To hell with magic. I would have done anything in this world to save you from the humans." Lily's heart broke for her ancestor. The pain on Juniper's face was crushing.

She wanted to call Juniper back to the spirit box, to get her away from this place, away from Simon, so she wouldn't have to face her own broken heart.

But this moment was for Juniper. She needed this confrontation, needed it so her soul could finally rest easy, and Lily's family needed a way to get past their hatred for vampires. The root of all their problems lately was this, the tragic love story between a vampire and a witch that had caused so much trouble down the bloodline.

Albert gripped Lily's hand tighter. It was like seeing what could have been for them. A deep love that ended in betrayal over misunderstandings. It could have easily been them.

But they were not like Juniper and Simon. Rather than jump to conclusions, they communicated, they talked out their problems. And they were a stronger pair because of it, even with their bumps in the road. That was something Juniper and Simon would never understand. Something Simon especially would never understand.

"I thought... I had heard word going around town about a vampire. They were arranging a party to find me. The only one who knew what I was then was you and the children." Simon finally found some strength behind his words, his voice accusing. He stood his ground and didn't shrink from Juniper now. Finally, some of that arrogance returned, as if he was bolstered by his absolute confidence that he was the wronged party.

Juniper advanced on him again so that there wasn't even an inch of space between them and craned her neck to look up at him. "So you heard rumors in the square and assumed it was me? And rather than come to me for truths, you killed me without question. You are a selfish coward, and I curse you!"

"Juniper, no—" Simon began, but the electric feel of magic permeated the room suddenly. Lily felt the magic building quickly against her skin.

"I curse you, Simon. I curse you by taking the one thing you hold most dear, so that you may know you are nothing, and will return to nothing." Juniper slammed her hand against Simon's chest and held it there. A bright crimson light pulsed from her hand into Simon's chest, similar to what she had done to Lily when placing the other curse. Lily and Albert shielded their eyes as the light grew in vibrancy.

But Lily could not drown out the scream that tore through the room. It was unearthly, like what Lily imagined a soul being ripped from a body sounded like. It was primal to the core and rang so harshly in her ears that she wanted to clap her hands against the sides of her head to try to push the sound from her mind. It was the kind of sound that would likely haunt her for the rest of her life.

The scream seemed to go on forever, but perhaps it was only seconds. When it stopped, so too did the light, and they were left in the dim lighting of the hotel. In the absence of the scream, the room felt eerily silent. When Lily opened her eyes, she saw Simon doubled over, his knees on the floor. He was curled in on himself; his breathing was loud and ragged. Above him, Juniper stood with one hand still outstretched. There was no kindness on her face, just a blank mask.

"What did you do to him?" Celia shrieked, a sound that broke through the pregnant silence. Lily had forgotten the rest of the family was still in the room. During the entire encounter with Juniper, they had remained on the edges of the room, probably confused by what had transpired before them.

Juniper's attention snapped to Celia, though her face didn't change. "I took away the one thing he held most dear: his vampirism. Too long has he lived, lording over those he has found, considering himself a god. Now, like me, he, too, shall become dust."

Soft crying filled the air. It took a moment for Lily to realize it was Simon. Still curled in on himself, he sobbed quietly on the floor. His skin, which was already slightly golden before, had brightened noticeably, the gold now a brilliant hue as life returned to his body. His shoulders heaved with heavy breaths between tears. But the titanic presence he had once possessed was gone, and he was just a simple man, crumbled and broken.

The rest of the vampires in the room stared down at their maker, all unsure of what to do, what to say. So, they said nothing, just continued to look down at the man who was their everything. Albert drew her close and wrapped an arm around her shoulders, but his focus was solely on Simon. Lily could feel his body tense against hers. She snaked an arm around his waist and leaned into him. If only she could know what he was thinking, but his face was blank, and there was no way to read his flat eyes.

The longer Lily stared at Simon, the more she started to feel light-headed. She felt so tired. All she wanted to do was sit down and rest for a moment. That's when her legs suddenly gave out, and her hold on Albert slacked. She slumped, and it was only Albert's hold on her shoulders that kept her from falling to the floor. He put his other arm around her waist and heaved her against him. "Darling, are you alright?" The panic in his voice was clear. So much had happened so quickly. He had to be emotionally overloaded.

Lily made to wave him off, but her arms felt so heavy. It took more effort than she was capable of to move them. "I'm ... fine. Just need ... to rest." Why did she sound so breathy?

"Your pulse is too slow. It's Juniper. She's pulling too much energy from you." Albert sounded like he was in teetering on full-blown panic. Somehow that made sense to Lily's muddled brain. Juniper's use of her power to reverse Simon's vampirism took more energy than Lily was able to easily channel. If she kept the connection much longer, the magic it took to keep Juniper's spirit connected to the living world would completely drain her, and she could easily become a magic-less husk.

Juniper finally turned her attention away from her diminished former lover and focused on her descendant. "It is too much for her to hold. Child..." She addressed Lily directly. It was becoming an effort to focus on the words directed at her. "You must let the magic go. Without the power of our family, you cannot hold me here on your own. Let me go, Daughter." Lily could barely feel the hand Juniper placed on her cheek, having missed completely Juniper's movement toward her.

Am I that cold?

It took more effort than it should for Lily to reach into herself, to find that warm glow within that connected her magic to Juniper. But when she finally did, she imagined a pair of shears severing the connection between them. It was easier than she had thought it would be, while everything else seemed to take more effort and concentration.

As if a projection had been turned off, Juniper blinked from existence as if she had never been there at all. And as Lily slipped into darkness, she vaguely felt the curl of Albert's hand around hers.

Lily wasn't dead. That was the first thing she noted. Her surroundings were much as they were when she entered her visions with Simon. There was endless nothing in every direction. The only thing was her own body, and as she looked up, there was Juniper. The elder witch smiled softly at Lily and opened her arms to her.

Lily wasted no time in rushing into her ancestor's embrace, letting the motherly feel of her hug warm her. One of Juniper's hands came up to stroke the back of Lily's head, and the two women stayed locked together for several long moments.

"I am proud of you, daughter of my daughters. I know this is not the outcome you had wished for, but

I hope it brings you peace all the same." She pulled from Lily a few inches to look down at her with that same soft smile.

Lily brushed a few tears off her cheek. When had she started crying? "I hope you find peace, too, Grandmother."

This was goodbye, and she knew her ancestor would find her final rest. Juniper placed a tender kiss on Lily's forehead, and then she was gone for good. Lily was left in the vision space alone. She expected to be jogged back into consciousness, but then the vision space shifted into a true vision.

She was surrounded by lush greenery. Tall tropical trees waved in a soft breeze. There were a few tilled fields on a hill. Off to her right, there sat a solid yet modest house with the glow of candles in the window. It was night, and there was no artificial light, but the stars and moon shone so vibrantly that it provided enough to see clearly.

The door to the house opened, spilling candle-light onto the ground. She recognized Juniper standing at the doorway, smiling at something ahead of her. When Lily turned, there was Simon walking up the lane, a matching smile on his face. He only had eyes for Juniper, and he looked so happy. *Like a man in love,* she thought. This must be before the betrayal.

As he approached, he reached out and pulled her into his arms for a passionate kiss, and Lily could feel the electrical pulse of magic flare up. Juniper radiated a type of magic that only came with great emotion.

"Our children have been waiting for you, my love." Juniper stroked one of Simon's cheeks with her thumb.

Simon's fanged smile was wide, not the predatory smile Lily had known. "I've brought them all gifts. But first, I believe I owe my wife another kiss." He drew Juniper close again, and Lily felt a twinge of embarrassment at how passionate and consuming their kiss was. But then they turned, wrapped their arms around each other's waists, and walked into the house, shutting the door behind them.

The last thing Lily heard before the vision faded was the sound of delighted squeals.

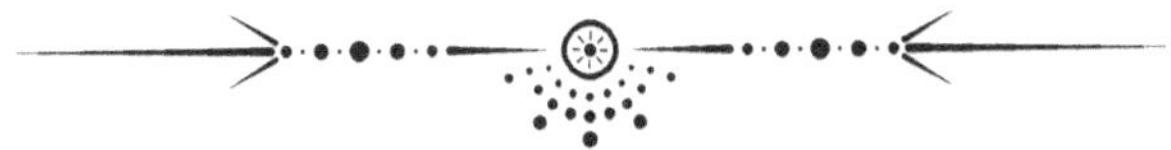

When Lily opened her eyes in the real world, she was looking up at the dark crimson ceiling. She took stock of her body. Nothing seemed off, nothing hurt, her heart rate was normal, and she no longer felt cold. She was lying down on something soft, one of the couches, probably.

Sitting up slowly, she looked around the room. She was alone on the couch, but across from her, on one of the chaises, the vampires, including Albert, were all huddled around a mass, sitting curled up on the furniture.

Simon.

They were whispering in soft tones to him, arms wrapped around him and each other while he cried. Though she knew he was a total bastard that didn't deserve her sympathy, Lily still felt sorry for him. In that brief glimpse into their life, she saw that he and Juniper had truly loved each other once.

As she straightened in her seat, Albert was already by her side, his movements too fast for her eyes. "Darling, how are you feeling?" The frantic tone from earlier was gone, but there was still a note of panic in his voice. He wrapped her in his arms and pulled her close. Lily let him hold her for a moment before she began to speak.

"I'm alright. Better now. Just had a chat with my dead ancestor, so I am ready to get out of here and sleep for a solid day." She smiled up at him and pressed her lips to his. Albert kissed her back gently, but he pulled away quicker than she liked. His head turned back toward Simon.

Lily followed his attention and stared at the still-huddled group. "Will he be okay?" Not that she wished ill on him, but he might actually deserve what he got.

Albert was silent for a few seconds. "I don't know. The family will take care of him for now. Someone could try to turn him again, I'm sure, but there's no telling the full extent of Juniper's curse. The transformation could kill him outright if they tried."

"So, he's really human, then. Guess he's going to have to figure out how to function without being an asshole with a superiority complex," Lily quipped as she let Albert pull her to a standing position.

The smile Albert gave her was strained. "I have no doubt that when he adjusts to his new state that he will absolutely return to his old self. Come on. Let's get out of here." He started to pull her away, but they stopped abruptly when Celia stepped in front of them.

"And where the hell do you think you're going? Your fucking witch girlfriend did this to Simon. She doesn't get to just walk out of here!" Celia bared her fangs. Her intention was clear: Lily wasn't going to leave the hotel alive if Celia had her way.

The tension filled the air for only a beat before Celia went flying from her place before Lily and into a wall across the room. In her place stood Sam with their arm still outstretched. "Fuck off, Celia. This had nothing to do with the witch. Simon brought this on himself."

Celia quickly got up from where she had crumpled on the floor. Aron was at her side in an instant to help her up while he glared at Sam. "You would spare her life while our master sits there helpless because of her. So, you are a traitor," Celia spat, shrugging off Aron.

Sam held their ground, even as Celia approached. "What happened to Simon had nothing to do with her or us. His problems were long before any of us. You know that better than any of us. And he is no longer my master. I'm free. Finally."

And just like that, Sam was gone; the only trace they had been there at all was the door closing slowly.

Aron walked toward Celia, but then stopped short. "I think ... I'm leaving, too." Celia whipped her head around so hard Lily was surprised she didn't snap her own neck.

"What do you mean you're leaving?! We can't just leave him like this," Celia shrieked at Aron. But he didn't meet her eyes. Instead, he kept them focused on Simon.

"I've stayed all these years because he terrified me. Made me feel like I would die out there on my own. I stayed because of you. I had hoped one day you could see we would be fine on our own if we just had each other. But now he can't hurt me, and I want to see the world on my own terms." Lily was surprised at the speech that came out of Aron. She had thought him pretty empty-brained from the few times she had heard him speak. Albert had always described him as a devoted but stupid lap dog.

Aron finally looked at Celia, his eyes pleading. "We could go together. Finally enjoy our time without all the hovering and questioning. Go to all the places Simon wouldn't allow us." He held out his hand to Celia as he smiled sheepishly. Hopeful and boyish was his smile as he waited for Celia to take his hand and go off to their happily ever after.

But all she did was look at his hand in disgust. "After all that Simon has done for us, you would leave him in his most desperate hour. You are despicable. Get the hell out of my sight!" She turned her back on him and walked back to Simon's side.

The smile dropped from Aron's face, and his eyes grew sad, the look of a man whose heart had just been broken. Unlike Sam, Aron walked slowly out the door, trudged really. He turned and gave Celia one last look, but she didn't even turn his way. Then he was gone.

All that was left were Lily and Albert on one side of the room and Celia, seated next to the still-crying Simon on the other.

Silence fell upon them like a thick blanket. Simon's tears were silent sobs now, and Lily looked up at Albert questioningly. Should they stay or go?

Albert turned his attention to Simon, and Lily knew he wanted to say a proper goodbye—needed to say it, his last bit of closure. She grabbed her bag from where it still sat on the couch, placed the now empty spirit box back inside, and then turned her attention back to Albert.

She grabbed his hand and pulled him toward Simon and Celia. The vampire glared up at them but did nothing more. Albert knelt down on one knee in front of Simon and, with a hand on each cheek, pulled Simon's face upward. His eyes were puffy and red from crying, and he looked an absolute mess. "You have done so much for me over the years, and I want to thank you. I have a friend in the city who can help you. He'll know someone who can get you through this transition. And then that will be the end for us. I never want to see you after this."

Simon grasped onto Albert's wrist; his face hardened, his tears forgotten for the moment. Some of his customary swagger was back. "I don't want your pity or your charity, Albert. Just leave and take that cursed witch with you." His eyes flitted toward Lily for half a second before they returned to Albert's face, like he couldn't bear to even look at her.

Albert dropped his hands and stood. With one last parting look, Albert grabbed Lily's hand and pulled her away. As they walked toward the exit, Celia called out to them, "One of these days, Albert, I am going to kill you."

Albert didn't bother to turn around, and Lily kept her eyes on the door. His voice was flat as he responded, "I look forward to it, Celia." And that was it. They were through the door, and it shut behind them with a soft click.

They said nothing as they made their way through the hotel and out into the night. Silence remained between them as the valet brought up the car and the entire trip back to Spirit Antiques to meet up with Brie and Ezra.

Finally, Albert parked the car in a darkened lot and turned to her. He reached for her, and with impressive strength and dexterity, he had her lifted over the console and straddling him in the driver's seat in half a second. His kiss was desperate and deep, claiming and frantic, the grip on either side of her waist bruising. But Lily didn't care. She grabbed at him, pulled herself closer to his body, and wrapped her arms around his neck, wanting to erase every bit of space between them.

They were moving without conscious thought and in what felt like mere seconds, clothing was pushed aside, and he was sinking into her. There was some discomfort, as she wasn't fully ready to take him, but he kept it slow at first, letting her rock against him at her own pace. But just like his kisses, it grew increasingly more frantic, and soon he was slamming up into her as she pushed down onto him. The windows started to steam from her heavy breaths, and their grip on each other tightened until it felt like they were trying to merge into one body.

Albert's long cool finger came down between them, and he began to work at her until finally, Lily's eyes rolled back and she screamed his name, the sound filling up the car. He followed with his own climax a few seconds later, spilling into her with undeniable force.

When they finished, Lily slumped against him and rested her forehead against his chest, breathing deeply. They sat there, with her still straddling him, him still buried deep within her, and said nothing as they just held each other. There would be time for words later, but right now, all Lily wanted was to hold him.

CHAPTER 22

Albert accepted the teacup from Ezra with a mumbled thanks. He felt so numb. Though he no longer felt the blinding obsessive love for Simon he once had, there was still sadness. It was as if Simon had died right before his eyes. To Simon, being human would be worse than death. And in a few short years, Simon would fade from existence. Albert had been so sure the one person who would evade death would be Simon. He was eternal.

But now he was human, mortal, and in the vampire world, that made him less than, made him just a blood bag waiting to be drained by those who had fewer scruples about what they ate.

Of course, he was grateful and relieved that Lily had made it through the encounter. What had happened to Simon was a tragedy, but no longer Albert's problem. But if anything had happened to Lily, Albert wouldn't have been able to go on. She was his everything. Not in the way Simon had been. Simon had made sure that Albert relied on him for everything. Made him feel like he could have nothing outside of his master.

Lily made him feel like he could survive anything, that he was stronger than even he knew. And maybe he could live without her. He just didn't want to because there was no point to life without her smile, without her endearing teasing, without her kisses.

Still, that didn't mean he didn't feel a hole where his maker's presence had once been. Because that connection had been severed the moment Simon became human. Even in all his years away from the family, Albert still felt the constant pull that was his maker, and now that pull was gone, and it would never be there again. A piece of him was empty now, and nothing would fill that void, not even his love for Lily. But he could live through that. Would live through that.

His gaze wandered over to where Lily sat on Ezra's couch, nursing her own teacup. Despite the numbness, he was too full of energy to sit. A quick swallow of the liquid told him there was more than tea in the cup, and he found himself grateful for the dash of alcohol to go with the hot liquid.

"You both lived. Seems like a win to me," Brie said, and her tone was breezy, like near-death confrontations happened all the time.

Suppose they do for her. Maybe for all of us.

Lily shrugged at her friend's words. "I guess. Though, I don't think it worked out well for Simon. Or Eiko, for that matter. Goddess, she was just a kid." Her eyes flicked over Albert and he could see the sadness and guilt. He felt the same thing. It was because of him that Eiko was even made, and her death was on his hands as much as anyone's. Lily wasn't to blame. It was Juniper's curse; Lily had no control over it.

"It wasn't your fault, darling. She was going to kill you. And you didn't ask for Juniper's curse. She forced it upon you in exchange for her help. Eiko was simply too young to control her impulses. She thought it would please Simon to defend his honor." Albert could say the words easily to Lily, though he didn't fully feel them himself. That poor child had been a casualty of Simon's hubris. How many others had suffered the same fate over the centuries?

Lily's head tilted to rest against the back of the couch, eyes closing against the reality of it all. "Thank you for saying so, but we both know it's a lie. It's another death on my hands."

Albert thought back to that night nearly a year ago, when she had taken on that feral werewolf. She was a force of nature, calling upon the strangling limbs and vines to do her bidding. They had never actually confirmed if the werewolf encased in vines had died, but the chances were slim. He was probably left there to rot since his master was dead. By now, the warehouse that had belonged to the warlock Moloc had been cleared out and likely occupied by some other evil creature that called Demon's Row home.

"So, what happens now?" Ezra asked, taking a seat next to his mate and resting his ankle on his knee.

That's a good question.

Lily's eyes were questioning as she looked over at Albert. She needed answers that he didn't have. It wasn't like they could forget everything that had happened in the last few weeks. Despite what they went through together, he had hurt her. He had been weak against Simon and had prepared everything for when he left. There was broken trust now, and he wouldn't blame her if she left him. They had swept all their personal conflicts aside to focus on the task of getting rid of Simon, on repairing the rift with Lily and her family. But they never addressed the issues between themselves. Lily may have put on a brave face for him and everyone else in last week, but he knew, below the surface, there was a deeper struggle in her. In truth, he worried that when they returned home, she would pack up her things and return to her family's farm. And he only had himself to blame.

But right now, she needed him to be the strong one, the one with the answers. And he could do that for her, even when he wasn't sure about anything else. "Now we can focus on truly repairing everything with Lily's family. I think I should try to find Sam and Aron; they are now out in the world on their own for the first time and might need some guidance. Not like Simon, of course, but maybe I could help them find better feeding sources. If you are willing to assist me, Ezra." His friend nodded because, of course, he would. That was what the antique shop was really for, after all, to help the magical community. Just like Ezra had been helping him for so long. He didn't expect Sam or Aron to stick around New Britain, and truth be told, he didn't want them to. But he could give them a good start in the world on their own.

He didn't mention anything that had to do with Lily and himself because that would be for them to figure out on their own, without an audience to bear witness. A look over at Lily confirmed she was in agreement with the plan with a simple nod, like she knew exactly what he was thinking.

"What about Simon?" Brie asked, leaning into Ezra.

Albert sighed deeply. *What about Simon, indeed?*

"Albert offered to help him, but he seems to be content to be a stubborn ass. He's Celia's problem now, since she's so brainwashed by him. It's not like he can hurt us anymore. Even if I see him in my visions, I don't think he'll be able to kill me again. But I doubt I'll see him, at least not like before, just in like a normal vision." Lily took a drink of her own tea and sighed. Albert watched as the tension eased bit by bit from her body, and he could hear her heartbeat's slow, normal rhythm.

Brie scrunched up her face. *An unbecoming look,* Albert thought. "Humans can still be dangerous. I mean, like, he could still come after you. He just doesn't have superpowers anymore. Just be careful, okay? People can totally go unhinged after something like this."

Albert hated to admit she had a point. He had underestimated Bridget in the past, and she had proven to be more capable than he had realized. She had killed an ancient, powerful warlock, after all, without magic. No doubt Simon would blame them for his mortality problem. Though he didn't have his power anymore, Simon still had connections. Still had Celia to do his dirty work for him.

Will we ever be truly safe from him? Will I ever truly be rid of him?

The problem was that Albert didn't know the answers to those questions. He wanted so badly to say yes, that Simon wasn't a threat to them anymore. But that wasn't really the case.

"Simon still has many friends. How many of them he will keep now that he's human is beyond my knowledge, but he won't be entirely abandoned. And there's still Celia to consider. She hated me before. Now I'm certain she absolutely loathes me and definitely wishes for my absolute destruction." It was a sobering thought, to be sure.

"We need each other more than ever right now. Celia and Simon won't just forget about this, and leaving Albert won't stop me from being a target. We'll just have to find a way through all of this. And besides..." Lily turned and smiled at Albert. It was genuine and toothy, and he loved her for it. "We'll outlive Simon no matter what. We'll make it through."

Hope bloomed in his chest. The hope that Lily would forgive him for fucking it all up. Hope that this wasn't the end of them. "Why don't we go home? We both could use the rest." Albert set his teacup down on the coffee table and watched as it refilled itself. He watched as Lily drained her own cup and flipped it upside down on the saucer, like he should have done had he remembered. She stood, and the other two followed suit.

As much as Albert wanted to rush straight out of the apartment and home, he waited patiently for Lily to hug Brie and Ezra. Brie whispered something into Lily's ear and then gave her a kiss on the cheek. Lily held out her hand toward Albert, and he crossed the room and grabbed her hand, threading his fingers through hers.

She tugged him out of the apartment and through the shop door. The grip on his hand was tight as she led them to the car, and she only relinquished her hold on him once he had opened the passenger door for her.

Albert walked slowly around the car and slid in behind the wheel. "Lily, I—"

But Lily's upturned hand stopped him short.

"Later, Bertie. We'll discuss everything after I've had some sleep." She sounded utterly spent; the night had finally caught up to her. They drove the rest of the way in silence, though it wasn't uncomfortable.

When they arrived at their home, Albert scooped Lily up from the car. She didn't fight him, just wrapped her arms around his neck and buried her face in his chest. The house was dark, but Albert didn't bother to turn on any lights as he carried her up to their room.

He laid her on the bed, immediately knelt before her, and began to remove her shoes. Lily watched him wordlessly, lifting her foot as he slid each shoe off. Piece by piece, he undressed her. It was soft and sweet. He wasn't looking for more, not tonight, anyway. They had already been through so much, and Lily looked absolutely exhausted. Albert's goal was to get her comfortable and let her sleep while he held her close. Together they pulled away the blankets, and Lily slithered between the sheets.

Making quick work of his own clothes, Albert slid in next to her and pulled her to his chest, wrapping his arms tightly around Lily's waist. Legs twined together, her back to his front, they laid in their darkened room, focused only on the feel of each other's bodies. Lily's heartbeat sounded like a timpani, loud and reverberating in the room. Her breaths hitched every now and then.

Albert nuzzled against her neck. "I love you, darling," he whispered into her skin.

She moved her hand, so it covered his hand on her waist. "I love you, too. Good night, love." The room was silent after that, and within minutes, Lily's breathing evened out into sleep.

But sleep would not come for Albert. He could only hold her and think. There was still so much that awaited them in the morning and the next few days. They would need to visit her family; no doubt they would want to know the outcome of all that magic they poured into Lily and the spirit box. The spirit box also needed to be returned. Juniper was gone now, but the box was undamaged and was probably bound for the Everett attic again until it was needed once more.

After that, he would talk to Ezra about additional protection charms for their home and to carry on their person and return what they already had. The chances of Celia coming after them seemed slim for now. She was smart enough not to do anything until she had Simon situated. But Celia was good at waiting. She would bide her time and wait for them to let down their guard. There was no way of knowing if Juniper's curse still resided in Lily or if it was a one-time thing, and he wasn't exactly willing to volunteer to test it. Maybe the threat of the curse would be enough to keep Celia away. He could only hope.

From there, he would devote all of his time to Lily, as much as she wanted him around. Though he wasn't much of a gardener, he would gladly do anything she asked him to do in the garden. He would haul her wares to her clients, bottle potions, which was her least favorite part of her job. Whatever she asked, he would do anything to prove he was worthy of her and would never again consider doing something without expressly speaking with her. Never again would he even consider the thought of leaving, even if he thought it was for her own good. Never in a million lifetimes would Albert ever know what was for Lily's own good better than she did.

On a normal night, Albert delighted in the hours of dark while the rest of the world slept, save for the nocturnal creatures. But tonight seemed to stretch into one long eternity. Never in over a century had Albert longed so much for the sun as he did holding Lily in their darkened room after everything they had gone through. No matter how much he willed it, the sun was still hours away from rising, and Lily was deep asleep. She needed the rest, but it was still a test of his will to keep from rousing her and hashing out everything right then. Plenty of time remained for them to speak once she had had a chance to sleep. How he wished he could sleep with her, find that dream space that would soothe his mind for a few hours. But it would not come for him. And since he didn't need to sleep, his body did not crave it. *Not that my mind would settle enough to sleep, anyway,* he thought forlornly.

He could leave the room, of course, go to his office and focus on something that wasn't his own thoughts. The thought of leaving Lily alone in the room, however, kept him in the bed, kept him wrapped around her, staring at the wall as he breathed in her scent and counted her heartbeats.

When the sun had just started to rise, Lily stirred in his arms. She stretched out her body while her eyes remained closed, like she was unwilling to greet the day. "Morning," she mumbled, extracting her legs from his to stretch out further, her body going rigid for a second.

Albert kissed her temple and pulled his arms away, giving her space to awaken properly. "Good morning. How did you sleep?" He cursed himself for asking; he knew very well how restless her sleep had been. Though she didn't awaken once throughout the night, she had twisted and turned in his arms. In those moments, Albert released his hold on her and let her move about until she settled again. There wasn't much else for him to do when she was in that state, even if he wanted to wake her.

Lily sat up slowly. "Like garbage. But at least there were no dreams or visions, just wasn't restful." He watched her get up off the bed and head toward the ensuite bathroom. The door snicked shut behind her, and he heard the water start in the shower. He let his head drop down and rested his hands between his legs on the side of the bed. Not that he expected sunshine and kisses from her, but it wasn't like Lily to say so little and walk away.

The bathroom door opened wide suddenly, and Lily bounded quickly across the room to stand between his legs, like she was summoned just by thinking of her. "I love you, you big dope. Get out of your own head and get your ass in that shower." She grabbed his chin, raising it up to face her, and kissed him fiercely. As she released him and turned to head back into the bathroom, there was an extra swing to her hips for his benefit.

Albert smiled softly and, for the moment, put aside his fears and eagerly followed Lily to the shower.

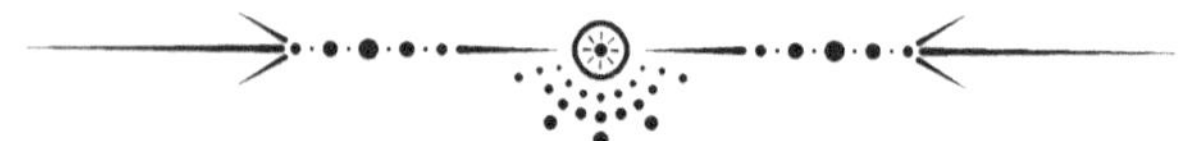

"Well, I'm glad to hear Mama Juniper kicked some ass!" Granny took a sip of her brandy and turned her attention back to the tarot card she was painting. A set of magnifying glasses sat perched on her nose as she leaned in with her paintbrush against the easel to continue the delicate filigree on the edges of what looked to be one of the cup cards.

"Mom!" Hyacinth chastised, but the older woman just snickered without looking up from her work. The more time he spent around Lily's granny, the more he adored the woman. Driving her daughters crazy seemed to be one of the old witch's favorite past times. Granny was nearly as old as he was, older probably, and despite looking elderly, she certainly wasn't slowing down. "What do you kids plan to do now? Any more ancestors we need to raise from the dead? I think there's some vampire hunters in my family tree if you need." Damien laughed loudly as he set down a tray of tea and pesto sandwiches. A stack of plates was handed around while Damien set down the second tray of food.

They sat in the Everett living room with Lily's family; luckily, only her nuclear family and her aunts were gathered, rather than the whole gaggle of Everetts, like during the séance. Lily had finished telling them about Juniper's appearance and Simon's fate. The collective look of pride from the Everetts was almost amusing. Lily's voice was even as she recounted the previous night, though the sound of her racing heart in his ears betrayed her cool exterior. She had taken a double dose of her anxiety medication after their morning shower, and even then, he couldn't stop himself from constantly watching her for any sign that her panic was rising.

"Maybe it would be best if he just left, since the vamp can't seem to keep her out of danger." Rose glowered from one of the armchairs. Albert had secretly hoped she wouldn't be around while they were there, but he wasn't that lucky. There would be no winning over Rose, no matter how much the rest of the family came to accept him. He could be fine with that because it didn't bother him that much that Rose hated him, but it hurt Lily, who only wanted her older sister to be happy for her.

Albert wanted so badly to snap at Rose. There was no reason for her to be so hostile toward him, and yet she still glared at him as if she was a moment away from staking him. He didn't realize he was clenching his jaw until Lily laid a comforting hand on his forearm. Thumb stroking over his cool skin, she answered her sister. "Maybe you should shut your mouth and get over yourself. Bigotry doesn't look good on you, Rose."

Ivy gasped and brought a hand to her mouth, her eyes darting between her sisters. Hyacinth clapped her hands loudly. "Girls, that's enough! You'll get along and like it, or I'll whoop you both. I don't care how old you are." Both Lily and Rose stopped their staring contest and turned toward their mother, though neither looked particularly abashed. "Now, Rose dear, you are going to need to get over whatever you have against Albert. He's part of the family now, and I'm afraid you're just going to have to deal with it. And Lily," she focused on her youngest daughter, "stop antagonizing your sister. I don't expect you and Albert to break up or whatever the kids are calling it these days, but you both are in for more trouble in the future, and I want to know what kind of plan you have so nobody ends up dead."

They didn't have a plan. Earlier that day, they had spent hours talking, but there was no concrete plan other than buffing up wards and charms.

How do you prepare when you don't know if and when something will happen? Don't even know what could happen? Are we just going to live constantly looking over our shoulders forever?

Albert had more questions than answers, more worries swirled through his head; he couldn't even focus on the good. That he had Lily and she had him, and together they could overcome anything. *Maybe it's a bit idealistic to think that way, but it's how she makes me feel.*

"We will take it one day at a time. It's either that or live in fear. Which isn't a way to live at all." Albert moved his hand to twine with Lily's and gave her hand a squeeze. The smile she flashed him hit him right in the heart, and for a second, he could almost believe that everything would be fine if she just smiled.

"Well then, everyone to the kitchen; we have some magic to brew!" Granny shouted suddenly, dropping the paintbrush she had been holding. The woman moved quicker than expected, and the rest of the family rushed out to keep up with her, all eager to get to their spell work.

Lily hung back in the living room and pulled Albert's hand to keep him with her. He stopped mid-step and sat back down next to her. She took his other hand in hers and angled her body so that they faced each other. "Bertie, I love you. And no matter what, I will always love you. So don't think that you have to prove anything to me. The last few weeks have been an emotionally stressful time for us. Not once did I think you didn't love me. Whatever is going to happen in the future, let's not let what happened with Simon shake us. Okay? We're in this together, and we both need to remember that."

The earnest look in her beautiful eyes was all it took for Albert to nod his head in agreement. "I would like that very much, my darling. But you are mistaken if you think I won't work every day to ensure you know just how much I love you."

Her arms were around his neck in an instant, and she pulled him close and kissed him passionately. "Well, who am I to argue with that?" She smiled against his lips. A call for them from the kitchen had them breaking apart and heading off to work some magic.

EPILOGUE

Lily clutched the paper coffee cup between her hands so as not to fidget. Albert sat across from her in the café, sipping on an espresso, watching her with intent.

"Why are you so nervous, darling?" he asked, placing a cool hand on one of hers. Normally, she would grab onto his hand, but now that it was winter and her hands always felt chilled, his cold digits sent goosebumps up her arm. The drawback of having a vampire mate: he never had warm hands.

She scrunched her nose. "I'm not nervous exactly, just perplexed. The vision showed this place, and the person I saw was vaguely familiar, but I'm not sure why I'm meant to be here." Her eyes drifted around the café, waiting for something to trip her magical senses. When nothing did immediately, she turned her attention back to Albert and smiled brightly. "But we'll find out soon!" She lifted her cup and took a long drink of the latte, which really did nothing to calm her nerves. *Maybe I should quit caffeine altogether.* It was a preposterous thought.

"Do you think your dad really is going to make me help make the Yule log again? Because last year was a disaster, and my practice logs are not getting any better. I am not meant to make desserts." Albert was trying to keep her anxiety from getting the better of her. Not that she was anxious. Well, maybe a little anxious, but only because her curiosity was piqued, and her latest vision decided to be as vague as possible.

"Oh, he'll definitely make you stand in the kitchen, maybe give you a spatula and bowl. But there's no way he's going to actually let you do anything again. Dad may love you a lot, but there are no friends in his kitchen once you have failed him." She started to laugh but stopped, the smile frozen on her face. Because suddenly, her magic lit up as her gaze roamed over to the café counter right as a familiar figure walked from the backroom.

Ivy's friend Cameron, the baker, walked up to the display counter with a tray of baked goods and slid it onto an empty shelf. He looked the same as he had years ago on their misguided, blind date, tall and solid, his chocolate-brown hair was slightly longer, settled midway down his ears. Even with the summer long over, he looked tan, as if even the cold couldn't keep him inside.

"Bertie." She tapped his hand excitedly but didn't look away from Cameron. "I think I figured out why the vision brought us here."

Albert turned in his seat toward where Lily was staring. "Are we introducing a third? Because, honestly, darling, that's not really for me." He was joking with her, of course, but in true Albert fashion, he delivered it in such a bored, deadpan way.

"No, Bertie, we're not adding a third. He's not for us. But I know exactly who he's for." Her smile was large and gleeful, and she heard Albert huff loudly.

"We're playing matchmaker now?" He sounded less than thrilled.

Lily drew her attention away from Cameron and back toward the vampire she loved. "Just call us Cupid, my love." She leaned across the table, and he met her for a chaste kiss.

As Albert drew away, he rolled his eyes, but then flashed her a quick, full-fanged smile. "The things I do for you, darling."

"You love it." She grinned back.

"I love you; there's a difference," he replied, grabbing her hand and pressing a cool kiss to her knuckles.

Lily luxuriated in the feel of his lips on her skin and sank into the intimate moment. But there was work to be done now that had nothing to do with their own romance. "Alright, love, it's time to go work some magic."

The End

BOOK CLUB QUESTIONS

1. There are a few interpretations of "blood" in Blood Magic. What does that mean for Lily? For Albert?

2. Juniper and Simon have a very sordid past. How do you feel about their romance and ending?

3. Blood Magic introduces plenty of new characters. Do you have a favorite?

4. Cameron = himbo (male bimbo, think Kronk from the *Emperor's New Groove)*? Discuss.

5. Do you think Albert made the right decisions to try to save Lily? Was his willingness to sacrifice himself and their happiness believable?

6. Did you find the relationship between Lily and Albert strong? Did they have good chemistry?

7. How do you feel about the bond between the Everetts? Did you find their family dynamic good? Toxic? Loving?

8. The vampire family breaks down after Simon's transformation. Do you see them as victims of Simon, or were they capable of taking care of themselves, choosing to stay?

Author Bio

Kait Disney-Leugers is an author of fantasy stories with lots of romance. Originally from Ohio, she has a degree in history from Ohio University. She now lives in Maryland with her husband and two kids and uses her history degree to be insufferable while watching historical movies and shows.

When not writing in the dead of night once everyone else is asleep, she enjoys playing D&D, trying in vain to get through her giant pile of books, and baking bread to 90s hip hop.

KYLE SORRELL
Munderworld
Potarium

LYRA R. SAENZ
Prelude
Falsetto in the Woods: Novella
Ragtime Swing
Sonata
Song of the Sea
The Devil's Trill
Bercuese
To Heal a Songbird
Ghost March
Nocturne

PAIGE LAVOIE
I'm in Love with Mothman
Dear Galaxy

ROBERT J. LEWIS
Shadow Guardian and the
Three Bears
Shadow Guardian and the
Big Bad Wolf

T.S. SIMONS
Project Hemisphere
The Space Between
Infinity
Circle of Protections
Sessrúmnir
The 45th Parallel

VALERIE WILLIS
Cedric: The Demonic Knight
Romasanta: Father of
Werewolves
The Oracle: Keeper of the
Gaea's Gate
Artemis: Eye of Gaea
King Incubus: A New Reign
Queen Succubus: Holder
of the Crown
Val's House of Musings: A
Mixed Genre Short Story
Collection

V.C. WILLIS
The Prince's Priest
The Priest's Assassin
The Assassin's Saint
The Champion's Lord

PARANORMAL & URBAN FANTASY

AMANDA FASCIANO
Waking Up Dead
Dead Vessel

BEAU LAKE
The Beast Beside Me
The Beast Within Me
Taming the Beast: Novella
The Beast After Me
Charming the Beast

The Beast Like Me
An Eye for Emeralds
Swimming in Sapphires
Pining for Pearls

CHELSEA
BURTON DUNN
By Moonlight

J.M. PAQUETTE
Call Me Forth
Invite Me In
Keep Me Close

JESSICA SALINA
Not My Time

KAIT
DISNEY-LEUGERS
Antique Magic

LYRA R. SAENZ
Prelude
Falsetto in the Woods: Novella
Ragtime Swing
Sonata
Song of the Sea

The Devil's Trill
Bercuese
To Heal a Songbird
Ghost March
Nocturne

MEGAN MACKIE
The Saint of Liars
The Devil's Day
The Finder of the Lucky Devil

PAIGE LAVOIE
I'm in Love with Mothman

ROBERT J. LEWIS
Shadow Guardian and the
Three Bears

VALERIE WILLIS
Cedric: The Demonic Knight
Romasanta: Father of
Werewolves
The Oracle: Keeper of the
Gaea's Gate
Artemis: Eye of Gaea
King Incubus: A New Reign

DISCOVER MORE AT
4HorsemenPublications.com

www.ingramcontent.com/pod-product-compliance
Lightning Source LLC
Chambersburg PA
CBHW021108100726
47797CB00003B/82